PRAISE FOR
THE GIRL IN THE ORANGE MAILLOT

"'No lie lives forever.' Police procedure, courtroom drama, compassion, superb writing, filled with numerous twists and turns—author Bailey Herrington incorporates many of my favorite subjects in *The Girl in the Orange Maillot*. Readers will love this mystery featuring protagonist David Elliott. My recommendation? Rest up before starting; you'll pull an all-nighter."

—**Donnell Ann Bell**, Amazon Bestselling Author of 2020 Colorado Book Award Finalist *Black Pearl: A Cold Case Suspense*

"Is the death of an abusive father and husband a cult killing? Or straight revenge? David Elliott and his wife, Judy, team up to try and clear a grieving son. This meticulously constructed thriller takes us to dark and harrowing corners of the human heart. Come for the twists, stay for the humanity . . . and the truth."

—**Richard Cass**, Author of *Mickey's Mayhem*, and Maine Literary Award Winner

The Girl in the Orange Maillot: A David Elliott Mystery

by Bailey Herrington

ISBN 978-1-64663-615-0

Published by

köehlerbooks™

3705 Shore Drive
Virginia Beach, VA 23455
800-435-4811
www.koehlerbooks.com

THE GIRL IN THE ORANGE MAILLOT

A DAVID ELLIOTT MYSTERY

BY BAILEY HERRINGTON

VIRGINIA BEACH
CAPE CHARLES

For Bill

"I am the wound and the knife!
I am the blow and the cheek!
I am the limbs and the wheel—
The victim and the executioner!"

Charles Baudelaire, *L'Heautontimotoumenos*

CHAPTER 1

Saturday, September 28, 1963

"Where are we going?" Molly asked. Thick underbrush bordered the narrow track they walked. The tree canopy cut the sunlight to a dusky murk. Small, dark birds perched among the leafy branches. Silent. Still. "I hear water. Is there a river around here someplace?"

"Chartiers Creek's about a hundred yards over that way," Ron said. "I want to show you something cool. It's only a little farther."

"This place gives me the willies." She shuddered, stepping as if walking on a narrow board over a canyon. Molly, a first-year student at the University of Pittsburgh, wore her shoulder-length light blonde hair tied off her forehead with a navy cotton band.

Ron stopped. "C'mon, don't be a wet blanket." He spread his arms, turning in a slow circle. "Look around. No brick streets. No greasers hanging out on the corners. No people shoving along the sidewalks, goin' who knows where for who knows what. No traffic noise. Here, just the creek gurgling and murmuring along. Crickets and other insects singing songs in the grass. The air smells clean and fresh, like clothes drying on a line in the backyard. Only you and me, walking on this old road—peaceful, no rush." He took her hand. "We have the place to ourselves." He leaned and pecked her on the nose. "Seriously, nothing's gonna hurt you out here." She gnawed at her thumbnail, hanging back a step, her eyes scanning the underbrush.

"Okay, I'll tell you what I want to show you. Remember telling me how excited you were to see the Meadowcroft Rockshelter last month? Well, I'm taking you to the ruins of a really old spring house. It must be at least a hundred years old. The walls are stone, and you can drink the water right as it comes out of the pipe."

"It sounds like it could be muddy. Maybe we should come back when I bring boots."

"When you step inside, it's like opening a refrigerator d—"

Molly grabbed Ron's arm, bringing him to a stop.

"What?"

She stood still, looking off to the right. "What's that over there in the field?"

"What?"

"Something's . . . no, dummy, look there." She grabbed his chin and forced his head sideways. "See?"

"Why would someone sleep out here in the weeds?" he whispered.

"Let's go back. I don't like the looks of this."

Ron giggled. "Come on. Let's have some fun." He picked up a quarter-sized stone and tossed it underhand. It landed on the man's chest.

They turned tail. After a few retreating steps, they looked back. The supine figure hadn't moved.

Ron poked Molly. "That's what I call dead to the world."

She wasn't listening. Her eyes were fixed on the prostrate form. "Something's screwy." Then—although she couldn't say why—she edged toward the figure until she was standing a few yards away. A gentle breeze wafted a faint, unpleasant odor. She scrunched up her face and squinted. Molly's heart jumped as she staggered back, her face white.

Ron hurried to her. "You okay?"

Her brown eyes fixed on the man in the weeds. "He—look at his throat!"

"Oh, God!"

The man's neck was torn and bloody. A horde of slippery white maggots churned beneath his chin. A dried lake of blood pooled under his head and left ear. His face was masked with a sheet of paper taped to his forehead.

Molly grabbed Ron's wrist, her fingernails pinching painful depressions into his flesh.

"This way!" He pulled her at sprinter's speed back along the country road, then veered off on a narrow rocky path. The steep terrain didn't slow their headlong rush. Throats burning, chests heaving, they burst into an open field, stumbling through ground-hugging tangles of thorny dewberry vines, racing toward a stone farmhouse, scattering chickens and ducks ahead of them. A woman opened the door before they reached the porch. The aroma of just-baked pies drifted from inside.

"Phone!" Ron gasped. "Need to call the police!"

"There's been a terrible . . . thing . . . accident!" Molly said between sobs.

"Would you like a piece of sour cherry pie, dear?" the woman asked.

• • •

An Allegheny County sheriff's deputy arrived at the house in minutes. He'd been patrolling less than a mile from the crime scene. He asked some questions, then told the pair to get in the car. After a brief drive, the deputy turned onto the old road the couple had been walking. When they arrived at the field, the officer said, "Stay in the car." An unnecessary command. He heaved his considerable bulk from the car and stood at the road's edge, eyes scanning the area. Since the crime scene was within the boundaries of Chartiers Creek County Park, the Allegheny County Police Department had jurisdiction. Back at the patrol car, he radioed their headquarters.

"Allegheny County Deputy 5467 reporting a 187 in Chartiers Creek County Park approximately three-quarters of a mile south of CR315 along Springhouse Trail." He listened to the crackling voice on the other end, then said, "Ten-four." He mopped sweat from his face.

"Can we go home now?" Molly asked, her voice shivery.

"Sorry, little lady. I need to ask you some more questions. Then you'll have to wait until the investigators get here."

They told him they had entered the crime scene at approximately 12:45 p.m., had not touched the body, and left in a hurry along the same pathway by which they had arrived. They gave their addresses and phone numbers.

"Would it be okay if we sat under that tree? It's pretty hot in the car."

The deputy produced a dark wool blanket. "Make yourselves comfortable. I expect we'll have to wait for at least an hour or more. Let me know if you get hungry. I keep a supply of pretzels and candy bars on hand. Don't have any water, though."

They sat, knees tucked against their chests, and leaned against each other, heads touching. Molly's eyes were screwed shut. Ron watched a beetle scuttling on the edge of the road, a large black ant speared between its pincers. *I need a drink,* he thought, *and I don't mean water.*

The afternoon shadows stretched long by the time two crime scene investigators from the Allegheny County Police Department drove up. The deputy struggled out of his car and introduced himself.

"Lieutenant Jakubowski, deputy. My partner, Sergeant Eggleston."

The deputy informed them he was the first and only responder and related the details of his interview with Molly and Ron.

Jakubowski asked the young couple why they'd been walking on the abandoned road. Had they seen anyone in the vicinity that afternoon? They had not. "Okay, nothing further for now."

The deputy handed their addresses and phone numbers to Jakubowski.

"After you take them to their car, come back here. I'll need you to keep watch over the crime scene while we search the wider area," Jakubowski told him.

When they arrived at Ron's car, the deputy turned to them. "This is an active crime investigation. Don't talk to anyone about what you saw until you hear otherwise. Discussing this with others may compromise the investigation. As witnesses to a homicide, you'll need to be available for further questions."

Ron nodded, then put his arm around Molly's shoulder. She was trembling.

"Take me home," she whispered. "Please."

• • •

Lieutenant James "Jake" Jakubowski stood at the shoulder of the abandoned roadway, taking stock of the scene. A tall, lean man in his mid-thirties, Jakubowski rubbed his crew cut. His partner, Detective Sergeant Harry Eggleston, stood behind the cruiser, head bent, scrutinizing the earthen track. He lifted an equipment bag from the trunk while eyeing the grassy verge of the road. The bag smacked against the trunk edge.

"Hey, pay attention!" Jake yelled. "You don't have the money to replace those lenses. Get your head out of your ass."

"Sorry, Jake."

"Here's the plan. We'll tape across this track and extend the area clear over to the edge of the woods. Then down to that outcrop of boulders, back across the track, and into the trees." Jake pointed to their left. "Let's use the field over there to set up. Paul Schrode is on his way. Should be here in less than an hour. He's the only medical examiner in this part of the state who's an expert on maggot activity. Did you round up the photo crew?"

"Yeah, they should be here soon."

The deputy sheriff returned and angled his car to block the path.

"Good. Let's get to it. There are no tire tracks except the deputy's. Nothing coming from that direction." He pointed. "This road narrows to a footpath about a mile that way."

Jakubowski and Eggleston followed the old road in both directions. The path to the south ended in a heavily wooded area. About a half mile to the north, they came to an empty, weedy parking area. A dirt road led up a steep hill to an asphalt secondary road. The detectives agreed this may have been the route the killers used to bring the victim to the place of execution. A thorough reconnaissance of the area turned up nothing relating to the crime.

Back at the crime scene, Jakubowski waved off the deputy sheriff with a thumbs-up. He surveyed the field before them. "We're going to have to start with a good-sized perimeter. You start over at that big tree." He pointed to an oak about forty yards from where they stood. "I'll begin where the track curves away to the left."

The two walked through the field, searching the ground with every footstep. As Eggleston reached a place beyond the body, he spotted something partially hidden in the grass. It looked like a bundle of dried leaves, about five inches long, tied together with what appeared to be a thin vine. One end of the bundle was charred. He flagged it and noted its location in his small notepad.

Eggleston came to the edge of a steep bank dotted with mature trees and bushes. About thirty or forty yards below him was Chartiers Creek, flowing in a large oxbow. The crown, or closed part of the oxbow, lay directly east, while the open end below the bow was due west. Thick woody plants and wild grasses covered both banks of the stream. Access to the creek appeared to be impassable. Unless the killer was a mountain goat, there was no chance he had approached the murder site via this almost vertical terrain.

Eggleston retraced his steps, eyes glued to the ground underneath the grasses and weeds. When he came abreast of the corpse, he saw a round metal pin about the size of a quarter in the grassy weeds. The insignia on the pin was a rendering of a human eye with a blue iris. He marked its location with another flag, then made a note describing the object and its location. Eggleston walked toward the road. About ten yards from the car, he stopped. A tiny, curved edge of green plastic lay hidden in a tangle of weeds. An untrained eye would have missed it. He crouched. Carefully, he parted the weeds. It was a plastic comb. Printed along its edge was the name and address of a barbershop. Eggleston picked it up and with a glance toward Jake, put it in a small paper evidence bag, which then went into the inside pocket of his jacket.

Lieutenant Jakubowski's first move when walking a crime scene was not to move. He would stand in place, looking many yards ahead. His habit was to see the entire scene before examining the area step by slow step, eyes riveted on the ground. Jake had developed the ability to see each blade of grass separated from all others.

The field before him contained a variety of weeds, grasses, goldenrod, and a scattering of clover. A place near the edge of the far-off trees caught his eye. It appeared different, somehow out of place.

Jakubowski's meticulous step-by-slow-step scrutiny of the intervening distance revealed nothing that could be tagged as evidence. He came to the spot he had noticed. At the top of the steep bank above the oxbow, a large shrub with yellow flowers spread beneath the tree line. Several of the twiggy branches on the right side of the plant were broken, dangling from threads of plant fiber. The blue-green leaves and flowers hadn't wilted, meaning the breakage had happened recently.

The damage was more extensive closer to the ground. Branches were snapped off and lay in a jumble. An animal or a human being had crashed into the bush. It was unlikely this had happened during daylight. He discounted all wildlife doing so, except perhaps—he smiled—a blind pig.

Jakubowski crouched, surveying the ground. Close to the shrub's base in the scuffed soil were two slight, almost parallel, indentations. He estimated them to be about eight inches apart. *Did someone fall to their knees?* He inserted a flag and made a notation. He stood. Two or three yards to his right lay a crushed cigarette butt. Jakubowski flagged the cigarette end. With a pair of tweezers, he lifted the butt to his nose. The smell of smoke was sharp. He put the cigarette back, then turned to face the murder site. This location offered a favorable vantage point to witness the killing.

Had someone watched the man be executed? And why? What would motivate a person to stand here smoking, as if casually watching a baseball game, and watch a murder? Jakubowski looked back at the battered shrub and the curious indentions. The killer would have noticed an onlooker standing this close, and smoking to boot. Even if it were nighttime, the smell of cigarette smoke travels.

The smoker may have had a hand in this. What if the smoker ordered the killing and watched to make sure there were no slip-ups? He wasn't familiar with this spot and ran into the bush in the dark, Jake reasoned. *We're possibly dealing with at least two suspects.* Hopefully the body would yield some clues.

The medical examiner drove up. Dr. Schrode climbed from the car. He removed his tie, shrugged off his suit coat, and stood beside his vehicle, waiting for Jakubowski and Eggleston to complete their initial walk-through.

The photographers arrived. At Jakubowski's direction, they documented the crime scene in wide-angle, medium, and close-up shots. The charred bundle of twigs and the insignia Eggleston had found were photographed and entered in the photo log.

Jakubowski and Eggleston scrutinized the body. The victim appeared to be in his early to mid-forties. A letter-size piece of unlined paper covered his face. The paper was taped to his forehead. Jakubowski spoke into a hand-held recorder.

"Victim is an adult white male; five feet, nine inches; approximately forty years of age; brown hair graying at the temples. Throat cut ear to ear. Vertical blood distribution. Victim found lying on his back; body oriented on a precise east-west axis, head to the east; hands folded on his chest. Clothed in a short-sleeve ivory button-down dress shirt, top two buttons open; brown leather belt; gray dress slacks; gray socks; brown Oxford shoes.

"Fastened to his forehead with adhesive tape is a typewritten message, which reads, 'N-A-Q-A-M.' Second word, 'M-A-L-A-K-H-I-M.' All caps. 'We have solemnly warned you, if you ceased not your heinous sin of fornication and sexual misdeeds that vengeance would overtake you sooner or later, and when it did come it would be as furious as the mountain torrent and as terrible as the beating tempest; but you have affected to despise our warnings and pass them off with a sneer, or a grin, or a threat, and pursued your former course. But vengeance sleepeth not, neither doth it slumber; and now vengeance hath overtaken you at an hour when you did not expect, and at a day when you did not look for it. For you, there shall be no escape, for there is but one decree for you, which is that your blood be shed on the ground as a sacrificial atonement for your sin. N-A-Q-A-M M-A-L-A-K-H-I-M.' All caps. End quote.

"No form of identification with the body. Thirty-five cents in change in left trouser pocket. Three keys on ring in right-hand pocket. Rolled-up copy of *Pittsburgh Post-Gazette,* Wednesday, September 21, 1955 edition in victim's left hand."

Eggleston placed the singed bundle of stems and the insignia pin in individual bags while Jakubowski encased the victim's hands in paper bags to preserve fingerprints for the lab.

"Okay, Paul, it's all yours."

Dr. Paul Schrode approached the body, swinging his artificial left leg through the weeds without apparent difficulty. "Interesting coincidence," he said to Jakubowski and Eggleston. "In the eighteenth century this section of Chartiers Creek, which is called the Wapakonee Oxbow, was the scene of a bloody massacre of the Aligawi tribe by the Delawares who were migrating east. The Aligawis happened to be in their way and were wiped out."

Jakubowski and Eggleston were too busy for a history lesson. Dusk was approaching. Eggleston wanted a cold beer and a sandwich. Ham and Swiss on rye, mayo and brown mustard, kosher dill pickle on the side.

Schrode spoke into a small tape recorder as he proceeded through his examination of the corpse.

"Saturday, 28 September 1963. 5:48 p.m. Heavy infestation of blowfly larvae activity in the area of the throat and dissipation of rigor mortis indicate probable date of death to be Thursday, 26 September 1963." Dr. Schrode made a few additional observations, turned off the recorder, and removed his examination gloves.

"Jake, this has all the earmarks of a ritual execution by some far-out religious group—the manifesto, the smudge stick, slitting the throat."

"Or maybe someone wants us to conclude that," Jake said. "How soon can you make your report available?"

"Give me five or six days."

"Come on, how about the day after tomorrow?"

"How about you take a long walk on a short pier?"

They laughed. "D'you have everything you need, Paul?"

"Yeah. I see my limo service guys have arrived. Time to take the deceased to the lab."

Jakubowski and Eggleston headed to their car. Just as they pulled open the doors, Dr. Schrode hailed them. "Wait. You need to see this."

The two detectives rejoined the medical examiner and his two assistants where they stood over the body.

Schrode nodded to his assistants. "Show them what you found when you lifted one side of the body."

They raised the victim's shoulder a few inches from the grass, revealing a knife. Jakubowski called the photo crew over to shoot it.

Eggleston donned his gloves and pulled a paper bag from his kit while Jakubowski recorded the find. "Folding hunting knife in extended position found beneath victim's body. Wooden full-tang handle, three-to-three-and-a-half-inch stainless steel blade. Blade and handle extensively soiled with what appears to be blood. Entered as Evidence Number 3. Conveyed to Paul Schrode, FOP, Medical Examiner, Allegheny County, Pennsylvania."

CHAPTER 2

Thursday, October 3, 1963

When Lieutenant Jakubowski picked up his phone messages at police headquarters, his first return call went to the county morgue. Family members had identified the body of the man murdered at Wapakonee Oxbow as Walter Harris of Ormsby, Washington County, Pennsylvania.

Jakubowski dispatched Eggleston to Ormsby to interview the Harrises and the Ormsby police officers assigned to the case.

The next day, Eggleston reported to Jakubowski.

"You want some coffee, Harry?"

"Not if you made it."

"I made it fresh yesterday—no, Tuesday. Should still be good."

"Uh-uh." Eggleston looked at his notes. "Here's what I got: The evening of Thursday, September 26, 1963, Mrs. Harris—her name's Regina—and her younger daughter Carin—age fifteen—became worried when Mr. Harris failed to return from a short drive to the Ormsby Post Office. They walked to the post office and found Mr. Harris' car in the lot, driver's door open. They searched the neighborhood but failed to locate Mr. Harris. After phone calls to friends proved fruitless, Mrs. Harris reported his disappearance to the Ormsby police." Eggleston flipped a page. "Neither the wife nor the two teenage daughters, Allison, seventeen, Carin, fifteen, had noticed any unusual behavior by Mr. Harris. He hadn't appeared to be nervous or uneasy. To the contrary, Mrs. Harris said her husband had just closed a lucrative contract for his firm, Ormsby Steel Fabricators. She said his mood the day he disappeared was very happy. They have no idea who would want to kill Walter.

"I questioned Harris' boss at Ormsby Steel Fabricators. He said, and I quote, 'profound shock and dismay' about the killing. He offered no pertinent information."

Jakubowski drained his coffee cup and made a face. "So, we have a guy who landed a big contract for his company. He's happy as a winner of the Irish Sweepstakes. He goes to the neighborhood post office where he disappears from the parking lot, leaving his car door open. Did you talk with the Ormsby police?"

"I did. They found no forensic evidence inside Harris' car. They identified a black rubber scrape on the pavement near the driver's door, probably from a shoe heel. Ormsby wants one of the shoes from the deceased to see if there's a match. They're interviewing nearby neighbors, but so far nothing."

"Okay. Keep on it."

• • •

Jakubowski received the autopsy report from Dr. Schrode the next day.

Estimated date of death: Thursday, 26 September 1963. Blood tests and examination of the organs reveal the presence of sodium thiopental, a barbiturate. Injection site: cephalic vein in the right arm. Contusion on the upper left jaw, one-half inch below the left eye socket. Deep abrasions penetrating to dermis on both wrists indicate victim may have been bound. Traces of cotton lint fibers present on interior of both cheeks, tongue, and hard palate suggest the use of a gag. Bloodstains on the clothing indicate vertical distribution of blood.

Cause of death: a deep, long, obliquely placed incised neck injury on the front side of the neck. The left end of the injury began below the left ear at the upper third of the neck and deepened, with severance of the left carotid artery. The right end of the injury stopped at the mid-third of the neck with a tail abrasion.

Weapon: a folding hunting knife, found under victim's body. Extensive type O blood residue on the blade and handle matches the blood type of victim. 'Bruce MacDonald' etched on one side of the blade, letters approximately three-eighths inch high.

Killer is right-handed, slightly taller than victim, and stood behind victim. Victim was standing erect at the moment of the killing, probably restrained by one, perhaps two persons. However, if sodium thiopental was injected thirty minutes or less before death, the victim likely was in a drug-induced stupor.

When he finished reading, Jakubowski pushed a button on his phone. "Harry, got a minute? I have the autopsy report on the Harris killing."

"Give me a few minutes."

Sergeant Eggleston was writing a personal letter. After hanging up, he resumed writing: *Please don't worry about me, Mother. I'm not in any danger. Working as a detective is more boring than dangerous. I wanted to write yesterday to tell you the good news about William, but this has been a very busy week for me. I know you are happy to hear about him. I hope this turn of events means Violet will be able to rest easy. I must get back to work, but I will call you Sunday evening. Love, Harold.*

Eggleston slipped the letter into an envelope addressed to a street in Parkersburg, West Virginia, sealed the flap, and put it in the inside pocket of his sports coat.

He entered Jakubowski's office without knocking and sat in the only chair.

"I read your follow-up report about the kids who discovered Harris's body," Jakubowski said. "Your sense is that their account of finding the body is straightforward and truthful?"

"Yeah. Neither offered any additional details or observations. The girl was still shook-up. Her mother said she hasn't slept well since."

"I'm not surprised. It had to horrify her—and him—to see that. Good work, Harry. One loose end tied off." Jakubowski handed the medical examiner's report to Eggleston. The sergeant read it and looked at Jakubowski. "I want you to dig into this *Naqam Malakhim* thing. Is it actually a cult, and if so, who heads it, who are the members, what the hell is their purpose, where's their center of operations, any evidence they've done this before?"

Jakubowski paused, looking thoughtfully at his partner. "Do I recall that six or so years ago you were dispatched to check out some crazy bunch who threatened to kill a woman unless she killed herself?"

Eggleston nodded. "Yeah, I remember. 1955. Eight years ago. Kind of hard to forget it. Three guys had formed a small pseudo-religious sect that believed in appeasement by the blood of sinners—or something to that effect. The woman they were badgering had been caught in the act of adultery. They didn't make a threat on her life, but they sure as hell were trying to get her to commit suicide to pay for her sin. We arrested them. But a few days later, the woman declined to press charges. The upshot was her family decided to take care of the situation themselves. They gave the woman no choice in the matter. She caved to pressure from her family."

"Are those three still around here?"

"One was killed in a car wreck not long afterward. The family told the other cult members to get out of Dodge or else. Apparently, they did. Leave, that is."

"While you're investigating Naqam Malakhim, see what you can find out about the other two. Their names must be in a file."

"Will do," Eggleston said. "Although that happened eight years back and didn't amount to much from a legal standpoint. That file may have been purged. At least we have the name of one person from this particular cult."

"We do? Who?"

"Bruce MacDonald. He owns the murder weapon. Talk about signing your own death sentence. This ties in with—"

"Hold on, Harry. You can't assume he owned the knife when this guy bought the farm. MacDonald may have been the original owner, but he could have sold it, or given it to someone, or lost it in a poker game."

Eggleston realized he had screwed up. To assume this or presume that had no place in any investigation. Jakubowski preached this all the time.

"Something bothers me about this," the lieutenant said, the reprimand over and done with. "Execution-style killings, including ritual executions by cults, don't usually hide the names of the victims. They want the public to know the victim didn't deserve to live because of his wickedness, that by killing him, they'd rid the world of a threat. But according to his surviving family and his employer, Mr. Harris seems to have been a model citizen—not a threat. We'll dig further into his background, but what we know so far doesn't indicate he committed adultery. This has all the earmarks of an execution by members of a cult, except the killers didn't name him. Why wouldn't they?"

Eggleston turned and looked out the window, wagging an index finger.

"What?" asked Jake.

"What if the killer *intentionally* gave us a clue to the victim's identity and the identity of the killer—someone who appears to be innocent but isn't?"

Jakubowski pursed his lips, then nodded. "Go for it."

"Okay." He leaned forward, his brown eyes intense, wide mouth fixed in a tight-lipped line. "The big local news story in the 1955 edition of the *Post-Gazette* we found in Mr. Harris' hand was the not-guilty verdict handed down the day before in the trial of Lloyd MacDonald. MacDonald had been accused by one Walter Harris of sexually molesting Harris' nine-year-old daughter. Walter Harris winds up with his throat cut. Bruce MacDonald's name is etched on the knife that killed him. No way is that a coincidence, Jake. Bruce kills Harris to avenge his dad."

"C'mon, Harry. Lloyd MacDonald was acquitted of all charges. What's the point of an angry amateur killing the schmuck who lost the case against his dad? Plus, this guy wasn't killed by an amateur. Whoever killed him knew what he was doing." Jakubowski stood. "Let's go talk to Bruce MacDonald."

• • •

The two detectives waited in their car across the street from Bruce MacDonald's apartment building. Evening rush hour traffic streamed past on Bower Hill Road.

"Did you see the communique from Mount Lebanon?" Eggleston asked.

"I saw it but haven't read it yet."

"Mount Lebo got a call from a woman who overheard Bruce MacDonald tell one of his buddies in a bar back in May that he was going to kill the guy who caused his dad's death. The elder MacDonald died of natural causes four months after his exoneration."

"So, he died in January 1956," Jakubowski said, rubbing his chin. "And now in 1963—seven years later—some broad in a bar says she heard MacDonald's son swear he's going to kill the man who lost the trial? Why in the hell would he let seven years pass before taking action?"

"Presumably because Harris and his family moved, and it took MacDonald seven years to find out where. If a person is committed to avenging a loved one, it doesn't matter how long it takes."

"Presumably? Did I hear you use the *P*-word? Haven't I drummed it into your head not to *presume* when we're investigating?" Jakubowski shook his head. "What makes this, uh, young woman in the bar think the Chartiers Creek victim is the same guy who took Bruce's father to court in 1955? Shit, Harris' body was found only a week ago. How did she even hear about it?"

"Her dad's a Mount Lebanon cop, and she overheard him talking to her mom about the killing. It was the Mount Lebanon force that arrested Lloyd MacDonald in 1955."

"Get her name and address. We'll interview her tomorrow."

A car pulled into the apartment house driveway and disappeared around the back of the building. Jakubowski looked at the information card. "That's MacDonald."

Young MacDonald invited them in, wearing a quizzical expression. Jakubowski showed him a photograph of his hunting knife. MacDonald confirmed it was his. He asked where it had been found. Eggleston answered tersely. Jakubowski watched MacDonald's reaction. *Genuine surprise. Disbelief.* He told them he'd lost the knife years ago. He had no idea how it could be the murder weapon. When asked, MacDonald gave a detailed account of his whereabouts on the night of September 26. And then he said something he immediately regretted. Bruce MacDonald admitted he hated Walter Harris for ruining his dad's life.

"Mr. MacDonald, that's it for now. We'll be in touch."

The following morning, Jakubowski and Eggleston drove to the home of Amanda Carmichael, the witness at the Hot Corner Bar. When Jakubowski phoned to schedule the meeting, she'd balked. She couldn't afford to miss her college classes. "Miss Carmichael, please let me speak with your dad." In less than a minute, the two police lieutenants had confirmed the meeting time and place.

By then, Amanda's attitude had softened, but not by much.

"Thank you for agreeing to meet with us, Miss Carmichael," Jakubowski said.

The corner of her pouty mouth twitched.

"According to a statement you gave to the Mount Lebanon police—"

"To my dad. I told my dad."

"Yes, to Lieutenant Michael Carmichael. You attested that on the night of May 10, 1963, you were a patron at the Hot Corner Bar on Forbes Avenue. Were you alone or with a friend?"

"With Mitzi. She's not really a friend—more like a classmate from high school, you know?"

"What's Mitzi's full name?"

"Gaynor." Amanda giggled. "I wish you could've seen the look on your face. Actually, it's Black."

Jakubowski looked at Eggleston whose features registered self-restrained innocence.

"Did Miss Black also hear Mr. MacDonald's remark?"

"No, but I told her."

Eggleston asked for Mitzi Black's address and phone number. Amanda looked them up in her datebook.

"Tell us, was the bar crowded that night?"

Amanda said it was.

"Was the room noise loud enough to make normal conversation difficult?"

She looked up at the ceiling. "Yeah, but I heard what he said. He and some Black guy were sitting at the table right next to me and Mitzi."

"Do you recall his exact words?"

"Yeah. I remember the way he said it, too. Like you could tell he was dead serious. By chance, I looked at him the exact moment he spoke. I was checking him out. He's good looking, you know? He got this frown and said, 'Rudy, I'm gonna kill Walter Harris if it's the last thing I do on this earth.'"

CHAPTER 3

Sunday, June 5, 1955

"Who is Walter Harris?" Lloyd MacDonald asked his wife, Lynn. She had interrupted his reading of Ernest Hemingway's *A Farewell to Arms.*

"You didn't listen to a word I said," Lynn responded, stating the obvious. When Lloyd read one of his favorite authors, he became totally engrossed. Maybe he would hear a bomb going off. But maybe not.

Lynn, slim and attractive at fifty-nine, stubbed out her cigarette. "The Harrises moved in next door yesterday. Remember the moving van? Walter, his wife Regina, and their young daughters, Allison and Carin, came from someplace near Cleveland. Shaker Heights, I think," Regina said. "So, this afternoon I did the good neighbor bit and took them the chocolate cake we had in the freezer and a bottle of Bordeaux."

"Not the Gallo, I hope."

"Not to worry. Walter said no thanks. Turns out they're fundamentalists. His wife told me alcohol is the tool of Satan."

Lloyd lowered his book. "She actually said that?"

"In a friendly but firm way, yes."

"At least we didn't waste a good wine. What does Walter do?"

"He's the new sales manager at Dornhoefer Motors." Lynn picked a bit of tobacco from her tongue. "Their kids seem nice. Allison—or Allie—is nine, and Carin—Carrie for short—is seven. Both girls are blondes, on the tall side."

Lloyd closed Hemingway and lifted his powerful body from the rocking chair. He walked across the library and tucked the book into its place on the third level shelf. At sixty-nine years of age, Lloyd stood six feet, one inch tall and weighed 190 pounds. His reddish hair resembled a frayed pad of steel wool. The balding area at the rear of his head was inexorably expanding in circumference. Lloyd's cheeks and jowls had begun to give in to gravity, but he remained a strong man, with thick forearms and muscular legs. Lloyd returned to his rocker and sipped the last of his martini.

"What's his wife look like? What did you say her name is?"

"Regina. She's about my height, with wavy, brown shoulder-length hair, good cheekbones, pinched brown eyes—"

"Pinched? Her eyes are pinched? What does that mean?"

"As if someone took her eyelids between thumb and forefinger and squeezed. She was wearing one of those overblouses that are trendy this year. Although she's carrying a few extra pounds, she has a good figure."

"You would have been a terrific detective, kiddo," Lloyd said. "Anything more to report on Mrs. Harris?"

Lynn gave a raspy chuckle, which ended in a fit of coughing. "She was wearing a very expensive gold necklace, dangling matching earrings, and multiple rings."

"Seems like the appropriate fashion choice for unpacking boxes." Lloyd smiled.

"Oh, and she bites her fingernails."

He laughed. "Next, you'll tell me she suffers eczema of the earlobe."

"How in the world did you know?" A smile bathed her face. She picked up the pack of cigarettes on the end table, tapped it against the back of her hand to shake out a smoke, then, with a look of disgust, tossed the Pall Malls aside.

"I'm glad Ginny and Bob's house finally sold after eight months. I told Ginny their asking price was too high. And that kitchen—" Lynn tossed her short blonde hair. There were times, though not often, when she thought about selling her management consulting business and renewing her license as a real estate agent. Doing so would mean less travel, which would be nice. On the other hand, she relished the challenges of owning her own business and the satisfaction of helping other small businesses succeed.

She looked at Lloyd. "I give you three weeks, max." Her smile morphed into a laugh.

"What?"

"Three weeks until you, the Jesuit, and Walter the fundamentalist, have your first debate about good versus evil. If I knew the exact date and time, I'd print tickets."

Lloyd snorted. "It'll never happen. Neither a Jesuit nor a fundamentalist will change his Biblical or theological beliefs. Walter and I will have to find other subjects to debate." He glanced at his watch. "I need to doublecheck my measurements for the vanity you bought to make sure it'll fit in the guest bath. You still want it to the right of the sink?"

"Yes, sir."

"Our blueprints call for a large mirror above the sink. Do you want me to remove the tri-fold mirror on the vanity?"

"What's a vanity without a mirror?" asked Lynn. "Next, you'll wonder if it really needs the stool. The answer is yes."

"Bruce—by the way—where is our son?"

"He's at Al's Diner. One of his Sig Ep brothers from Ohio State arrived this morning to interview for a job with U.S. Steel."

"Anyway," Lloyd resumed, "Bruce and his merry band of wood butchers will be here tomorrow morning to begin the rough carpentry work in the guest bath. So, I've got to make sure the vanity will fit."

"Trust me, it'll fit. I checked its dimensions against the wall space from sink to closet door on the blueprint."

"That's good enough for me."

For four years, Lloyd and Lynn MacDonald had been designing, planning, and constructing a major addition and renovation to their Mount Lebanon home and carriage house. Their plans included removing nonbearing walls to expand the kitchen and laundry room and constructing a three-story octagonal tower addition. The tower would provide an office for Lloyd, a craft workshop for Lynn, and a sunroom.

They'd enlisted twenty-two-year-old Bruce and a few of his former high school buddies to work on the project. Lloyd paid them a generous wage of five dollars an hour and taught them basic house construction skills.

Gradually the work crew expanded as other teens learned of the opportunity. A general contractor had constructed the tower the previous year. The work in the kitchen and laundry room had been completed, and efforts now focused on the guest bath and the rooms in the tower.

Lynn picked up an embossed invitation from the coffee table and traced the letters with her index finger. "I'm convinced David's graduation on Friday only happened because of you, sweetheart. I think he feels that way, too, since you were the first person he hugged after the ceremony."

"That was a nice surprise," said Lloyd.

David Elliott graduated from Passavant College, a liberal arts school located in western Pennsylvania. He majored in American literature and captained the Passavant Paladins baseball team.

The previous summer, David took a summer job in Las Cruces, New Mexico, to be close to his true love, Judy. The idyllic situation exploded in violence, murder, and attempted rape. David and Judy suffered shell shock and serious physical and psychological injuries. Judy's traumatic ordeal required intensive psychiatric therapy for several months. On the advice of a therapist, David delayed his return to college his senior year. His friend Bruce MacDonald persuaded him to join the crew working for his dad.

Always generous with his time and attention, Mr. Mac spent hours listening to David and stayed with him during flashback episodes. Ultimately, his wise counsel gave David the emotional strength to return to school.

"I was chatting with Judy on Friday before the graduation ceremony, and she told me she still has flashbacks."

"I'm not surprised after hearing what David shared with me."

"What you did for David was so special, dear. You gave him back his life. You're a treasure."

"Thanks, sweetheart. I'm just glad I could help him."

"I'm going up to bed." Lynn moved to kiss her husband on top of his head, but Lloyd pulled her onto his lap and kissed her mouth.

"You know what I think? The vanity can wait."

Lynn smiled. "I agree."

While Lynn put the empty martini glasses in the kitchen sink, Lloyd switched off the lights. They were two steps from the second floor when the phone rang.

"Very rotten timing," Lloyd grumbled, then retraced his steps to the kitchen. "Who's calling at this hour?" He picked up the receiver. "Hello?"

"Hello," said a woman. "Forgive me for calling so late? This is Regina Harris, your new next-door neighbor? You must be Lloyd?"

Lloyd thoroughly disliked the affectation of up-speaking—ending sentences with question marks—even sentences that required a period. "Yes. Welcome to Mount Lebanon. What can we do for you?"

"I wonder if I may speak with Lynn, if she's still up?"

"Lynn's . . . uh . . . busy at the moment, Mrs. Harris. Is there something I might—"

"I'm in sort of a bind? My daughter Carrie is in the hospital with appendicitis, and she's going in for surgery in about forty-five minutes. Walter—my husband—and I wondered if you could watch Allison until one of us—"

"Oh, here's Lynn, Mrs. Harris. So sorry about Carrie."

Lynn favored her husband with a look that said, *Chicken*, then took the phone. "Regina, what's up?" Lynn listened, looking at Lloyd. "Of course, bring her over. She'll be fine in our spare bedroom. Pack her toothbrush and things. We can plan for you to pick her up tomorrow morning."

Two minutes later, the bell rang. Lloyd grunted. He knew taking Allison for the night was the right thing to do, but he resented the interruption at that particular moment.

In spite of himself, he empathized with Allison. Nine years old, a new house, a new neighborhood, her sister in the hospital, strangers taking her in for the night.

He stooped to the girl's eye level while Lynn and Regina headed upstairs. "I'm glad to meet you, Allison."

"This place is really old," she said.

"More than a hundred years old. Let me show you to your room for the night. It's just up these stairs." At the top, they turned a corner and stood in the doorway of the spare bedroom. Lynn had turned down the light blanket and sheet. "Here you go, Allison," said Lloyd with a smile. "You can put your things in the top drawer of the dresser."

Lynn pointed to the hallway. "Your bathroom is right across the hall. We'll leave the nightlight on for you. Mr. MacDonald and I will be sleeping just down the hall. See that door? That's our room." Lynn touched the bear Allison clutched to her chest. "Who's this?"

"Biggy. Mom bought it for me 'cause I didn't want to move here."

"He's darling," said Lynn, passing over the girl's explanation.

"All right, Allie," said Regina. "Hop into bed and say your prayers. Your daddy and I need to get to the hospital."

"Is Carrie going to be alright? I mean, she won't die or anything, will she?"

Regina hugged her and tucked her under the covers. "Of course not. Carrie will be just fine. Now, say your prayers, and don't forget Grandmother Avery . . . and Carrie, of course."

"I don't wanna stay here!" Allison wailed, thumping her fists against the mattress.

Lloyd and Lynn stepped into the hall while Regina comforted her daughter.

When she joined them outside the room, she lowered her voice. "Allie's a little upset. Would it be okay if the door stays open?"

"Certainly," said Lloyd. "Lynn and I are right down the hall if she needs us. Now you run along. I'm sure the surgery will go well."

When Mrs. Harris left, Lynn locked up, then joined her husband in their bedroom. "Tomorrow we'll pick up where we left off when we were so rudely interrupted," said Lynn, caressing Lloyd's cheek.

• • •

The next morning, Lloyd met Allison coming out of her bedroom. "Good morning, Allison. I hope you had a good sleep. Here's a very important question. What's your favorite thing to eat at breakfast?"

"Pancakes."

"Hey, that's my favorite, too! After you brush your teeth and wash up, come down to the kitchen. I'll be making the best pancakes in the world—or at least the best pancakes in this house. You can help me if you want to."

When Regina Harris arrived to pick up her daughter, Lloyd and Allison were laughing about their maple syrup-coated fingers and debating who had eaten the most pancakes.

"Okay," Lloyd chuckled. "You won the pancake-eating contest, Allison. I hope you'll come visit us again."

"Thank you, Mr. Mac. I had a really good time."

Regina Harris gave Lynn a look of surprised disbelief.

"What can I say? He has a way with kids of all ages." Lynn waved a hand at the blueprints covering one wall of the new kitchen. "Lloyd charmed a bunch of teens and hired them as his construction crew. He teaches them the basics of house construction—carpentry, painting, and the like. If they show an interest in literature or philosophy or science, he loans them books from his library and gives them time off to read. Within reason, of course." She rinsed the plates and put them in the sink.

"Actually," Lloyd said, "I get more satisfaction when one of the gang expresses an interest in literature. Nicky, Nicole Palmer, one of the regulars here and one of my best workers, is reading *King Lear*. She's shared some excellent insights into the behavior of the Lear sisters."

Regina stared, uncomprehending.

"Yes. Well, anyway, Nicky pointed out some things I hadn't noticed."

Car doors slammed. Lloyd glanced out the window. "Bruce and his buddies have arrived. Please excuse me, Allison and Regina. I need to put them to work upstairs."

"Can I come see you again, Mr. Mac?"

Lloyd turned and smiled at the girl. "Of course!"

"When?"

"Allison Harris! You're being impolite. Apologize to Mr. Mac."

"I'm sorry, Mr. Mac."

"I accept your apology, Allison. Now I must get to work. I'll see you next time."

CHAPTER 4

Monday, June 13, 1955

Summer weather arrived in southwestern Pennsylvania on the heels of four days of heavy winds and rain. But the days following were ideal: clear skies, warm breezes, great weather for cleaning up downed branches, and the last of winter's leaves from lawns and flower beds.

Lynn MacDonald, equipped with a leaf rake and a two-wheeled barn cart, was clearing the ground beneath the large oak at the rear of the house. She liked raking. The activity required zero concentration, freeing her mind for serious thinking and planning.

Her current planning focused on the newly constructed room which would become her crafts and sewing room. Lynn already knew where she would store the upholstery fabric, and the countless fittings for the earrings and necklaces she made. She had insisted that Lloyd build large cabinets to accommodate bolts of cloth and her prized Singer sewing machine, which, she had told her best friend, Carolyn, could do everything except suture wounds. She bent to scoop up a rake-full of branches when someone called her name.

Lynn brushed her hair out of her face. "Hi, Regina. Haven't seen you in a while. Are you settled in?"

"There are boxes in the basement to be unpacked, but I've got the important things stored. If Walter would take the time to get his stuff stowed, I'd be happy. How's Lloyd?"

"Lloyd's fine. He's making good progress laying the subfloor in the sunroom. His crew of kids are great workers. One or two of them have turned out to have real talent as finish carpenters."

"That's nice," Regina said absently, not really caring. She bent and picked up a branch and tossed it into the cart. "I wonder if I could ask a favor?"

"Sure." Lynn smiled. "You can always ask."

Regina's expression told Lynn the woman had no sense of humor.

"Just kidding, Regina. What's up?"

"I have a doctor's appointment tomorrow afternoon?" Her annoying habit of ending sentences with question marks reminded Lynn of the first time her sister scraped a bow across violin strings. "I wonder if you would be able to watch Allie and Carrie for a couple of hours?"

"I'm leaving tomorrow morning for a client meeting in Michigan, but maybe Lloyd would do it. You'll have to ask him. Just follow the noise of the hammer to find him."

Regina Harris stood in the library, waiting for the sound of a hammer. She stepped closer to the wall of books on her left to read the titles on the spines. *Great Expectations, The Red Badge of Courage, The Spiritual Exercises of St. Ignatius of Loyola, The Adventures of Huckleberry Finn*—hadn't that book been banned? Regina was almost sure it had by some church or preacher. She moved to her left. Her eyes landed on a shelf above her head, a shelf labeled, *Banned and Challenged Books.*

"*The Catcher in the Rye*," she said to no one. She knew it had nothing to do with baseball. Walter had read it in college. He told her it was filled with vulgar words. Impulsively, she removed it from the shelf and began reading from chapter two.

"'Life is a game, boy. Life is a game that one plays according to

the rules.'

'Yes, sir, I know it is. I know it.'

Game, my ass. Some game. If you get on the side where all the hot-shots are, then it's a game all right—I'll admit that. But if you get on the other side, where there aren't any hot-shots, then what's a game about? Nothing. No game."

"Hello, Regina. I didn't hear you come in."

At' the sound of Lloyd's voice, Regina clapped the book shut and hastily returned it to the shelf. Her heart thudded so loudly he must've been able to hear it. "Oh! You startled me. I'm sorry. I was just looking—"

"What's to be sorry about? Do you like J.D. Salinger?"

"Who?"

"Salinger. He wrote the book you were looking at, *The Catcher in the Rye.*"

"No. Well, uh, I mean—I don't read much deep stuff?"

Lloyd reached past her and retrieved the book. "I guess *The Catcher in the Rye* is deep stuff, as you call it. Holden Caulfield, the main character, is a sixteen-year-old who sees adults and the adult world as phonies." He held the book out to her. "You may borrow it, if you wish. Who knows? You may discover you *do* like J.D. Salinger."

"Oh, thanks, but no thanks? Maybe some other time?"

Lloyd turned to put the book back, smiling at her discomfort. "Were you looking for me?"

"Yes. I was listening for the sound of a hammer so I could find you. Lynn suggested that." She looked at her sleeve and picked off a piece of lint. "I was wondering if you could watch the girls tomorrow for a couple of hours? I have a doctor's appointment. It shouldn't be more than a couple of hours, but probably less."

"What time tomorrow?"

"My appointment's at one-thirty." Regina gnawed at a fingernail. "It'll take me about thirty minutes to drive out to Oakland, so I'll bring them over a little before one?"

“I can handle that, Regina,” said Lloyd. “My crew and I are working in the sunroom. Have the girls bring over coloring books, or their favorite books to read. I’ll set up a card table in Lynn’s study. It adjoins the sunroom, so I’ll be able to keep my eye on them.”

CHAPTER 5

Sunday, June 26, 1955

"You know," Lloyd said as he dried his prized Sabatier slicing knife, "Sunday suppers may be my favorite meal. How can you beat the combination of crisp celery, sweet onions, tomatoes, cold cuts, and crusty bread? Not to mention chocolate ice cream."

"Not to mention what braunschweiger and salami do to your diabetes." Lynn gave him a pointed look.

Lloyd hung the dish towel on the oven door. "Shall we sit outside on the patio? It's a peaceful evening."

"Maybe later. I have something to discuss with you." Lynn led the way through the short hall to the library.

When they needed to talk things over, the MacDonalds gravitated to the library. Floor-to-ceiling bookshelves took up two adjacent walls, holding Lloyd's collection of literature, science, philosophy, and religious texts. A floor lamp and caramel-colored leather easy chair flanked a mullioned west-facing window. Opposite the bookshelves, a fireplace invited occupants to make themselves comfortable in the low upholstered chairs. Above the mantle hung an oil painting of the eighteenth green of the Old Course at St. Andrews. A brick-red wool rug completed the picture of quiet restfulness.

Lynn sat and turned to Lloyd. "I think we need to put the brakes on the Harris kids' visits, honey. They've already been here more times than I can count, and it feels like the Harrises are taking advantage, just a bit. The girls tracked mud through the kitchen today. When I scolded them about it—*gently*—Carrie said she was sorry, but Allie just looked at me.

"And the other day, when I went into the crafts room, my pinking shears were on the floor. You know I wouldn't leave any of my sewing tools on the floor. We've told them they aren't allowed to wander into our private rooms."

Lloyd removed the briar pipe from his mouth to get in a word, but Lynn wasn't through.

"Besides, we're not really close friends with Walter and Regina. Her, I can tolerate, but Walter gives me the pip." She leaned forward, forearms on her knees. "He put the moves on Amy Bannister at the concert last week."

"What?"

"I saw him. Amy shot me a *rescue-me* look. When I got to them, Walter moved off—but that's not the main point. Those kids are beginning to think they can drop in any time they feel like it, which isn't surprising considering Regina uses us—particularly you—as her unpaid babysitters. Regina doesn't have the guts to put her foot down. She's not going to say anything to them, especially Allison. She's what, nine? And she already runs that household."

"Allie? I think you're overreacting, sweetheart. She's very bright. Like any nine-year-old girl, she's beginning to test her limits."

"How would you like it if Allison and Carin waltzed in here and pulled a first edition from a shelf and left it on the floor? I'm damn tired of having my private spaces overrun by those kids, and by extension, Regina and Walt. They're turning us from good neighbors into doormats."

Lynn reached over and gripped his hand. "Honey, you're the

most intelligent man I know. A true Renaissance man. But you're too trusting. People see this and take advantage of your good heart. Do I need to mention Justin Zimmer at Leblanc Tennant, who wound up taking credit for your innovative catalysis?"

"Come on, sweetheart. That was long ago. Water under the bridge."

Lynn fixed him with a knowing smile. "Lloyd, dear, you won't change. It's who you are, and I love you just the way you are. Just—" She squeezed his hand and kissed his cheek. "Just be careful. Okay?"

"Okay." Lloyd stared at his clasped fingers, then lifted his head and held Lynn in an earnest gaze. "I'm sorry I've been insensitive to your concerns about this. You're right to be upset. It's just that Allie and Carrie seem to need an adult to share things with. Evidently, their parents don't take time to listen to them."

"You may be right about that, but we're not their parents. That's on Walt and Regina. It's okay. I'll take care of it." She looked at him and shook her head, marveling at the complex makeup of Lloyd's character—a renowned scientist who relied on analytical evidence and a fervent idealist who thought the best of everyone. How could such contradictory positions coexist in a single individual?

Lloyd was about to switch off the floor lamp, but Lynn remained in her chair. "Shall we sit out on the patio now, hon?"

"Sure. I just want to finish the Sunday crossword. What's a six-letter word for a *confused mixture*? I already tried *medley*, but it doesn't work."

"Women," Lloyd offered, then ducked a flying pillow.

CHAPTER 6

Tuesday, June 28, 1955

Lynn glanced at the sky above the carriage house. Sunshine slid among a loose gathering of harmless clouds. She welcomed the change from the recent rains. Lynn climbed into her car but spotted Walter Harris coming out of his house.

"Hi, Walt! Got a minute?"

"For you, Lynn, anytime." He grinned; his pale blue eyes focused on her legs.

You little jerk, she thought.

The neighbors met at the forsythia hedge separating their driveways.

"It's rather a delicate situation," she said. "You're aware that Allie and Carrie spend a lot of time over here. They're great kids, and we like them, but could you consider having them drop over on a less frequent basis?"

Walter smiled but narrowed his eyes. "Have they done something wrong?"

"No, of course not. And please don't misunderstand me. I didn't say they weren't welcome in our home, and we're happy to watch the girls when Regina or you need to be somewhere. But they've been here the last four days, and while Lloyd loves to talk with them, he has work to do, and the kids who work for him often need hands-on direction."

Harris looked at his watch, dismissing her. "I'm sorry if my girls are bothering you. I'll speak with my wife. Have a nice day."

"Wait a second, Walt. You didn't hear me correctly." Lynn's irritation spiked. "I said—"

"Oh, I heard you correctly. Gotta run." Harris turned away, got into his car, brought the Cadillac to life, backed out to the street, and was gone.

Lynn watched him take off, hands on her hips. "Walter, you're a little bastard," she muttered.

She decided to take this up with Regina. If she stonewalled her or sided with her husband, Lynn and Lloyd would declare their home off limits to Allison and Carin.

As Lynn neared the carriage house, Regina emerged from her back door. Lynn recognized the opportunity. She was about to call out to her, but Regina went back into the house. She reappeared, lugging a short step stool and a bucket of water. Regina set the stool and bucket beneath the kitchen window.

Window washing? Lynn thought not. Her neighbor wore a pink blouse, a strand of pearls, a navy pencil skirt, and high heels.

Lynn approached. "Hi, Regina. Got a minute? I'd like to get your thoughts on something."

"Oh, hi. Sure. As long as it won't take long. I don't want the water to get cold."

My gosh. She is going to wash windows.

Lynn presented the situation of the girls' frequent visits. Regina apologized and agreed to limit the stopovers. She thanked Regina for understanding and made her way to her car. Simple.

Forgive me, Lord, but I have to see this. Through the windshield, Lynn watched Regina wring out a rag and mount the stool. Even in high heels, she came short of the windowpane. The rain-softened ground caused the stool to list to port. Regina grabbed the windowsill.

"Allie!" she yelled. Lynn clutched the door handle, intent on helping, but Allie and Carrie rescued their mother, laughing at her outfit more than her predicament.

When Lynn returned from the supermarket an hour later, Allie, clad in a T-shirt, overalls, and sneakers, stood on a ladder washing windows. *Maybe Regina's not a total milquetoast after all.* Lynn smiled.

She maneuvered the car around Rudy Williams' truck and parked in the garage beneath the carriage house. Rudy and Bruce had been close pals since junior high school. Lynn pressed the grocery bag against her hip and walked to the house. Rudy had a rare blend of intelligence and common sense, which Lynn appreciated. She put the groceries on the kitchen counter and stared out the window. Really, Rudy was just plain nice. Bruce was lucky to have such a good friend.

• • •

The thick bandage on Bruce MacDonald's left thumb cost him his grip on the end of the measuring tape. It slid closed. "Shit! Sorry about that, Rudy."

"If you had a nickel's worth of ability with a hammer, you'd have two healthy thumbs."

Bruce retrieved the tape. "You've got a lot of nerve to criticize me, or anyone. Did you forget stepping into the pan of paint while showing off your pathetic dance technique last week? I thought all Blacks were born with rhythm."

"I'm the exception that disproves the stereotype," Rudy said good-naturedly. He marked the floor with his pencil. "Twenty-two and three-eighths on the nose. Snap the line, bud." Bruce snapped the chalk line. Rudy clipped the tape to his belt. "Lisa Brown could dance. But I don't need to tell you." As soon as the words left his mouth, Rudy noticed the faraway look in Bruce's eyes. "Hey, man. I'm sorry."

Bruce waved off Rudy's apology. He reached for the sheath on his belt and found it empty. "What did I do with my knife?"

"You used it this morning to cut open the carton of molding from the lumberyard. You laid it on the windowsill. I'll get it." When he returned, he flipped the folding hunting knife over in his hand. "Man, this is a beauty. I've always wanted a knife like this. Don't make a habit of leaving that lying around where I might see it." He handed it to Bruce.

"Yeah, I'll start to worry when you tell me you've changed your name to Bruce MacDonald. Now, what did I do with those damn plans?"

"Your hip pocket."

Bruce reached back, patted the pocket, and pulled out the folded floor plan. He spread the paper on the top of the workbench. "We need to cut that plywood sheet to fit this area to the left of the door, and then we're done in here."

"You cut. I'll hold and guide. Then I'll handle the hammer, Brucey baby."

When they had finished and cleaned up the sawdust, Rudy said, "Look, it's none of my business, but do you feel like telling your best friend what happened between you and Lisa? I know it wasn't a problem about Black and White with either of you. You guys were so right for each other."

Bruce led the way to his bedroom and shut the door. He motioned Rudy to the easy chair, while he pulled out a desk chair and sat, left ankle resting on his right knee.

"I loved Lisa, and she loved me. We talked about getting married after graduation. Not in a fantasy way. For real. We knew it wouldn't be a walk in the park, given the present social and racial attitudes in this country." He picked up a pencil from the desk and held it between his fingers, gazing intently at its point. He flipped the pencil back onto the desktop. "Our discussion had only begun. We agreed to pick it up again after spring break."

"Last year?" Rudy asked. "Wasn't that when—"

"Yeah. The first night back, we took a walk along the river. I tried to make small talk, but her replies were sort of lifeless. I took her hands and asked her what was wrong. Actually, Rudy, I thought Lisa wasn't well, you know?"

Bruce gazed out the window for many seconds. Rudy, the wise friend, waited.

"Finally, she looked up at me, crying. I tried to hold her close, but she held me off. Then she spilled it all. When Lisa told her parents she was seriously dating me, a White guy, they hit the ceiling. Said they hadn't sacrificed to put Lisa through college just to see her marry someone before she entered medical school—not to mention a White guy two years younger. Shit, they even phoned Lisa's favorite aunt so she could weigh in. Lisa said she argued back, but in the end, they wore her down. And that was that."

The friends sat in silence. Rudy pondered several possible replies but discarded each of them. He understood words couldn't reach Bruce at this moment.

Bruce put his hands on his knees and stood. "Come on. Let's find Dad and ask him what he wants us to do."

As they ambled down the hall, Rudy asked, "What did your dad and mother think about your breakup with Lisa?"

"They were surprised and sorry. They only met her once, during homecoming at Ohio State a year before last. They took us to dinner. Mom and Lisa hit it off like they'd been friends forever. When Lisa broke the news to me, Mom was the only person I wanted to talk with about it. She refused to let me blame Lisa or her parents. God knows I did, but Mom helped me to see things from their perspective." He sighed. "It's kind of weird. I took to heart what Mom didn't say more than what she said. She didn't say it was all for the best. And she didn't try to reassure me by telling me there are plenty of fish in the ocean."

"Your mom is special, bud." Rudy smiled. "Hey, you want to go to the movies tonight? Me and Alex are going to see *To Catch a Thief*."

"I wish I could. I like Cary Grant films, but I'm doing a favor for our next-door neighbor."

"Harris? I hope the pay's good."

"It is."

• • •

Regina had planned the evening carefully. The girls were taking swimming lessons at the high school and wouldn't be home for another hour. Walter's favorite dinner—chicken tetrazzini—would be ready the minute he came in the back door. Her husband wasn't a romantic, but she wore a black Audrey Hepburn sheath dress beneath her apron. A single strand of pearls graced her throat, and her wrists and neck exuded the faint scent of Joy by Jean Patou.

Regina heard the back door open and close. Walter waltzed into the kitchen and practically sat on top of her. "What time do you have to pick up the kids?"

"Bruce—you know, Lloyd's son?—agreed to pick them up for me. I gave him a twenty and told him to take them to Connie's Ice Cream before bringing them home."

Walter raised an eyebrow. "Aren't you the sly one."

Regina couldn't decide if Walter's amorous signals resulted from the perfume or the chicken tetrazzini.

"You must have gotten Lynn straightened out about Allie and Carrie. She's a pushy broad, telling me how to manage my kids."

Regina let his remark pass. "Lynn and I agreed the girls would visit no more than once a week unless we need them to watch one or both girls. She was extremely nice, and I understand why she made the request. Everything's just fine." Regina cleared her throat. Time to proceed with her agenda before the sex. "Listen, Walt, before we . . . you know." She gave him her best effort at a sexy look. "I have something to discuss."

He shot her an irritated look.

"I ran into Kim Jarecki at the A&P yesterday. She manages the county food bank? They provide food for more than three thousand individuals and families throughout Allegheny County." Regina twirled a piece of her hair. "Kim's looking for a full-time employee to find more food providers—restaurants, supermarkets, and so forth? She knows I worked for the Portage County Home Extension

Association in Ohio and asked me to apply. I told her I'd love to work with her but would have to talk with you first."

Walter scowled. "No way. First off, you don't have the brains to hold a job. Have you forgotten you quit that position in Portage County? I told you before your first day you wouldn't make it."

Regina attempted to speak, but Walter pointed at her. "You keep your mouth shut and listen. Second, I don't want you to work outside the house. How do you think people will react to see you working full-time? I'll tell you how. They'll say I'm not making it at Dornhoefer. And if they believe that crap because of my dumb-shit wife going off to work, how long before it results in fewer sales?" He twisted and yanked off his tie. "And then how long before Dornhoefer puts a pink slip on my desk?"

"But you kept hounding me to quit in Portage." Regina's voice quivered. "I was doing—"

"Shut up! Third, don't you listen to Preacher Palmer? 'A woman's place is in the home,' he says. 'A woman must be the servant of her husband.' Preacher quoted that from St. Paul in the New Testament. That's the way it is in this house, and that's the way it's going to stay. Your job is to keep me happy in bed, wash and iron my clothes, feed me, and raise the girls. Like St. Paul wrote, to be my servant. Got that?" He jumped up. "You tell that Jarecki dame to mind her own business." Harris glared at his wife. Anger convulsed his countenance. "You ruined this evening. Not the first time, either. I'm going out."

Regina scrambled to stand. "Where? Wait!"

The door slammed behind him.

• • •

Lynn joined Lloyd, who was seated on their paver-brick patio enjoying a glass of scotch. He had showered off the day's sawdust and wore his favorite Northwestern University cap, an orange tee, and faded red shorts. His sandaled feet were crossed at the ankles. She smiled at Lloyd's color blindness. Lynn color-coordinated his clothing in his dresser and closet, but Lloyd usually ignored this and pulled on whatever suited him. She bent and kissed him.

"Hi, sweetheart." He beamed up at her. "How about a scotch?"

"Too peaty for me. I'll get some wine in a bit." Lynn dropped onto the settee and retrieved cigarettes and a lighter from her purse. She shook out a cigarette, tapped it on the back of her hand, and placed it between her lips. The unlit cigarette bobbed as she rattled off a summary of the day's meeting with a prospective client in Cleveland.

"They wanted me to work up details on a feasibility study, write the case statement for them, and give them the names of the key prospective donors and campaign volunteers." Lynn thumbed the lighter to life and drew the flame to the tobacco. She inhaled, then let the smoke drift lazily from her mouth. "I should give them the keys to the treasure chest so their people can do the capital campaign in-house, too? Do they think I'm stupid or something?"

She leaned toward her husband, arms on her knees, the words tumbling out like the trill of a house wren. "Sue referred The Ashton Group to me. Wait till she hears this. It'll be a cold day in hell before she recommends them again."

Lloyd sighed. "Well, I'm glad you found out beforehand. Sounds like they've never used a management consultant."

"More like they don't want to pay a consultant." Lynn stood. "Now I could use a drink."

When Lynn returned with a glass of wine, Lloyd said, "The crew finished laying the subfloor in the sunroom today, and Barnes Lumber delivered the flooring. Bruce and Rudy lugged the bundles to the upper hallway. They earned their money today. Maple flooring is heavy."

"Did Nicky work today?"

Lloyd nodded while sipping his scotch.

"She's a really nice kid," Lynn said. "And cute. Look out when she hits her twenties. The guys will flock to her like bees to flowers."

Lloyd grunted. "Which will drive her father nuts. He keeps Nicky on a short leash. After she read my copy of *Brave New World*, she told me he would have had a fit if he knew she'd read it."

"Are you kidding me?"

"Nicky said Reverend Palmer heard from someone that the book is against religion, traditional family values, and includes explicit sex scenes. He told her it was 'disgusting' and 'morally reprehensible.'"

Lynn shook her head. "Poor kid. She's going to rebel, big time. It's only a matter of when."

"Nicky caves to her father—and her mother—too readily for any rebellion to happen in the near future. Actually, from what she tells me, her mother doesn't give her much support when Nicky and her father disagree."

"You know her better than I do, but I see signs of Nicky beginning to believe in herself, and you're responsible for that." Lloyd waved away her compliment, but she persisted. "Since Nicky's been working here, she's blossomed. Thanks to your teaching and encouragement, she's uncovered some carpentry and painting skills she didn't realize she had. Plus, a growing love of literature." Lynn's speech accelerated when a topic engrossed her. "She's going to take off like a shooting star and leave her parents wondering what the hell happened to their acquiescent little girl."

Lynn reached for her cigarette, then thought better of it and stubbed it out. "Does she participate in any extracurricular activities at school? Music? Athletics? She looks like an athlete," she said, thinking of Nicky's broad shoulders and long legs.

"I've seen her running. Great form and effortless speed. It's not fair that girls and young women aren't permitted to participate in interscholastic sports. Although, it wouldn't do Nicky any good if they were. Blanton Palmer refuses to allow his daughter to wear uniforms, especially uniforms with shorts."

Lynn frowned. "For God's sake, why are girls and women always sex objects when it comes to these religious nuts?"

"It goes further than that. Apparently, Blanton Palmer believes wearing a uniform—other than the uniform of the US military—demonstrates an allegiance to human institutions. He told Nicky that's a sin. He maintains that one's loyalty belongs solely to Almighty God."

"What?" Lynn screwed up her face. "He really believes that?"

"That's what I hear." Lloyd walked to the edge of the patio. He banged the bowl of his pipe in the palm of his hand and scattered the ashes. He fetched a tobacco pouch from his shorts pocket, then loaded his pipe, tamping the tobacco with a finger. He rummaged through his other pockets. "Nuts. Left my lighter upstairs." Lynn tossed him hers, and he fired up his pipe.

When he returned to his seat, Lynn said, "Change of subject. Jim and Bev invited us to their annual block party a week from tomorrow. I said yes. Is that okay?"

"Sure. What do they want us to bring? I could make my famous cucumber salad."

"I told Bev you'd make dessert."

"Perfect. My buttermilk pineapple sorbet always gets rave reviews." He grabbed Lynn's thigh. "Did you ask Bev to wear the white sundress that shows off her—"

Lynn narrowed her eyes at him and pretended to scowl. "You're nothing but a lecherous old man."

"Watch that 'old man' stuff." He winked. "Let's go in. The mosquitoes have found my bare legs."

CHAPTER 7

Monday, July 5, 1955

Bruce and Nicky climbed the stairs to the sunroom. Mr. Mac had teamed them to assemble and sand bookcases, which would be varnished and wall-mounted. Bruce liked Nicky, and he liked working with her. She had an engineer's eye for how things worked. When things didn't, Nicky figured out a way. She was also attractive and fun. Silently, Bruce thanked his dad for providing such excellent working conditions.

"I thought Dad said there were instructions on how to put this together."

Nicky crouched, looking at the pieces of wood. She handed one to Bruce. "Do you think this could be the bottom shelf?" She glanced at him, smiled, then averted her eyes.

As they fitted shelves to the sides, Nicky hummed a melody.

"Do you like that song?"

"Yes. It's catchy and upbeat, but I don't know the title. I've heard you whistling it."

Bruce chuckled. "Really? Rudy threatened to tape my mouth shut if I didn't pipe down."

"Music makes any work go better," Nicky said. "What's the name of the song?"

"*Walkin' My Baby Back Home.* Johnnie Ray's vocal rendition made it one of the top tunes two or three years ago."

Nicky leaned to take a screw from the packet. Her hand brushed Bruce's arm. "Oh, sorry." She glanced at him, then lowered her eyes. Nicky fastened the screw. "Will you teach me the words?"

"Sure. Gee, but it's great after stayin'—"

"Can you sing it? That's the best way to learn a song."

"Nah, I don't sing very well."

"Come on, Bruce. I promise not to laugh."

He looked at her. Nicky smiled, her eyes bright, dancing. "You asked for it." Bruce cleared his throat. He sang two or three bars then broke off. He looked at Nicky before staring out the window. In the silence, the noise of a power saw came from a lower floor. "It's been a while since I've sung that. Guess I'm out of practice."

Who was she? Nicky wondered. *And what happened between them?* "I understand," Nicky said. "You have a nice voice. Who knows? With some practice . . ." Flustered, Nicky picked up the sander. "What grade of paper should we use first?"

• • •

It was a perfect summer day. The morning fog had burned off, and the temperature was heading toward the upper eighties. But Allie found little joy in it.

Tiffany had called to cancel their plans to swim at the country club. Her mother had awoken with a severe toothache. After a painful emergency dental procedure, Tiffany was recruited as chief nurse, thereby scotching all recreational activities.

Allie's mother and sister had left early to shop the post-Fourth of July sales in Pittsburgh and wouldn't return until late afternoon. Allie called her close friend Cissy Ellsworth, but there was no answer.

"Crap," she muttered—her favorite new word, courtesy of Tiffany.

Allie had the day to herself. She thought about walking to Washington Road, Mount Lebanon's main street, strictly forbidden by her parents, but dismissed it as boring.

"There's nothing to do in this stupid town," she said aloud. Allie retrieved a bottle of Pepsi-Cola from the fridge, snapped off the cap, and swallowed too much. She coughed and spluttered. "Crap!" Allie slammed out the back door into the yard and perched on the picnic table.

A circular saw whined from the MacDonald house. Mr. Mac and his kids were working somewhere on an upper floor. Maybe if she stopped in, he'd tell her more about chemistry; maybe he'd even demonstrate an experiment. The MacDonalds' kitchen door stood open. With luck, the screen door might be unhooked.

Allie set the Pepsi-Cola bottle on the picnic table. She walked up the steps to the MacDonalds' rear patio, opened the screen door, and entered the house. A quick look-see revealed no one on the main floor.

She stood in the open pantry between the kitchen and dining room, gazing at the rows of wine bottles. Her parents didn't drink wine. At least she hadn't seen them do so. Allie peeked around a corner to make sure no one was near, then carefully pulled a bottle from the rack. The label read, *Duckhorn 1952 Three Palms Vineyard.*

What the heck's a Duckhorn? she wondered. Allie held the bottle at arm's length to admire the deep red color. The weight of the bottle fooled her; it started to slip from her grasp. Just in time, she recovered it. Hands shaking, she put the wine bottle back in its place.

Allie's heart raced. *A close call!* She returned to the kitchen, then stealthily moved up the back stairway to the second floor. The noise of construction and voices of the workers came down from the third. She proceeded through the hall, looking into each room.

She came to a bedroom. And what a bedroom! Beautiful throw pillows were tossed against the headboard of a large bed. The pillows matched the colors of the bedspread.

Allie went to the dressing table and opened the top left drawer. A wonderful array of cosmetics filled it—creams, lotions, lipsticks, colognes. She was about to lift a cologne mister from the drawer when she heard a sound behind her. She shut the drawer and turned. A young man stood in the doorway.

"What're you doing in here? You have no business snooping in Mrs. MacDonald's things. Get out! Now, kid!"

Allie, head down, mouth dry with fear, scuttled into the hall.

"Who the heck are you? What's your name?"

She ran past him and down the stairs and hurried out the door. It could have been worse. At least he hadn't recognized her. And Mr. Mac hadn't seen her. Allie hurried to her house, her breath gradually returning to a normal pace. *Mrs. Mac has more beauty stuff than Horne's department store,* Allie decided. Her dad had said they were rich. He was right.

• • •

The Harris family had just finished a casual supper of hot dogs and baked beans at their picnic table when Bruce strolled into their yard.

"Hi, Bruce." Regina smiled. "May I offer you some iced tea?"

"No, thank you, Mrs. Harris. Mr. Harris, may I speak with you privately?"

Allie froze. Walter Harris screwed up his face. Reluctantly, he led young MacDonald around the side of the house. Allie, eyes wide, watched until they were out of sight.

"What's on your mind?" Walter asked.

"Mr. Harris, this afternoon, Alex, one of the kids who works for Dad, found a girl rifling through my mom's cosmetics drawer in her bedroom. He didn't recognize her, but his description convinced me it was Allison."

Harris glared. "What? You come here and accuse my daughter of sneaking into your house and you're telling me you didn't actually see her yourself?"

"Sir, Alex described her—light blue tank top, tan shorts, and blonde hair worn in a ponytail. Listen, I didn't tell my parents about this, and I'm not going to. My dad enjoys talking with both Allison and Carin. I see no reason for him to know about this. I figured if I came and spoke with you alone, you'd handle it. Please explain to Allison that it was wrong for her to be in our house without permission. But please tell her that she and Carin are welcome to visit when they have our permission." Bruce gazed at his shoes. "I know kids make mistakes, and I hope Allison will understand."

"Anything else you want to say, Bruce?"

"No, sir."

"You can be assured that I will take care of this with Allison."

When he got home, Bruce wondered if he had done the right thing.

• • •

Later that evening, Walter took Allison aside. He told her he was very angry with her because of what Bruce had told him.

"Go to your room this minute," he ordered. "You will have one hour of private time to think about what you did and to ask God to forgive you. You will not turn on any lights. Do you understand, young lady?"

Allison nodded, her eyes wide with fear.

"I will pray to Almighty God to instruct me as to the means of punishment you justly deserve. At the end of one hour, I shall administer your penalty."

Allison started to cry. She knew what was coming. Being banished to her room meant the punishment would be severe—and painful.

From that moment on, Allison hated Bruce MacDonald.

CHAPTER 8

Saturday, July 9, 1955

Regina stood before her bedroom mirror, studying the third sundress she had tried on. This one was a floral print with a halter top. *Too dressy? Too revealing? Should she throw a light sweater over her bare shoulders?* She needed to decide soon. Walter wanted to arrive at the party at three. The bedside clock read fifteen minutes before the hour.

Regina felt uncomfortable in groups, especially among people she hadn't met. She had reminded Walter of this at breakfast.

He'd pointed his fork at her. "Get this straight. You *will* go to this party. Understand? This picnic is a business opportunity. The Ellsworths are well connected to the movers and shakers in Mount Lebanon and Pittsburgh. Ellsworth is vice president of financial planning at U.S. Steel, and you will not screw this up. End of discussion."

Regina heard Walter dashing upstairs.

"What's taking you so long? You've been up here for close to an hour." Walter took in her woebegone expression. "Don't start with the *poor me, the scared rabbit* routine. This is my opportunity to become one of the inner circle. You will go with me, and you will mingle and meet. Understand?"

"Yes, Walter. Does this dress look okay? It's not too—"

"Who cares? This isn't about you. Let's go."

As he dashed down the stairs in front of her, Regina raised her middle finger.

• • •

The block party hosted by Jim and Bev Ellsworth brought together the four families whose homes circled the cul-de-sac on Pleasant Lane and other friends from nearby streets.

Folding tables and chairs were set up in the side yard, shaded by two oak trees. Jim tended the grill. Shrimp kabobs, ground beef patties, bratwurst, and hot dogs followed one another onto the smoking-hot surface. Two tables placed end to end were laden with cheeses, finger foods, vegetable salads, baked beans, coleslaw, fruit salads, and at least four versions of potato salad. Bev, wearing the famous white sundress, bustled to and from the house, making sure every guest had a cold drink. Two couples, beers in hand, played a competitive game of bean bag toss in the backyard. Some of the kids danced to the music of JD the DJ.

Lynn noticed Regina standing off by herself in the side yard, looking forlorn.

"Regina! Hi!"

"Oh, Lynn. Hi." Her dispirited voice indicated she would rather be anywhere but there.

"Have you met Bev?" Without waiting for an answer, Lynn took Regina's arm and steered her to where Bev was talking to a man wearing a Stetson straw hat with a wide yellow band. "Bev, this is Regina Harris. Regina, Bev Ellsworth, our hostess."

"Hello, Regina." Bev flashed her a brilliant smile. "I'm glad to meet you. Lynn's told me a bit about you—all good things, to be sure. This is Glenn Dietrick. His wife's around somewhere. Glenn, be a good boy and retrieve Emily, will you? I'd like her to meet Regina.

"Emily's the librarian at the Carnegie Library on Washington Road. She's also a board member of the Women's Auxiliary for the

Edna Tarbell Transitional Housing Facility in Pittsburgh."

"Really?" For the first time that day, Regina beamed a real smile. "I volunteer at the safe house on Thursdays? How'd you know I'd want to meet—" Regina Harris glanced at Lynn, whose countenance displayed total innocence. "You're something else, Lynn." She grinned.

Glenn approached them, accompanied by a woman who defied the stereotypical image of a librarian. Emily Dietrick, slightly taller than her husband, walked with the easy grace of a model, and her good looks encouraged that assumption. After introductions, Bev excused herself to resume her duties as hostess, and Lynn wandered off to find a glass of wine and friendly conversation, knowing Emily would benefit Regina, and not only as a board member at Edna Tarbell. Lynn had seen Emily crack the shell of more than one timid soul. A glass of chilled white Bordeaux would be just the way to congratulate herself.

Across the yard from the drinks table, she saw Lloyd talking with Dave Marberry, the architect. *Dave's getting a progress report,* Lynn thought, smiling. *Poor Dave.* Lloyd was really bending his ear. *Should I go on another rescue mission*? Lynn sipped the perfectly chilled wine. No, she'd done her good deed for the day. Dave would have to fend for himself.

Still looking on with vague amusement, Lynn watched Walter join Lloyd and Dave. That clinched her decision. "Lloyd, honey, you're on your own," she muttered. Lynn moved off to join a group of laughing neighbors.

Lloyd enjoyed neighborhood picnics. They afforded him the opportunity to check up on recent news of friends, along with the progress of their kids.

Lloyd stood out at these gatherings, if for no other reason than his attire. While the other guests at the Ellsworth party wore clothing defined as casual chic, Lloyd sported a faded purple Northwestern University cap and an umber T-shirt with a small hole under the right arm. He had answered Lynn's objection to the shirt with unassailable logic: "No one's going to lift my arm to look at my armpit." Rumpled tan shorts, shorter than the fashionable length, and leather sandals completed his ensemble.

Lloyd finished his progress report to Dave.

"Sounds as though you're nearing the end of your project," Dave said.

"Yeah, and nearing the end of the bankroll, too," said Lloyd, a touch ruefully.

Dave smiled but said nothing as Walter came up to them.

Walter nodded to Dave, then directed his attention to Lloyd. "I assume you're discussing your marvelous addition. You have my complete admiration. I wouldn't have the foggiest idea of where to begin. And you've done most of it without the benefit of contractors. Simply amazing."

Lloyd offered him a slight smile. "Walter, this is my friend David Marberry, the brilliant architect who designed our home addition. Dave, Walter Harris, my new next-door neighbor."

"Welcome to Mount Lebanon," Dave said. "It's a nice community with a wonderful school system, the best in the state according to some reports."

"Is that so? I doubt it's better than Shaker Heights schools. They're ranked one of the top five school districts in the United States."

"Yes, that's what I've heard. So, you formerly lived in the Cleveland area, I take it. Are you a native of Ohio?"

"I wasn't born in Ohio, but my family has lived there since 1939." Walter turned back to Lloyd and picked up where he'd left off about the MacDonalds' project. "Not only would I not know the first steps to take, but unlike you and Lynn, I wouldn't be able to cough up enough dead presidents to finance the first floor."

"Dead presidents?" Dave lifted his head to look at Walter through the bottom of his bifocals.

"Moola. The bank." Walter raised his brows. "Money, Dave. Money."

Lloyd changed the subject, mentioning Walter's position with

Dornhoefer Motors. "His wife, Regina, is here somewhere. Their two daughters are delightful. Allison is what, nine?"

Walter nodded. "My younger daughter, Carin, just turned seven."

"I haven't seen them this afternoon," Lloyd noted.

"They're visiting Regina's parents in Cleveland. Coming home this evening. Anyway, as I was saying, Lloyd, about your addition—"

"Sorry to cut you off, Walter, but I deal with that enterprise seven days a week, and I'd like to relax and enjoy the party and neighbors. Why don't you come over some evening this week and I'll give a tour?"

"I'd like that. Give me a jingle when it suits you." Walter smiled widely. "If you guys will excuse me, I'm going to circulate and meet the neighbors, especially the one in white." Walter winked and moved away.

Lloyd and Dave watched him as he strode in Bev's direction. "Walter, you're over-matched," Lloyd said. They laughed briefly. "Dave, your glass has a hole in it." He lifted his own empty glass. "Mine, too. Let's fix this situation." Lloyd clapped Dave's shoulder, and they made their way to the bar. Glasses refilled; Lloyd tapped his to Dave's. *"Slainte mhath!"*

Dave tilted his head. "What did you say? *Slange ee vah?"*

"A Scottish Gaelic toast. Translation—to your good health!"

"And to your good health, Lloyd. *Slainte mhath!"*

The friends tipped their glasses.

"I dislike generalizations," said Dave, "but to me, Walter fits the definition of a salesman." He caught Lloyd's eye and added, "A car salesman, to boot."

Lloyd pushed back the brim of his cap and grinned. "I can't disagree. He's okay, just trying hard to get past being the new kid on the block. I hope he does well. Selling big-ticket cars in this economy can't be easy."

"I agree." Dave consulted his watch. "Time to find Joyce and thank Jim and Bev. We have tickets to the Pirates game tonight. They play the

Phillies. They'll probably lose again, but that kid Clemente in right field is sensational." He smiled in his bashful way. "Nice talking with you. I'm glad the addition is nearly finished. It's been a long haul."

"Yes, it has. We're tired of cleaning up dust and scraps, but it won't be long now until Lynn and I are relaxing in the sunroom. We're going to throw a party when everything's done. You and Joyce head the invitation list."

"We accept in advance. Sorry. Gotta run. Take care, Lloyd."

"Enjoy the game!" said Lloyd.

• • •

In the sunset's afterglow, Walter and Regina made their way home.

"I hope the girls are okay. Mother said she and dad would have them home before six," Regina said. "I didn't think we'd stay this long. Dad refuses to drive after dark, so they're probably on their way back to Cleveland by now."

"The girls will be fine on their own for a brief time." Walter glanced sideways at Regina. "You seemed to have a good time. Aren't you glad I insisted that you go?"

"I did have fun. From the people I met and talked with, I think this will be a nice neighborhood for our family. Emily Dietrick seems especially friendly and interesting. Emily's the librarian at the Carnegie Library."

Walter remembered Emily as an attractive long-legged blonde. He'd have visited the Shaker Heights Public Library more often if she'd been the librarian.

"And she's on the board at the Edna Tarbell Safe House?" Regina continued. "From what she told me about the program and staff, I'm glad to be one of their volunteers."

"What does her husband—Glenn, isn't it?—do for a living?"

Regina bit her lower lip. "Gee, I don't think she said."

"I wish you had asked," he scolded. "There was no way I could meet and talk with everyone."

"You seemed to find time to talk with Bev and the other good-looking women," said Regina, surprised by her assertiveness.

"You're right. They have husbands, and the best way to get to them is to befriend and schmooze their wives. Why must you always think when I talk with women I'm trying to—"

"Please, Walt, let's not argue. I don't want to spoil today." With a swipe of her foot, she scuffed a small branch off the sidewalk. "I had fun. You had fun. End of discussion."

He made no reply but put his arm around Regina's waist. He kept it there until they reached their house.

CHAPTER 9

Saturday, July 16, 1955

Allie sat on the picnic table waiting for her mother and sister. *Crap! How long does it take to get ready to go swimming?* She scanned the yard, eyes moving from the bush to the flowers, then back to the bush. Something was lying in the grass under the bush.

Curious, she vaulted off the table and hurried to it. Allie picked it up, ran back to the picnic bench. She stuffed it into her beach bag just as her sister and mother came out of the house.

"We're ready," Regina announced.

They piled into the family car, heading for the neighboring borough of Dormont for their first swim in the huge slope-sided Dormont pool. When they emerged from the bathhouse, Allison and Carin stood at the pool's edge, gazing around in wonder.

"Mom!" Carin pointed. "This pool is bigger than Turkeyfoot Lake in Akron!"

Hours later, Regina and her daughters returned home. Carin had spent most of the afternoon lying on a sun lounge. Now she deeply regretted her decision.

"It hurts, Mom!" Carrie yelled, close to weeping. "Do something, Mom!"

Regina ushered her into the bathroom and began to fill the tub with cool water. "Take off your maillot, Carin. When the tub fills up, get in and lie back. The water will make it feel better." She retrieved a jar of skin moisturizer from her bedroom vanity and placed it on the counter.

"What's that stuff?" Carrie eyed the jar apprehensively. "Will it burn?"

"No. It's moisturizer. I'll put some on your skin after you soak for a while. Get in. I want you to stay there for at least ten minutes. Then I'll pat you dry and apply the cream."

The initial pain of the cold water on her sunburned skin quickly changed to relief.

Allie watched from the doorway. "I warned you not to stay on your belly, dummy."

"Allison, that's enough out of you. We don't need your criticism." Regina waved her away. "Go!"

When her mother turned back to Carin, Allie stuck out her tongue. She went to her bedroom, unzipped her bag, and took out the object she had found under the bush. It was heavy. She rubbed her fingers over the smooth surface. Holding it in one hand, Allie considered where to hide it. Then, in a flash of inspiration, she thought of the perfect place. *Nobody will ever find it there,* she said to herself.

Allie pounded downstairs and banged out into the yard. She climbed onto the picnic tabletop. Allie flicked a fly from her orange maillot. *Why doesn't Mom call it a swimsuit like all the other moms and kids?* She pulled open the fabric and looked at her naked chest. *When am I going to have breasts like Tiffany? I look like a boy!*

The high-pitched whine of a power saw and the thud of a hammer on nails interrupted her self-examination. Mr. Mac and his kids were busy on the third floor. Allie lifted off the table and made her way to the MacDonalds' back door. She knocked softly, not expecting anyone to answer, then pulled the screen door open. Allie made sure the door didn't bang against the frame when it closed, then padded, barefoot, up the rear stairway from the kitchen to the second floor.

She paused on the landing, listening. The only sounds came from the floor above. She heard Mr. Mac say something. Someone started the saw. Allie cautiously looked around the doorway, trying to listen over the noise of the saw. Satisfied she was alone on the second floor, she stepped into the MacDonalds' bedroom. Pausing just inside, she listened again. Convinced she was safe for the moment, Allie moved to Lynn's vanity and slid open the top left drawer.

The drawer contained all the vials, bottles, jars of makeup, skin care products, and perfumes she remembered. After stealing a glance toward the door, Allie picked up a small bottle of amber liquid. She opened it and breathed in the aroma of—was it violets or roses? She sniffed again—*roses.*

She poured some of the syrupy oil into her hand, more than she had intended. Rattled, she shoved her hand beneath the maillot, rubbing the fragrant oil on her buttocks, and wiped her hands on the back of the swimsuit. Allie replaced the cap and was putting the bottle back in the drawer when she heard footsteps on the stairs above her.

She closed the drawer and raced for the back stairs. A voice called out, and the person on the stairs stopped to answer. Allie escaped unheard, unseen.

As she approached her back door on shaky legs, her mother appeared. "Allison, where have you been? Go to your room and change. Your father will be home soon. I need you to set the table for dinner."

Allie swallowed hard. "I'll be there after I shower."

"You won't have time," said her mother. "Please hurry and change."

"Why can't Carrie set the table?"

"Your sister's in bed. Her back and legs are burned rather severely. I want her to take it easy. She's going to the emergency room after we eat."

"Wimp," Allie mumbled.

She shed her maillot and used a wet washcloth and a towel to sponge off the rose oil. She thought the smell seemed fainter. It would have to do. She donned a T-shirt and shorts. Carrie's door was closed. She thought about taunting her sister but went on to the dining room.

While she placed plates and silverware, her father arrived in the kitchen. Based on his voice Allie realized he was upset about something.

"When that moron Jackson lost the sale," her father was saying, "we came up one lousy car short of our July sales quota. Dornhoefer's furious. He came to my office and told me to turn things around or else I could start looking for a job pushing a broom."

"Crap," Allie muttered. Without her sister to share the brunt of his anger, her father would have only her and her mother to pick on.

Before taking his first mouthful of meat, he put down his fork and turned to look at Allison, sniffing the air like a bloodhound. "What do I smell? Are you wearing perfume? Haven't I told you you're too young to use perfume?'

Allison shrank.

Walter faced his wife. "Did you give her permission to use some of yours?"

Regina, with a mixture of fear and bewilderment, shook her head. "No."

He pointed a finger at Allie. "What's going on, Allison?"

"I . . . I don't . . . I mean, I can't—" Her father terrified her when he acted like this.

He grabbed her wrist. Allison gasped.

"Walter!" Regina stared at him with wide eyes.

"Shut up!" he shot back. "You answer me, girl, or you're going to wish this day had never happened."

"Daddy!" Allie cried out, sobbing now, fearing the worst. If he found out she had sneaked—

"Mr. Mac . . . I . . . He . . ." She wailed and put her head down on the table as sobs shook her.

Regina sat bolt upright, mouth hanging open, eyes wide.

Walter stood suddenly; his chair tumbled backward. In two steps, he stood over his daughter, eyes blazing. "What are you saying? Did he put that stuff on your body?"

Allison howled. She tried to speak but could only cough and gasp, tears and mucous soaking her face and arms.

"You're scaring her!"

"Shut up, Regina!" Walter bent over Allison. "Tell me what happened, Allie," he said just above a whisper. He put his hand on her head. "It's alright. I'm not going to punish you, honey." Placing both hands on her shoulders, he gently pulled Allison upright.

She looked across at her mother, silently pleading for help, but she got none.

"Let me see if I can guess what happened. You went to see your friend, Mr. Mac, who likes you and teaches you and your sister things about chemistry. Is that right, dear?"

Allie stared at her mother, who looked away. "Uh . . . uh," She croaked, still fighting to recover her breath, her terror rising.

"And because he likes you, Mr. Mac told you he would show you how to make yourself smell pretty. So, he rubbed perfumed oil on your bod . . . on you."

Allie burst into fresh tears, shaking her head back and forth.

"What else did he do to you?" Her father boomed.

"Nothing!" she yelled. "Nothing. He didn't—"

"That's enough, Walt!" said Regina, finally moving to Allison.

"What's wrong?" Carin shouted from the top of the stairs. "What's the matter with Allie?"

"Your sister's all right, Carrie," Walter called, keeping his voice calm. "Your mother and I will handle it. Just go back to your room for a bit." He turned his harsh gaze on Regina. "Take Allison to the den and stay with her. Give her some water, maybe a couple of aspirin. I'll be back in a little while."

"Wait, where are you going? Walt!"

He didn't answer or spare them another look. The back door opened, then closed.

• • •

Lloyd MacDonald hung up the phone. He'd been talking with Lynn, who was in Morgantown for a weekend reunion with a close friend and college classmate. He had shared the good news that he, Bruce, and Rudy had finished flooring the third-floor sunroom. Once the floor was sanded, stained, and sealed and the room was painted, their addition would be complete.

Lynn had responded gaily, praising Lloyd for seeing the huge project through from beginning to end. *"Has it only been four years?"* she'd asked. They'd joked that it seemed more like four decades.

Before he showered off the sweat and dust, Lloyd visited the liquor cabinet and poured himself a Scotsman's portion of single malt whiskey. He recorked the bottle and was placing it on the shelf when the front doorbell chimed. Lloyd picked up the glass, sniffed the whiskey, and went to the door.

"Walt! Come in! Sorry, I'm rather unpresentable. Just heading to take a shower. Except for Lynn and the kids who worked today, you're the first to hear—"

"This isn't a social call, MacDonald." Harris stayed on the porch. "Did you rub perfumed oil on Allison's body this afternoon, Lloyd?" he asked, almost nonchalantly.

"Good Lord, no! What are you talking about?"

Walter pointed his index finger at Lloyd's face. "From now on neither Allison nor Carin will be allowed in your house or yard. I forbid you to speak to either of them, or to my wife," he said, his voice measured, surrealistically calm.

"What the hell are you talking about?" Lloyd asked again. "Where'd you get this cock-and-bull story? You know I'd never even think of touching your daughters! Who told you this? Surely you and Regina can't believe I'd do anything to harm your girls." Lloyd stared at him with a crinkled brow. "Walt, for God's sake," he implored, "what's going on?"

Harris turned and walked off the porch.

Dumbfounded, Lloyd watched him disappear around the corner of the house. After a moment, he slowly closed the front door and without knowing why, locked it.

He wandered into the kitchen and sat at the table, trying to recall the last time he had talked with Allie or Carrie. Lloyd couldn't say exactly when, but it hadn't been today. Bruce and Rudy had worked with him all day, except for about thirty minutes in the morning when he went to the basement workshop to put a new wooden handle on his hammer.

Lloyd picked up his glass but his hand shook, spilling scotch on the table. Using both hands, he drained the drink in two swallows. "Get hold of yourself," he said aloud. "You've nothing to be afraid of."

But Lloyd knew this was not necessarily true. Innocent men and women were accused and convicted of crimes all the time. He went back to the liquor cabinet, poured a full glass of whiskey, and brought the bottle to the table.

Lloyd sipped his whiskey. "Allie probably got into her mother's cologne and lied about it to escape punishment," he said to the nearly empty cut crystal glass. "She'll realize that was wrong, confess, and Walt will send Regina over here to make apologies and that'll end it."

Lloyd rubbed his eyes, wishing he really believed that scenario. He glanced at his watch. He needed to eat something and take a shower. He didn't want to go into an insulin tailspin brought on by the alcohol.

After eating a plate of salad greens and leftover cold chicken, he showered, finishing with two minutes under a spray of ice-cold water. He donned pajamas, put on a terry cloth robe, and went into the library, intending to resume reading *A Farewell to Arms*. After reading and rereading the same three sentences, Lloyd laid the book on the end table. He took off his glasses to rub the corners of his eyes. Unbidden, Walter's words and the eerie way he'd said them bubbled to the surface of Lloyd's mind.

He picked up the phone.

"Hi, honey," he said in what he meant to be a cheerful voice.

"Lloyd, are you okay? We just talked an hour ago. I'm always glad to hear from you, but—"

"Walter came to the front door a while ago."

"Our front door? Okay, what happened?"

Lloyd related the story, which Lynn interrupted with frequent questions and expletives.

"Listen, I'm coming home tonight. I'll tell Louise there's been a crisis at home and ask to reschedule later this summer. She'll understand without asking questions. We planned to meet in the lobby for drinks in a couple of minutes before heading out for dinner. I'll ring her with the news and pack up. I should be home in two hours."

"No, honey. That's unnecessary. I just needed to hear your voice. I'm fine. Look, this will blow over tomorrow. Monday, at the latest."

Calling her had been a mistake. Her immediate decision to cancel her time with her friend and drive home tonight only reinforced his knife-edge anxiety. In the end, he succeeded in persuading Lynn to stay put.

• • •

Lloyd climbed the stairs and made his way to Bruce's room. Through the closed door he heard the sound of Bill Haley and His Comets' lively up-tempo hit, "Shake, Rattle and Roll." He remained just outside the door, listening through the tenor sax and guitar riffs, the final chorus, and the drum-banging finale. Then he knocked.

"Come on in, Dad," Bruce called.

Without bothering to preface the situation, Lloyd told his son of the accusation Walter Harris had made.

Bruce's face registered bewilderment, disbelief, and anger in rapid succession. He jumped up, slamming his desktop with his fist. "That son of a bitch! I'll break his damn neck! And Allison. She's a sneaky little snoop!" Bruce shook his head. "About two weeks ago, Alex said he chased a girl from your bedroom. From his description,

I knew it was Allison. I told Walter, and he said he'd take care of it."

"You didn't say anything to me about this."

"I didn't want to bother you. Besides, you've befriended her and Carin, and I thought why let this incident cloud that friendship? Honest, I thought she wouldn't do it again. But she did." Bruce pounded his fist into his palm. "And after all you and Mom have done for her and her sister. She's nothing but a—"

"Bruce," Lloyd said gently, "she's only a child. Think back. When you were her age, do you remember snooping in our dresser drawers out of curiosity and telling your mother a fib when she caught you in the act?"

Bruce appeared not to have heard the question. Instead, he clenched and unclenched his hands. "Just let Rudy and me take care of this. We'll—"

"No, son. Please. Sit down. For all we know, this is nothing more than Walt jumping to conclusions. We don't know if Allison was in the house this afternoon. She probably got into her mother's cologne, and her parents smelled it on her. Like any kid, she told a lie to avoid being punished. I expect by tomorrow, Walt and Regina will come over to apologize. This has hurt me—that's a fact—but I believe—"

"Dad, I admire your trusting nature. It's a rare and wonderful quality. But in the face of a false and serious accusation, it could be a dangerous flaw." He leaned toward his father, trying to capture his gaze. "Analyze and deal with this the same way you'd evaluate a problem of organic chemistry. Think of this accusation as a volatile chemical that may explode . . . that's how I see it. You once told me that a chemist couldn't guess about a problem because that was asking for trouble. It's the same thing with this. It may blow over, but it may blow up."

Lloyd listened, his arms dangled between his knees, hands clasped. Bruce went on.

"You didn't ask for my advice, but here it is anyway. Don't trust Harris or his family. The fact that he accused you of molesting his daughter proves he's dangerous. Look, unless they're braindead, he and his wife know you could never mistreat his kids. Treat this bastard the same way you treat toxic chemicals. Don't underestimate him, Dad."

Bruce stood, arms wide. Lloyd readily accepted his bear hug. "I love you, Dad. We're going to fight this. Harris is going to rue the day he messed with us." Bruce kissed him on the cheek.

Lloyd couldn't risk saying anything. He squeezed Bruce. Then he left, closing the door behind him. In the hall, he leaned against the wall as tears coursed over his cheeks.

Downstairs, Lloyd lit his pipe, but the usually mellow sensation of the smoke in his mouth was replaced by a bitter harshness. He emptied the bowl into an ashtray, then turned out the lights and turned in.

For hours, Lloyd fought for sleep, his mouth dry ashes, his mind racing and reeling. He wished he hadn't insisted on Lynn staying in Morgantown. Her presence would have comforted him, although he knew she would've been spitting mad. With a weak smile, Lloyd pictured his firebrand wife ripping back and forth across the floor, swearing like a bandit biker. Maybe she wouldn't have induced a peaceful night after all.

After uncounted trips to the bathroom, Lloyd gave in. He turned on the bedside lamp, shoved his feet into slippers, and went down to the library. It took some searching, but he found the novel he wanted: *Silas Marner* by George Eliot. In just six pages, Lloyd fell asleep.

• • •

By the time Walter returned from his confrontation with Lloyd, his dinner had cooled. He pushed his plate aside. Allison hadn't eaten, despite repeated entreaties from her mother. She sat at the table, dazed. Unresponsive. Walter applied honey, asking if there was anything he could do for her, was she feeling better? Allison seemed not to hear.

He switched to vinegar. He took her chin in his hand and jerked her face to the side, so she had to look at him.

"Listen to me," he said. "Mr. MacDonald rubbed perfume on your back and your bum. That is what happened, and that is what you will say whenever you are asked. That is the story, and you will stick to it if you know what's good for you. Do you understand?"

Allison stared, eyes wide with terror.

"Isn't that how it happened, Allison? What's the matter? You don't want to talk about it? Not in front of your mom? We can go to your room and have some private time right now, just you and me, if you want to tell me different." She wrenched her head in a frenzied attempt to twist from his grasp. "No, I didn't think so." Walter released her. "Go take a bath and get ready for bed."

• • •

The living room lights burned late in the Harris home. Walter and Regina had been locked in verbal combat for hours.

"I just can't believe Lloyd would harm either of our daughters in this way," Regina said.

Walter unlaced and removed a shoe. "He didn't," he said, scratching the bottom of his foot.

"What?"

"Remember a couple of weeks ago when Bruce came over and asked to talk with me?"

Regina remembered.

"He told me your daughter had been caught pawing through Lynn's beauty stuff. When I smelled perfume on her tonight and saw her terrified reaction, I put two and two together. Allie couldn't stop thinking about the fancy things she saw. Today, while you were busy taking care of Carin, Allie went back to Lynn's bedroom. I imagine she got scared she'd be caught again, so she was hurrying, not paying attention. She spilled some perfume, which she rubbed on herself."

"Did Allie tell you all of this?"

"No, but how else could it have happened? You said you can't believe Lloyd could have done such a thing. I know the type of guy who messes with kids. Lloyd's definitely not the type."

Regina looked at him, her hand covering her open mouth.

"Don't give me that look. You have to take advantage when an opportunity to score gets handed to you." He laughed. "You should've seen Lloyd's face. I scared the crap out of him."

"Walter, you lied. You wrongly accused a nice man of a serious crime. Please, it's not too late. For your own sake, go over and tell him you made a mistake, that—"

"Nothing doing. And I warn you, Regina, don't even think of telling him. I convinced Allison to say Lloyd put that perfume on her. She knows what to say if anyone asks her."

"My God, Walt! What have you done to our daughter?"

"Don't you mean 'what have I done for our family'? Why do you think I'm doing this? The MacDonalds are loaded. He won't want to contest this. It's his word against an innocent girl's. He'll settle out of court for big bucks—enough to finance our daughters' college educations, at least."

"It's a sin. Can't you see that?"

Walter feigned hurt surprise. "Since when is it a sin to make things better for your family?"

"It's wrong because of how you're doing this. Think what this will do to Lloyd and Lynn. They've been good to us, to Carin and Allison. Lloyd really likes them. This will kill him."

Walter tugged on his shoe and retied it. "Stop. You're making me cry." He walked to the window, pulled back the drape, and looked out at the darkness.

"Tell Lloyd. Or I will." Regina glared at Walt, who let the drape slip from his fingers.

He turned. "No, you won't. I falsely accused him of a serious crime. Are you so stupid to think Lloyd and Lynn will just laugh it off? Let bygones be bygones? Their attorney will stomp me into a little piece of hamburger meat. Dornhoefer will make sure I'll never get a position with another car dealership unless it's putting air in tires. I'll likely go to jail. The cushy lifestyle you enjoy—two cars, fashionable clothing, fancy friends—gone. Kiss the house goodbye. You and the girls will have to live with your parents. We're the ones who'll get killed."

"You can't say for certain Lloyd will sue us. If we don't go to the police or spread this lie, if we keep it just between our households, why would he—"

"You dumb shit," he cut in. "Do you think Lloyd just sat around twiddling his thumbs after I left? He told Lynn. Bruce, too. Lloyd holds the Ace of Spades. He's innocent. He already called his attorney, or he'll call him tomorrow at the latest."

"He might not. He might think—I don't know—he might think that this is some misunderstanding, that we'll acknowledge our mistake and apologize, which he'd accept. I'm sure of it."

"Right, that will happen—when lobsters learn to whistle." Walter stood above Regina, seated on the sofa. "I'm done talking. Unless you want to lose everything we have, everything I've done for you and the girls, you'll keep your mouth shut. Understand?"

She bowed her head. Her hand went to the pearls around her neck. "Yes."

CHAPTER 10

Sunday, July 17, 1955

A robin warbled his rain song from the oak tree. A squirrel did a masterful high wire act on the phone line leading to the carriage house. Rain drummed the windows and puddled the grass and soil. At breakfast, Lloyd and Bruce discussed the next day's work schedule as if nothing had happened.

Lloyd needed the distraction of work right away, but it was Sunday. Tomorrow, while Bruce and Rudy filled nail holes in the sunroom floor, Nicky would sand, wipe off the dust, and put the prime coat on the French doors and two windows. Seventeen-year-old Nicky had a professional's touch for painting trim. Lloyd wanted her to apply the finish coat to the doors and windows.

"Have you signed the contract with the painters yet?" Bruce asked.

Lloyd sat staring into his coffee cup.

"Dad?"

Lloyd lifted his head. "Sorry, Son. No. It's scheduled for this Friday."

"What if we painted the sunroom? Nicky knows how to cut in around the ceiling and edges, and Rudy and I could finish it in a day—less than a day. It'd save you and Mom some money."

"That's an inviting thought. You three could handle it." Lloyd emptied his cup and took it to the sink.

"Are you expecting someone? You keep looking out the window."

"Nope. Just watching the rain. Lord knows we've had more than our share the past few days." He returned to the table.

"So, we'll do it, then?"

Lloyd had picked up a teaspoon and was examining it as if he'd discovered a rare fossil.

His son looked at him with concern. "Are you all right, Dad?

Lloyd placed the spoon on the table, aligning it with the edge of a place mat. He tried for a reassuring smile. "Sure."

"What's your answer? About us painting the sunroom, I mean." The younger MacDonald began to worry his father was in the beginning phase of insulin shock. He looked intently at him.

"Tell you what," Lloyd said after a few seconds. "Let's see how the work goes this week. I want the floor finished before starting on the paint. And that's a big job. Using a floor sander and getting the stain and sealer coats on—we're going to have our work cut out for us. With the humidity as high as it's been the last couple days, drying time will take longer than usual—two, maybe three weeks, I think."

The kitchen doorbell buzzed. Lloyd flinched as if to evade a blow.

"Hey, Nicky," Bruce called. "Come on in. Door's open. You're looking good for a soaked kitten."

"Thanks, I think. How's the practice going?" she teased.

"I think I'm ready to invite you to attend the premiere performance," Bruce said, then added, "It'll have to wait awhile, though."

Nicky's smile faded. She tilted her head to the side, puzzled. "Okay."

If she noticed Mr. Mac had avoided giving her his usual friendly hug, Nicky gave no sign. "Sorry about tracking in the wet stuff. Father's still closing up at church, so I ran over to see if I could borrow *Jane Eyre*. I'm almost finished, and with this rain, I'll have it done by this evening and return it when I come to work tomorrow.

We're nearing the finish line, right, Mr. Mac?"

"What's that? Oh, yes. I hope there'll be no, uh, problems, or anything to keep us from—" His voice trailed off.

"Don't you worry, Mr. Mac. You've got the first team with you," Nicky said brightly.

Lloyd managed a slight grin. He led the way to the library, where Nicky retrieved Charlotte Brontë's masterpiece.

"Thanks, Mr. Mac. Sorry to run, but I need to get home before Father. See you tomorrow!"

Nicky looked at Bruce. "So long," she said, then hurried outside. *What did his eyes show?* Nicky brooded. *Anger? Yes, a lot. Melancholy? No doubt about it. Mr. Mac isn't himself either. What's going on?* she wondered. Rain pelted her. Nicky took off, *Jane Eyre* clutched to her breast.

• • •

Lynn returned that afternoon. As Lloyd had expected, she was furious. Bruce joined them in the living room. Lynn listened as Lloyd repeated the details of his conversation with Walter Harris. When he finished, she jumped up, heading for the back door.

Lloyd intercepted her. "Don't go over there, honey. They'll use your anger against us."

"I'm going to raise hell, and I want Walt and that chickenshit Regina to feel the full brunt of it. I'm not going to let them even *think* they can get away with this."

Bruce came over and put a hand on his mother's shoulder. "I know how you feel, Mom. I'd like to squash him like the poisonous little spider he is. But Dad's right. That'll just throw gasoline on the fire. Raising hell might push Harris over the edge."

Bruce and Lloyd watched her wallop a pillow decorating a nearby chair as she ripped back and forth across the floor. She had smoked three Pall Malls and a fourth was clenched unlit between her locked lips. Lloyd stayed out of her way, hoping the temperature would cool before a more violent explosion happened.

Bruce took advantage of a momentary lull in the eye of Hurricane Lynn as she searched for her cigarette lighter. "Tell you what," he said, rubbing his hands together. "Let's go to Bridgeville and have dinner at Wright's. No seafood restaurant does scallops better, not to mention their crab bisque. My treat."

Afterward, Lynn realized Bruce's idea had been a good one, even though Lloyd had to help cover the bill. She wouldn't admit it aloud, but she knew Walter Harris held all the cards. Provoking him would have been a serious mistake.

CHAPTER 11

Friday, July 22, 1955

The door chimes rang while Lloyd was shaving. Rain pelted the bathroom window, punctuated by lightning and rolling thunder. Toweling off the lather, Lloyd descended the stairs to the living room. As he prepared to step onto the landing and make the turn down the final set of stairs, Lloyd saw his visitors through the fanlight above the door. Two Mount Lebanon police officers in raincoats waited on the front porch.

It had been almost a week since Walter Harris made the astonishing accusation that Lloyd had rubbed aromatic oil on nine-year-old Allison, and Lloyd had begun to hope it had blown over.

Steady, Lloyd told himself as he made the last two steps. *Don't jump to conclusions. You don't know why they're here.*

He pulled open the door. "Good morning," he said.

"Good morning, sir," said the older officer. "Are you Mr. Lloyd MacDonald?"

"Yes."

"I'm Sergeant Armstrong, and this is Officer Blackmon." Both men produced identification wallets and held them out for MacDonald's inspection. "May we come in, sir?"

"Of course." Lloyd stepped aside. He closed the door behind them. He noticed he still held the shaving towel and self-consciously tossed it onto the steps.

"Lloyd MacDonald," said Sergeant Armstrong, "we have a warrant for your arrest, issued by Judge Frederick Tate, on the charge of sexual abuse of a minor, Pennsylvania Code 2907.05."

"You can't be serious. Sexual abuse? That's preposterous! Who made the charge?" Lloyd knew, but he wanted to hear the police say it.

"Sir, please put on a shirt and shoes and get your personal identification. Officer Blackmon will go with you until you're ready."

"You mean I must leave right now?"

"Yes sir." To his partner he said, "All right, Blackie."

"Let's go to your bedroom, sir," Blackmon said with a hand on Lloyd's arm.

In the bedroom, Lloyd put on a shirt. He fumbled with the shirt buttons but eventually finished the task. He was all thumbs tying his shoes.

"Your identification, sir. You will need your driver's license."

Lloyd shoved his wallet into his rear pocket, and they went back to the front entrance, where Sergeant Armstrong waited.

"Bruce," said Lloyd, "He's my son. He went to the grocery store to buy some milk. I need to write him a note."

"Turn around, Mr. MacDonald."

As Lloyd swung to his left, Armstrong grabbed his right wrist, pulled his left arm into place, and handcuffed him.

"Wait a minute!" Lloyd protested, "I'm not a criminal, for God's sake. I'm not going to fight or run. This isn't necessary!"

"Here, Mr. MacDonald. I'll drape this jacket over your shoulders," said Blackmon.

The officer escorted Lloyd out the door and across the porch, holding on to his belt. Armstrong walked a few steps behind.

At the Mount Lebanon Police Department, Blackmon unlocked the handcuffs, and Sergeant Armstrong brought MacDonald to stand before another officer seated behind a desk. The officer repeated that Lloyd was being booked on a charge of sexual abuse of a child. "The child in question is Allison Harris, age nine, daughter of Walter and Regina Harris." Lloyd, when asked, gave his full name, address, and date of birth. Then he was fingerprinted and photographed. They confiscated his wallet and set of keys. Lloyd signed the inventory form.

This is a dream, thought Lloyd, *a bad dream*. He pushed his glasses to the top of his head and rubbed his eyes. *No, it's real. Get hold of yourself*, he said to himself. *Think*.

A short, blocky, dark-haired man wearing a blue shirt open at the collar approached. "Mr. MacDonald, I'm Detective John Arkelian. I want to ask you some questions. Let's go where we can have a private conversation. Just follow me, sir."

"After I phone my wife," Lloyd said firmly. "Where's a phone I can use?"

"There's no need for that, Mr. MacDonald. This is routine stuff."

"Not for me it isn't," Lloyd retorted. "I'm entitled to call my wife, am I not?"

Arkelian narrowed his eyes. "All in good time. May I call you Lloyd?"

"No. Look, detective, I'm not answering your questions until I get in touch with my wife, and not even then without benefit of counsel."

Lloyd managed to reach Lynn at Carstairs Arts and Crafts in Wexford, a town about twenty-six miles north of Pittsburgh. She advised him to sit tight, not to answer any questions, and told him she loved him. Then she phoned their attorney.

"That's absolute bullshit," he said. "Anyone who knows Lloyd knows it's bullshit. You know I'm not a criminal attorney. But I can recommend one. Meredith Goldsmith. She's bright. A tough bulldog. Meredith fights tooth and nail for her clients. There's no one I'd rather have in your corner."

• • •

The thunderstorm blew off to the east, leaving Mount Lebanon with shiny wet streets and puddled sidewalks. Ninety minutes later, Meredith Goldsmith, a red-haired thunderstorm, strode into the Mount Lebanon Police Department to meet with Lloyd MacDonald. Goldsmith, tall, graceful, with long curly hair pulled back in a ponytail, presented her credentials to the policeman behind the desk.

Detective Arkelian appeared and introduced himself.

"Hello, Detective Arkelian," said Goldsmith. "My client's waiting. I need some time to confer with Mr. MacDonald. Is there a room we may use?"

Detective Arkelian took in Goldsmith's green eyes and her alabaster complexion. She was the type of redhead born without a freckle. "Of course, counselor," he said with a smile.

"Has Mr. MacDonald had anything to eat? It's nearly one-fifteen, and as you know—or you should know—he's diabetic."

"Uh, no, he hasn't eaten."

Meredith Goldsmith's fierce green eyes snapped between the detective and the officer behind the desk. "That's unacceptable. I need the use of a phone and a copy of the local business phone book to order some food. Unless you want to have my client go into diabetic shock here in the station."

The officer hastened to accommodate her. Meredith dialed the number of a local deli and placed an order for chicken salad and a fruit plate to be delivered to the station.

Goldsmith eyed the officer. "When the food arrives, please bring it to Mr. MacDonald without delay." She filled a paper cup with water from the cooler. "Okay, detective, how about showing me that room?"

She followed him to a small room furnished with a wooden table and two plastic chairs. In a few minutes, Lloyd MacDonald was ushered into the room by a uniformed police officer.

"Please remove his handcuffs. He's not a threat, and he's going to be eating lunch."

"I wasn't told to do that," the officer said.

Meredith jumped to her feet, brushed past him, and strode into the hall. "Arkelian!"

Detective Arkelian appeared.

"Please tell the officer to remove the handcuffs."

He nodded to the uniformed cop, and Lloyd's hands were freed. He rubbed his wrists, encouraging the blood to return.

After the two policemen exited, Meredith extended her hand. She introduced herself and explained how she'd come to be his attorney. For the next hour, while Lloyd drank the water and ate the chicken and fruit, she asked questions and took extensive notes. Meredith sized up his physical and emotional state. Lloyd looked tired, about at the end of his rope.

"Okay, Lloyd, I have enough information for now. Let's get you out of here. First, we're going to tell Detective Arkelian you're not answering any questions. In fact, I don't want you to say anything at all unless I tell you it's okay. You and your wife will have to post bail. The charge falls under the category of a third-degree felony. I'll demand to get copies of the affidavit Mr. Harris filed against you."

Lynn was waiting for them in the visitors' area. She had withdrawn $15,000 from her business checking account—the amount required for bail—to secure Lloyd's release. The three of them left the police station. Lloyd blinked in the afternoon sunlight, scarcely comprehending what had transpired. He wanted his pipe and a stiff whiskey, but most of all, Lloyd wanted to sleep.

"Let's sit on the bench over there in the shade. Just for a few minutes. I know you need to get home and rest." With a handkerchief she wiped off the raindrops.

Lloyd sat heavily, staring into space. Lynn reached over and took his hand. Briefly, Goldsmith related the possible next steps, which included assignment of a prosecutor, scheduling a date for a preliminary hearing, and getting Lloyd's trial on the court docket. Lynn smoked, inhaling furiously. *Calm down*, she scolded herself.

Pay attention. Being enraged won't do us any good. Listen to her.

Meredith released her ponytail and shook out her curls. "I'm going to request a meeting with Judge Tate to get your bail amount reduced. The probable cause evidence presented by the police is an incoherent nine-year-old girl and a one-piece swimsuit with a faint aromatic stain on the rear. Neither Harris nor his daughter presented any evidence that you improperly touched her. I know his attorney. He always pushes the envelope."

She looked tenderly at Lloyd and Lynn. "Listen, I'll be honest. You're facing a long, difficult time with this. You're going to find out who your real friends are, and there'll be some surprises, guaranteed." Meredith took Lloyd's other hand and squeezed. "You can count on me to fight for you. But you've got to fight, too. As for Harris—anyone who would put their daughter through this is dangerous and despicable. We're not going to underestimate him. He's out to get you and everything you have."

• • •

Bruce met them at the kitchen door. It was obvious his parents had been put through the wringer.

"I won't let this happen to you, Dad. Harris is evil. He needs someone to knock some sense into him, and I know just the guys to do it. He'll find out what happens to anyone who—"

"Son, stop. This isn't who you are. I know you're angry, but even expressing these ideas doesn't help. We have to channel our anger into how best to use the justice system to win this case."

"I don't know about you guys," Lynn said hastily, "but I'm starving. Let's have a late lunch, or an early supper. I made some potato salad and stuck it in the fridge this morning. Bruce, while I put the final touches on the salad, will you set the table and fill a pitcher with ice water?"

When he finished eating, Lloyd excused himself, claiming he needed a nap. After he made his way upstairs, Lynn and Bruce cleared the table and stowed the dishes in the sink.

"Let's go to the library," Lynn said. "I need to flop and have a cigarette."

She and Bruce sprawled in the chairs before the fireplace. Lynn lit up, blowing smoke toward the ceiling. For a long minute, neither spoke.

"I'll kill him. I swear I will. He's a dangerous lunatic." Bruce smacked his knee with his fist. "He knows damn well Dad didn't do this. He wouldn't even think—couldn't—" He covered his eyes. Tears seeped between his fingers.

Lynn stubbed out her cigarette. "You seem determined to commit murder."

Bruce raised his head. "Don't try to talk me out of it," he snapped.

"It would be a terrible mistake, but I'm not going to argue with you. I do want to get your thoughts, though. What's your plan? How do you propose to kill him, and where? And when?"

"I don't know, most likely shoot him next time he comes out of the house."

"Well, that will be a short murder investigation. The taxpayers will like that. Maybe you and your dad could share a cell," Lynn's tone had an edge she didn't intend.

"I haven't worked out the details, Mom. Listen, this is weird, talking with you as if I'm planning . . . I don't know, a surprise party or something."

"Well, it is a surprise party of sorts," Lynn said. "You've got a lot of things to think about, decisions to make before you act."

"Such as?"

"How will killing Walter Harris help your dad? Or me? What do you think it would do to us as a family for the rest of our lives, Bruce? Your goals, your future, your *life* would be over. In effect, killing Walter Harris will kill your dad and me. That despicable excuse for a man isn't worth the cost, Son. I know you're angry and worried about your dad. But please, honey, I couldn't bear to lose you. We'll win this case. Please, Son."

She sobbed and buried her face in her hands. Bruce knelt next to her chair and wrapped his arms around her, holding her close.

• • •

That night, Lloyd suffered through the first of what would become weeks of sleep-deprivation. His mind raced, taking him places he didn't want to go.

Okay, thought Lloyd, *suppose for the sake of argument I'm a pervert and wanted to assault Allie. Would even an obsessed, deplorable pervert try anything with two teens working in the same house? Absurd.* He hated even thinking it, but the truth was, there had been no opportunity for Lloyd or the boys to hurt Allie. He made a mental note to tell Meredith that Bruce and Rudy had been working nearby that day.

Nauseated by the hypothetical, he willed his rampant thoughts to focus on Harris.

Why? What motive could Walter and Regina Harris have in persecuting him? How could Regina think such a thing of him?

Or does she?

Regina had asked Lloyd to watch Allie and Carrie while she ran errands only the day before the alleged incident. She'd even thanked him for his patience with the girls and for his genuine interest in them.

As for Walter, Lloyd knew him to be greedy and envious. Harris' own words, not only to Lloyd, but to Dave Marberry and other neighbors, revealed this.

But was that reason enough to make a serious criminal charge against Lloyd? Reason enough to drag his little girl into this mess? Lloyd wasn't a psychologist, but even he could see that Walter's behavior was heinous. Didn't he realize the psychological damage he may be doing to Allie? And Carrie as well. And for what?

As he lay next to Lynn, who managed to sleep, though fitfully, Lloyd went over the infrequent conversations he'd had with Walter Harris since he'd moved in.

About a month earlier, he and Lynn had entertained the Harris family at a backyard cookout. While the girls captured lightning bugs in a jar, Lynn had taken Regina inside to show her latest craft project. The two men had remained on the patio.

Walter had complained about the high property taxes in Mount Lebanon. As Lloyd recalled the conversation, he'd pointed out to Walter that the return on tax revenue for Mount Lebanon residents was a nationally acclaimed school district.

How had Walter responded?

Lloyd looked at the bedroom ceiling, concentrating as the conversation took shape in his mind. Walter had said something along the lines of, *"It's all well and good for you to think like that with the lifestyle you lead, but you don't have the problem of paying college tuition for two daughters."*

The remark had surprised him. From Lloyd's random observations, the Harrises enjoyed a comfortable, if not extravagant, lifestyle. Regina and Walt had entertained Lynn and Lloyd just once. Lynn had remarked that Walter's suits and shirts were tailored. Even Lloyd had noticed Regina wore expensive clothes and jewelry.

They had two cars—perhaps not unusual for the manager of a car dealership, but Lloyd couldn't think of any other family he knew who had multiple vehicles. Not even Jim and Bev.

Some weeks ago, Walter had tried to persuade Lynn it was time to buy a new car, suggesting he could see her in a Cadillac Coupe DeVille or a Brougham. When she told him she wasn't interested in a luxury car, Walter had asked, "Why not? You probably have the money to pay cash for a Coupe DeVille."

And at Jim and Bev's party, Walter had insinuated his level of income was below that of Lloyd and Lynn. *How had he put it? Walter joined Dave and me and wanted to talk about the addition to our home. He claimed that unlike Lynn and me, he wouldn't have the money to finance the first floor.*

That's it, Lloyd concluded, raising himself onto an elbow. *Greed.*

Harris wants a large financial settlement. He probably doesn't care if I'm acquitted or sentenced to a prison term as long as he gets our money. If the criminal case doesn't work for him, he'll pursue a civil suit.

Somehow, this realization calmed his mind, and he lay back and slept.

CHAPTER 12

Thursday, July 28, 1955

Lynn and Lloyd overslept, and after a hasty breakfast, Lynn kissed Lloyd, reminded him to take the cod from the freezer to thaw, grabbed her purse and keys, and hurried to the door.

It was opening day of the annual Western Pennsylvania Antique Dealers Exhibit at the Venango County Fairgrounds in Franklin, Pennsylvania.

"Carolyn and Arlene will be fidgeting by the time I get to Franklin," she said over her shoulder. "They always want to be there when the fairground gates open. Love you, dear!"

As Lynn headed out of Mount Lebanon, she felt none of her usual enthusiasm at the prospect of exploring the wares of the dealers. Lloyd's plight occupied her mind.

She liked Meredith Goldsmith, and had complete confidence in her ability. However, Lynn worried this ordeal would take its toll on them, especially Lloyd. He was physically and emotionally strong. His intelligence would be an asset as he faced this trouble. Still, this had rocked his deep-seated trust of others. Maybe she should have called off today's outing.

"No, damn it," she said aloud, "I need to get away from it." She couldn't help Lloyd if she was running out of gas. To emphasize the thought, Lynn pushed the accelerator.

• • •

Lloyd emptied the coffee grounds, rinsed the glass pot, and put the breakfast dishes in the sink. While he waited for Bruce and Rudy to get back from the tool dealer with the rented floor sander, Lloyd studied the blueprints, even though he'd committed them to memory. Dave had perfectly interpreted the written schematic Lloyd and Lynn developed. These four years of working to convert the prints into a finished project had been fun and rewarding. He placed his hand on the blueprint. *I'm not going to allow that greedy liar to stop us,* he resolved.

He glanced out the window. A young man dismounted his bike and booted the kickstand. He bounded up the steps. Lloyd opened the door, smiling broadly.

"David! David Elliott. How great to see you! Come in. Did Bruce shanghai you into working today?"

"No, sir. Dad told me what happened, and I had to see you." The young man's eyes fastened on Lloyd. "If you don't mind my saying, Mr. Mac, this guy lied through his teeth. Grandmother Elliott used to say, 'No lie lives forever.' I believe that. But most of all, I believe in you. There isn't a mean or malicious bone in your body. You healed me last fall when I was a helpless wreck. Hell—I mean, heck—just by listening to me all those afternoons and nights, you helped me find myself. I'll never be able to thank you enough. I don't know if there's any way I can help—testify as a character witness, write letters to the editor—but if I can, just say the word. I haven't touched base with any of the other kids, but I know everyone who worked here would walk barefoot over live coals to help you."

Lloyd touched his eyes with a handkerchief. "Sorry. Must've gotten some sawdust in my eye. Thank you, David. I deeply appreciate your kindness and willingness to help. I'll tell Meredith Goldsmith, my attorney. She may want to contact you. She's a fighter like you,

Dave. If you hadn't fought through the psychological demons you were dealing with, nothing I could have said or done would have amounted to a lead nickel." Lloyd rested a hand on David's shoulder. "Have I heard correctly that you're about to leave for Gettysburg Seminary?"

"Yes, sir. Matter of fact, I have to register August 12. Classes start the following week." David nearly blurted out how nervous he was, since he hadn't read the Bible much, and was in no way saintly. He stopped himself. *What are you, nuts? You're going to whine about nerves over seminary classes when he's facing possible disgrace and prison?*

Instead, he said, "When I find out my address in Gettysburg, I'll let Bruce know so he can inform your attorney that I'll come back to testify if she wants me to."

The rattling clank and bark of Rudy's rusting pickup rolling down the driveway interrupted their conversation. Lloyd picked up his work gloves and opened the door. Rudy and Bruce slid the heavy sander to the tailgate.

"Hi, Bruce! What say, Rudy? Need some help?"

It required the strength of all three young men to lug the machine to the third floor. When they had recovered their normal breathing, Bruce asked David if he was staying to help.

"Geez, Bruce." David chuckled. "Don't you remember what a master carpenter I was? How many pounds of nails I bent? How many board feet of lumber I cut too short or too long?"

"No, I remember, pal. I just thought Rudy and I could use some laughs." Bruce grinned. "I'll get the tools and sandpaper rolls," he said to Rudy, then clattered down the stairs, David with him.

"Seriously, Dave, thanks for talking with Dad. He's doing pretty well, considering. He has a damn good attorney, and he and Mom believe in her a hundred percent." Bruce clapped him on the back. "Hey, do you think you'll have a chance to have a beer with Rudy and me some night before you head to Gettysburg?"

"I think that can be arranged." David smiled. "I'll give you a call." With a wave, he took off for home on his bike.

• • •

Before Bruce had a chance to make it back inside, two Mount Lebanon police officers approached the rear patio. Bruce shouted, "Dad! Will you come down, please?"

Lloyd appeared at the back door, and Bruce slipped in behind him.

"Good morning, Mr. MacDonald. I'm Officer Green, and this is Officer Ross." He held up a paper. "This is a search warrant, which gives us permission to search your premises." Officer Green extended the warrant to Lloyd, who refused to take it or even look at it.

"I'm calling my attorney," he said evenly. "Kindly wait there."

"Sir!" Officer Ross called, but Lloyd closed the door.

"Dad, don't do anything foolish. We need to let them in. Call Goldsmith." Bruce opened the door again.

The officers, who both carried plastic bags, split up. Ross headed for the carriage house, while Green headed upstairs.

"Okay, Lloyd," Meredith said. "Stay calm. Please put one of them on the phone."

Her conversation with Officer Green was brief.

"Judge Tate issued the warrant yesterday evening," Meredith told Lloyd. "It's legitimate, but I'm going to lodge a protest. This is nothing but a fishing expedition. They don't have any specific items they're looking for. That stretches the purpose of a warrant too far. Tate's going to hear about it.

"When they collect whatever they think is relevant, the law requires them to show you what they have and present you with a detailed list, which you sign if you're satisfied. And Lloyd? Be cool."

The high-pitched howl of the belt sander filled the house. Lloyd sat, elbows on the table, his clasped hands supporting his chin. Officer Ross entered; his examination of the carriage house completed. His bag held only one item—a pair of soiled cotton gardening gloves. Ross passed through the kitchen and headed up the stairs.

Twenty-five minutes later, the two officers stood before Lloyd. Bruce had followed them to the kitchen and stood next to his father.

"Mr. MacDonald, we're finished here for today," Officer Green said. "We have confiscated these items." He set them on the table one by one. "One pair of stained cotton gloves, two spray bottles of skin moisturizer, one jar of makeup removal cream, three bottles of cologne, one perfume mister tube, one two-ounce bottle of perfume with a misting top, and one tube of, uh—"

"Vaginal lubricant," Lloyd deadpanned.

Green dumped the contents of the second bag onto the table.

Lloyd started. "What's this? Why have you bagged my underwear?"

"Five pairs of white briefs. For the record, sir, we are not obligated to give reasons." "Five pairs of white briefs with residue of an unidentified substance." Officer Green turned to Officer Ross. "Do you have the inventory form?"

Ross put the paper on the table in front of Lloyd and handed him a pen.

CHAPTER 13

Friday, August 5, 1955

Lloyd picked up the extension in the library. "Hello, this is Lloyd."

"Hi, Lloyd. It's Meredith. Just wanted to share some information. As I mentioned to you and Lynn, the state's attorney assigned Patrick Walsh as the prosecutor to handle our case. I don't know him, so I'll ask around to learn what I can about him; is he a tight ass . . . sorry, Lloyd. I mean—"

"I know what a tight ass is."

"Right. Also, is he overly ambitious, or is Walsh a reasonable attorney we can expect to be fair? Usually, it takes two or three weeks for a prosecutor to decide whether to prosecute you for the charge. Walsh also has the authority to add charges or remove them. Next, the defense attorney would reach out to the prosecutor to see if something might be worked out—you know, to plead guilty to a lesser charge. I'm not going to do that. You're not guilty of anything. Period. End of discussion."

"Thank you, Meredith, for pursuing this course."

"One thing more about the timeline. If Walsh is a typical prosecutor, he'll ask for an arraignment hearing in about three weeks to a month. Perhaps sooner. The arraignment is when the defendant pleads guilty or not guilty. You won't have to appear, because I'm pleading you not guilty."

• • •

Lynn got home just after four and tossed her purse and car keys on the kitchen counter.

"May I fix you a drink?" Lloyd asked.

"Just ice water."

"I brewed a pitcher of MacDonald iced tea if you'd rather have it."

"Perfect, sweetheart."

He poured two glasses and moved toward the door.

"No, not on the patio," Lynn said. "I don't want to sit where those two girls can see us. Let's go into the living room."

Lloyd related the gist of his phone call with Meredith. Lynn agreed that pleading guilty to a lesser charge was out of the question.

"Meredith's a godsend," Lloyd said. "She's tough. Nobody's going to push her around. We're in good hands."

Lynn agreed. "This tea hits the spot. I like the inclusion of orange juice and fresh mint."

Lloyd reported it had been a good week of work. Bruce and Rudy had made steady progress with the belt sander. Nicky and Bruce had assembled, sanded, and applied the first coat of varnish to the bookshelves, which would be mounted on the walls of the guest bedroom and Lloyd's office in the sunroom.

He chuckled. "I think Nicky has our son flummoxed. She flirts in the most subtle ways, and he doesn't know what to make of it."

"Nicky has a crush on Bruce, but he doesn't see it yet. He will eventually, if he's anything like you."

"I would've had to be blind not to see your flirtations," Lloyd needled.

She picked up a newspaper to throw, but a column headline caught her eye. The current edition of the weekly *Mount Lebanon Respondent* included a brief article about Lloyd's arrest. Lynn crushed the paper between her hands and threw it on the floor.

"Hey," Lloyd said. "Meredith told us to expect the publicity. Our friends will realize this is a false accusation. Those who don't know me may conclude I'm guilty, but since I don't know them, it's no skin off my nose."

Lynn got up from the sofa and stormed out to the kitchen window to check out the source of the repeated dull thudding sounds coming from outside. Allison and Carin were kicking a soccer ball in their backyard. "That lying little shit. I'd like to kick her into the middle of next week."

Lloyd went to her side and put an arm around her. "Honey, take it easy. It's going to be alright." But his family's emotional state, including his, belied his reassuring words. He was under no illusions. Being charged with a felony, especially a felony involving a nine-year-old girl, was the most frightening thing he'd ever faced.

"It's Friday," Lloyd reminded Lynn. "Our date night. Let's go to Pescado's for some Mexican and margaritas. Lord knows I could use a margarita or three."

"I don't think that's a good idea, sweetheart. We've got this accusation hanging over us and yet we're seen dining and drinking at a local restaurant as if nothing's happened?"

Lloyd pursed his lips and shook his head almost imperceptibly. "On the other hand, we eat at Pescado's practically every Friday night. Will our friends and other Pescado's regulars think we're scared—or guilty—if we don't show? Some of them are bound to talk about it."

"I'm not suggesting we become hermits. But maybe it's a good idea to stay here tonight. Besides," she said brightly, warming to her point, "your burritos rival Pescado's. You make your stellar beef-and-bean burritos, and I'll mix us some killer margaritas." She pulled his apron out of a kitchen drawer and tossed it at him.

As he minced an onion and added it to the simmering ground beef, Lloyd felt sure his wife had made the right call.

• • •

A few blocks from the MacDonald's kitchen, a young man in a plain-vanilla Studebaker pulled into a convenient parking spot on a brick side street and killed the engine. Before the war, this neighborhood along Washington Road had been three blocks of two-story houses, a few suffering from neglect. Commingled with the modest homes were small family-run stores—Miller's Grocery, Mangini Shoe Repair, Karol's Tavern. In 1950, the homes and businesses fell to the postwar redevelopment movement. In their place stood a national chain supermarket, department store, a movie theater, and a bank. Karol's Tavern was the sole survivor, adjacent to a glitzy car dealership.

The occupant of the Studebaker rolled down the window to get some fresh air and a clearer view of two men talking on the other side of the brick street. One of the men, his white shirt sleeves rolled to the elbows and his dark tie loosened, carried the conversation.

His companion seemed to have tired of the talk. He looked at a streetcar motoring past, checked his watch and his shoes. He leaned against the fender of a seafoam green-and-white car. The movement caused the shirt-sleeved man to thrust out both arms like a father jumping to catch a falling toddler. He quickly caught himself and stuffed his hands into his pockets.

A third man exited the glass-walled building plastered with gaudy signs announcing *GREAT DEALS!* and *REDUCED PRICES!* He walked at a no-nonsense pace toward the two. He appeared to be in his early thirties. From the expensive cut of his suit and his demeanor, it was obvious to the young man in the Studebaker that the boss had arrived on the scene. The onlooker studied the tableau, paying particular attention to the man of authority and the way he interacted with the bored individual. He laughed at something the disinterested man said and rested a hand on his shoulder. With that, the three men turned and strolled in the direction of the sprawling one-story glass-front building.

The Studebaker's occupant scrutinized the trio until they went inside. He leaned to his right to get his wallet. He withdrew a creased and faded photograph, which he considered for several minutes. His lips tightened. "Yes," he whispered.

The young man snapped his index finger against the photograph. He tore it into small pieces and started the engine. As he drove home, he let the photo shards fly out the open window.

CHAPTER 14

Saturday, August 6, 1955

Saturday dawned hot and muggy. After breakfast, Lloyd and Lynn gathered canvas tote bags and headed to the garage and carriage house. On Saturday summer mornings, area farmers and local food producers set out their produce and goods under tents on the Mount Lebanon Lutheran Church parking lot.

Lloyd and Lynn enjoyed the opportunity to talk with friends almost as much as checking out the fresh fruits and vegetables. As he walked to the carriage house, Lloyd saw Allie and Carrie sitting on the picnic table in their yard. He started to wave but caught himself in time. Neither girl gave any sign they had seen him.

Lynn kept up a steady stream of conversation until she backed the car out of the garage, turned, and traveled the long driveway to the street.

Lloyd shook his head. "I just don't understand it."

"What, the price of tomatoes?" She patted his thigh. "Now listen, honey, there's only one reason for this. Harris wants to take us for every cent we have. That's it. Pure and simple. And," she smacked his leg with her fist, "that's all I want to hear about it. Got it?"

"Got it. But I'm not convinced it was his only reason."

Lynn shot him a warning look. Lloyd stared out the window, his Northwestern cap pulled low.

Mount Lebanon Lutheran Church was a ten-minute drive, during which Lynn talked animatedly about her latest find among the cluttered rooms of the old Lawrenceville bank, now stuffed with antiques. The former bank building was her favorite hunting ground for items that, at first glance, Lloyd considered to have no practical purpose, only to see Lynn fashion something useful or artistic from them.

Lynn arrived in the second row of the parking lot just as a car backed out of a spot.

"Our lucky day, Lynn. Francesco's Pasta is here." He pointed to a Ford station wagon.

"Let's get some of their yummy rosemary and olive pasta," Lynn said. "You can make spaghetti pepperoncino."

"Good idea," Lloyd enthused. He mentally inventoried the contents of their pantry and refrigerator.

Lloyd favored this Italian dish over several others for practical reasons. Spaghetti peperoncino tasted fantastic, and it was uncomplicated—a snap to make. The combination of ingredients presented a rich blend of earthy flavors. Neither the fish nor the vegetables overpowered the sauce. The first step of this dish entailed sweating thin strips of onion in extra-virgin olive oil in a covered skillet, which allowed the onions to cook in their own juices. The use of fresh homemade spaghetti provided a richer taste than packaged versions.

"We need to pick up a couple red bell peppers and a yellow onion or two." Lloyd had the rest of the ingredients he needed, including fresh parsley from Lynn's herb garden.

They walked toward the tents, passing a young cornetist playing "St. Louis Blues." Lloyd dropped a couple of dollars into the open trumpet case.

"Not exactly Louis Armstrong, but then again, nobody is," Lloyd said to Lynn.

The market was crowded with people seeking fresh produce,

baked goods, and other comestibles. Someone called their names. Bev Ellsworth. She gripped the handle of a shopping bag overflowing with produce.

"Listen, you guys," she said as she approached. "Jim and I are with you. If you need us for anything, anytime—" Bev looked at Lloyd. "It's a fucking lie, and your friends know it is." She hugged Lynn with her free arm, then kissed Lloyd's cheek. "Remember, anything." Her eyes were glossy with tears as she turned and hurried off toward the parking lot.

Lynn stared after her. "Bev Ellsworth, whom I've never heard say anything more vulgar than *heck*, just tossed off the F-word!"

"I thought that's what she said." Lloyd shook his head and laughed. "To hear Bev come out with that flat-out astonished me."

Lynn giggled, took his arm, and moved toward Bennett's tent and their red peppers. Standing next to them around a table heaped with fresh vegetables were their neighbors who lived a few doors up the street.

"Morning," Lynn said.

The woman turned her head, saw Lloyd, nodded tersely, then said to her husband, "I don't fancy the look of those beans. Let's try the A&P."

Lloyd watched them go, his head cocked, lips compressed.

"Forget it." Lynn patted his arm. "Get the peppers and onions you want."

Lloyd stared at the bin of red peppers. Watching her husband's inflamed face, Lynn marveled that the peppers didn't roast into a blackened heap under his gaze. He lifted two firm red bells and handed them to Mrs. Bennett.

"Oh, and two medium yellow onions, please."

When she had bagged them and received the money, Lloyd smiled and said, "By the way, Mrs. Bennett, those green beans look great. Let us have a pound, please."

Francesco's Pasta station wagon was ringed with pasta lovers. No surprise. Francesco expertly prepared just about every form of pasta known to Italy.

"Why don't you sit on that bench under the beech tree?" Lynn suggested. "If they don't have rosemary and olive, what's a good substitute?"

"Basil," said Lloyd. "If they don't have it, then regular angel hair will do."

As he walked to the bench, he felt his pockets for his pipe and tobacco pouch, only to realize they were in their car. A woman and young girl strolled toward him, talking earnestly. When they were only a few yards away, the woman looked up, saw Lloyd, grabbed the girl's hand, and made a wide detour. Lloyd stopped. It was Mrs. Konstantine. *God, she looked at me as if I were a child eater. Guess I'll have to stay out of her checkout line at the A&P.*

He recalled Meredith's blunt declaration that they would discover who their real friends were. He knew she had spoken the truth but experiencing it this morning smacked him hard.

Lynn came to Lloyd, holding a paper bag aloft triumphantly. "Basil," she announced. "I got the last of their supply. I figure we'll freeze what you don't—" She lifted her husband's face. "What's up, babe? You okay?"

"Sure, I'm fine." He managed a smile. "Just thinking. The sunroom floor . . . stain color."

Lynn sat and nuzzled him. "Listen, we got what we came for. Let's head home."

• • •

Lloyd's spaghetti *al peperoncino e tonno arrostiti* filled the kitchen and dining room with enticing aromas. Surprisingly, they were ravenously hungry.

"A very fine meal, my dear." Lynn lifted her glass of wine in a toast. "I always think of this dish as gutsy. Does that sound weird?"

"Not in the least. In fact, your use of 'gutsy' is on the mark if you mean courageous as a synonym for gutsy. I had to be courageous while making this."

Lynn sat back. "I hesitate to ask, but what about this delicious

Italian fare required your courage?"

"Including a whole can of anchovies in the sauce. If you, the champion anchovy despiser, saw me sautéing anchovies, you would have landed your famous left hook on my jaw."

"I refuse to believe you put anchovies in that heavenly sauce. I would've tasted those salty excuses for fish. If you had added anchovies, I wouldn't have eaten even one fork full. And I would have smelled them as soon as you put the serving dish on the table. So stop your kidding."

Lloyd went to the trash receptacle, retrieved the empty can of Crown Prince Flat Anchovies, and held it aloft.

"You bugger!"

The light mood didn't last.

• • •

That night, Lloyd's agile brain refused to allow him to sleep. What would he and Lynn do if the jury believed Harris's accusation and found him guilty? What would they do after Meredith appealed? Even if he never went to jail, chances were they'd be bankrupt. A lifetime—two lifetimes—of working, investing, and saving, all wiped out because of one man's lie.

Lloyd wasn't an avaricious person or a liar. He had difficulty understanding those who were. Walter and his family attended Reverend Palmer's Sola Scriptura Church every Sunday and Wednesday evenings.

How does Walter's false accusation match his supposed Christian beliefs and values?

It doesn't, Lloyd concluded. There was nothing in Scriptures or theological teachings that remotely condoned or promoted bearing false witness.

He rolled to a sitting position on the bed's edge, his feet searching for and finding his slippers. Lloyd stood and walked down to the library. He switched on the lamp beside his favorite chair and retrieved a slim volume from a bookshelf.

Prayer Thoughts, passages 26–50, *Selected Writings of St. Ignatius of Loyola*. Lloyd put on his reading glasses and opened the book.

In Prayer Thought 30, Lloyd read that St. Ignatius expressed sincere sympathy for individuals dealing with unspecified trials and tribulations. Lloyd studied the next sentence. He reread it. Ignatius believed God sends us trials to help an individual grow in faith in the Lord.

Lloyd took off his glasses and chewed on an earpiece tip. He had trouble believing God sent him this mess as a "special gift" to help him practice patience. God allowed events like this to happen because His entire relationship with mankind is based on free will. *No way do I think a loving God deliberately sends crap like this to anyone.*

He resumed reading but shut the book after scrutinizing Prayer Thoughts 37 and 38. In 37, St. Ignatius advised his followers to study and learn the intentions of one's neighbors to avoid condemning their actions based on first impressions and superficial observations. Ignatius inferred that one may learn that a neighbor's intentions are innocent even when they appear guilty.

In Thought 38, Ignatius asserted that if God sends a person a lot of suffering, spiritual and physical, this is a sure sign that God is making you into a saint. You want to be a saint? Then you've got to want to do a bunch of suffering.

Lloyd turned off the light and sat in darkness for many minutes. Shaking his head, he climbed the stairs, shucked off his slippers, and stared out the window.

"You okay, dear?"

"Right as rain, sweetheart. See you in the morning."

CHAPTER 15

Sunday, August 7, 1955

The Studebaker moved slowly down the street. The young man at the wheel scanned the buildings and houses. "There it is. Sola Scriptura."

He drove into the church lot at the rear of the building, then walked to the front entrance of the dirty gray-brick structure. The cornerstone indicated the imposing edifice had originated as Four Gospels Baptist Church, 1903. He sat in a pew near the rear and casually looked around at the congregation. *Excellent,* he mused.

Reverend Palmer's sermon focused on the Holy Bible as the "inerrant Word of God."

After the service, Palmer made his way to the newcomer, smiling, hand extended. "In the name of Jesus, I welcome you," he beamed. "I am Blanton Palmer."

"Hello, Reverend. My name is Charles Craft. I recently moved to this area. I saw your advertisement in the paper yesterday and decided to visit. A mighty powerful sermon, Reverend. Yes, sir, mighty powerful."

"Thank you. What brought you to Pittsburgh, Mr. Craft?"

"My job. I do private research for a corporation."

"U.S. Steel?"

"I'm not at liberty to divulge the name. The work requires secrecy."

"How interesting. You're sort of a spy, then?"

"I'm not at liberty to reply, Reverend."

"Very well. Excuse me for prying. Will you join us for our coffee hour, Mr. Craft?"

"Sure, and please call me Charles."

Blanton Palmer made sure Charles met most of the members at the coffee hour.

Palmer recognized that Craft had not been reared a fundamentalist, so he was surprised to see him among the congregation the following Sunday and a month's worth of Sundays after that. Charles Craft became a member of Sola Scriptura Church in October and was baptized in the Spirit.

Reverend Palmer and Craft adopted a habit of meeting monthly for coffee and conversation. Craft didn't consider Blanton Palmer a friend. He disapproved of Palmer's treatment of his wife and daughter, and women in general, but he kept his opinion to himself. The two men discussed a range of topics, most often religious and Biblical themes. At one of these get-togethers, Craft said he had recently heard something about an obscure practice called blood atonement. Reverend Palmer furnished Craft with detailed information about the subject. Palmer's impassioned delivery made it apparent he thought certain crimes merited execution by blood atonement.

As usually happens with informal meetings between individuals, after a few months, Palmer and Craft met on a less frequent basis. Craft's work became more demanding, with unpredictable hours. He still attended worship at Sola Scriptura, although he avoided more than a nodding acquaintance with other members.

Palmer himself faced personal problems. His daughter Nicole had graduated from high school and was showing obvious signs of rebellion against her father's strict rules. Palmer's wife kicked over the traces and began divorce proceedings. The subsequent divorce forced him to resign as minister of the congregation. Early in 1963, Blanton Palmer moved to the small town of Ormsby.

CHAPTER 16

Tuesday, July 9, 1963

David Elliott often observes that there are no coincidences. There are only connections.

A young woman of seventeen sat at a table in the Eata Hamburg Hot Dog Shop in a midsized town in southwestern Pennsylvania. Her face and figure warranted a second look. She frequented the eatery, but never ordered food or drink. Sometimes, she leafed through a magazine. Most often, she just sat or rested her head on her folded arms. After an hour or more, she would leave. The kid who grilled the burgers and dogs didn't care that she wasn't a paying customer, as long as he had an unobstructed view of her legs.

This Tuesday morning, the young employee sat behind the counter reading a comic book. The door opened. A man came in. He approached the young woman's table and addressed her by name.

"I don't know if you remember me. I used to see you at church up in Brentwood." He pulled out the wire-back chair across the table from her and sat. "I'm Charles Craft. It's a pleasant surprise to see you. How have you been?"

"People who say that don't really care how you feel. Besides, it's none of your business. But yeah, I remember you. You look different without the beard."

"How's your family?"

"Damn, you're nosy. Quit asking things you don't want answered." She made as if to go.

"But that's where you're wrong. I'm extremely interested in your family. How's your father these days? Has he made any false accusations against any neighbors lately?"

"What the hell are you talking about?"

The kid lowered his comic book. Craft told him to do his reading in the kitchen. Craft's tone made it clear it was not a choice.

"I apologize," Craft said, returning his attention to the young woman. "It did happen eight years ago. Perhaps you've forgotten, although I don't believe that."

She jumped up. Before she could take a step, Craft clamped his hand around her wrist. "Please sit down. You need to hear me out."

Without another choice, Allison Harris settled back into her chair.

"First, do you know the kid in the kitchen?"

She shook her head.

"Does he know who you are?"

"No."

Craft released her wrist. "You're entitled to some background. I lived near Mount Lebanon in 1955. I do private security work for a corporation. It's essential in my job to know things, to find out things people don't want found out. You'd be amazed at the interconnections among situations and events that, on the surface, have no apparent relationship."

Three guys came in looking for something to eat. The kid came out of the kitchen, his eyes on Craft.

"Anyone home at your place?" asked Craft.

She shook her head.

"Let's go."

"I'm not going anywhere with you."

"I have a way to end your . . . private times once and for all. Guaranteed."

"How do you know about—"

"Make up your mind, Allison. It's today or never."

Impulsively, Allison stood.

• • •

Craft parked three houses away. Inside the Harris home, he checked the second-floor rooms. When he came down, he held a photograph. "Where'd you get this?"

"Nicky Palmer took it years ago."

"I'm taking it. I don't want it lying around."

"Suit yourself. He won't care."

He insisted they sit in the front room near the door, where he had a clear view of the street and the driveway.

"Does the name Mary Lou Mezzacappo ring a bell?"

"No. Should it?"

"Mary Lou is—was—a prostitute on the North Side. She's dead now. Nice woman. Sang soprano in St. Ann's Church. Worked as a secretary for a firm in Pittsburgh in the fifties. She had some dirt I needed to shovel. In 1955 Mary Lou decided to expand her profession to the South Hills. The cops in that area decided they already had a surplus of prostitutes and arrested Miss Mezzacappo. Turns out, Walter, your old man, knew her. One night, Walter told Mary Lou he wanted to do 'private time' like he did with his daughter. This was during the MacDonald trial, and Mary Lou sang this song to the police, hoping for a deal. She was stoned at the time. Talked a lot of nonsense—claimed two of her regulars were Martians who forced her into a spaceship—so the police dismissed her story. Stupid mistake. But you and I know she told the truth about Walter, don't we?"

Allison stared at Craft, her mouth agape. "How did you—"

"Find this out?" Craft shrugged. "Connections. My connections tell me Walter still likes his private time. The bruises on your arm tell me my sources were right. My connections also tell me you wish you could go away and never see him again."

Allison got up and went to the front window, arms crossed. "You don't know what I wish." She turned and shot Craft a look that could blister skin. "Why the hell are you telling me all this, anyway?" She snatched open the front door. "Get out of here, you—"

"Close the door and sit," he said, gently. "You have to hear me out. It's important to me, and to you." Allison looked at Charles Craft. There was something in his eyes, his quiet but insistent way of speaking that drew her in. Allison shut the door and seated herself on the sofa, never taking her eyes from him.

Craft nodded his thanks. He leaned forward, forearms on his knees. "You see, I've got this problem . . ." He spoke to her for many minutes. Occasionally he paused, waiting until he regained control of his emotions. When he finished, he looked at her. "I'm asking you to help."

Craft's account stunned Allison. "My God," she whispered. "My God."

For the next hour, Craft sketched the rudiments of a plan. Important details remained, but he didn't see them as difficulties. They could wait. Allison said Carin would be home in ten minutes. Craft stood in the open door, his hand on the knob. "You're sure you want to help solve my problem?"

Allison's expression was serious and unwavering. "Yeah, I do."

"Okay." He handed her a sheet of paper with handwriting on both sides. "Type this on a blank piece of paper exactly as I wrote it—capital letters and all. We'll meet again next week. I'll tell you where and when. Your other job is to convince your friends to sign on. Be damn careful how you approach them." He fished a small amber bottle with an aerosol dispenser from his pocket. "Here. For Walter's next private time. Just one application to his private parts will stop his clock."

"Seriously?"

"Seriously."

"Wait," Allison said. "You've waited years for this. Why didn't you do anything about this until now?"

"Get your Bible and read the third chapter of Ecclesiastes, verses one through eight." Then he jogged down the front steps and was gone.

CHAPTER 17

Monday, August 8, 1955

Lloyd sat at the kitchen table staring at the rain, which had been pouring since daybreak. He lifted his coffee cup to his lips but set it back on the table. The contents were ice-cold. Bruce's voice startled him.

"Dad, can you come up to the sunroom? We need your decision on the paint."

"The paint?"

"Rudy and I tested the floor this morning. The seal coat is totally dry. You did a fantastic job with the stain. It looks terrific, and now that the—"

Lloyd got up, went to the sink, and poured out the coffee. He returned to the table and sat.

"Now that the urethane coats have dried, we need you to make a decision on when to paint. Nicky's coming today and if you give the okay, we can probably finish by—"

"The paint's still in the basement."

"Rudy and I took the primer to the sunroom this morning, figuring you'd give the go-ahead. The two of us can roll on the prime coat. Nicky's coming later. With her priming the trim and sash, we can finish the prime today. It should dry overnight, and we could finish putting on the first coat tomorrow. Nicky will cut in around the doors and windows, then Rudy and I will roll paint on the walls. There should be nothing to it. Besides, Rudy's gotta go back to school the week after next, so we need to take advantage of the time he's still available."

"Sounds to me like you've made the decision already, Son."

"Well, I think you need to make the final decision."

Lloyd smiled and clapped Bruce on the back. "Let's take a look."

The sunroom floor had turned out beautifully. To Lloyd's eye, he didn't think professionals could have done a better job.

He stepped over to one of the windows. "Okay, you two eager beavers, the job's yours. Before you start throwing primer around and stepping in paint trays," he smiled at Rudy, "I want you to apply strips of adhesive tape around the windows, doorframe, and the base."

As Lloyd began to show them what he wanted, he caught sight of Walter Harris pulling out of his garage. He continued to stare even after the car had moved out of sight.

"Dad?" Bruce asked. He followed Lloyd's gaze. "Earth to MacDonald. Alien craft no longer in range, sir."

Lloyd appeared not to have heard him.

"Once we get the tape on, we'll put down the cover cloths, maybe even tape them to the baseboards so they won't slide," said Rudy. "We got this, Mr. Mac."

Lloyd turned from the window. "Okay. I'll be in the library if you need me. I'm expecting a call."

When Lloyd had gone downstairs, Rudy asked, "Is your dad okay?" He knew, as did all of Mount Lebanon, of Lloyd's arrest.

"I dunno. He's not himself." Bruce shook his head. "That's a stupid remark. I'd really be worried if he continued to go through his routine as if nothing had happened. He hasn't lost his fighting edge, but he's become preoccupied with some theological conundrum, which isn't unusual. Dad loves to debate questions of theology and doctrine with his friends. It's second nature to him."

"Maybe he's trying to wrap his head around what's happening, you know, trying to assimilate this from the vantage point of his faith. Hell, this has to have been a severe shock to his value system."

"I'm afraid that he's . . . that he's accepting this as something God sent him as, I dunno, a form of discipline. I don't understand Dad's Jesuit theology. More to the point, I don't buy into it. But he needs to channel his energy and thoughts to winning this case. He can't afford any distractions."

"Yeah, you're right. His rights, his reputation, his family, his future, they're all on the line." Rudy laid his hand on Bruce's shoulder. Their eyes met. "You mark my words, your dad's gonna come out of his corner for every round like Sugar Ray Robinson."

"I hope you're right, pal. Thanks." Bruce turned on the radio and tossed Rudy a roll of two-inch-wide adhesive tape. "Here. You want to do the windows while I tape the baseboards?"

Rudy was on the second window when Bruce began to sing along with Johnnie Ray's version of *Walkin' My Baby Back Home.*

"Whistling that tune wasn't enough torture for me; now you're singing it? I have to admit, you sing better than you whistle."

"I've been practicing."

Nicky's voice reached them from the stairs. "Do I hear someone singing? Sounds like Johnny Raymond."

"Johnnie Ray," Rudy corrected. "On second thought, he does sing more like Johnny Raymond, whoever he is."

Nicky placed two brushes and a putty knife on a sill and shucked off her baggy slacks.

"I didn't know your father allows you to wear shorts," Bruce stammered, staring at her legs.

"He doesn't. I figured it would be hot working up here today. What he doesn't know won't hurt me." She smiled. "Does it bother you guys that I'm wearing shorts?"

"Nope." Rudy shook his head.

"Yeah . . . that is . . . I mean, no. I mean yeah, you should wear whatever's comfortable." Bruce spluttered. His ears grew hot. "Dad asked Rudy and me to sand the drywall joints."

"Okay," said Nicky. "I'll spackle the nails. Spackle dries quickly, so I'll sand them, too." She mounted the stepladder. "Nuts. I left my putty knife on the windowsill."

Bruce handed up her knife, making sure to touch her hand.

Nicky smiled. "Thanks. That was nice of you."

"Need anything else?"

"Not right now. I'll let you know." Nicky smiled.

Rudy watched them with a knowing grin spreading until it reached his eyes. Nicky's father might have thought he kept her on a short leash, but he couldn't stop her from being a woman.

CHAPTER 18

Thursday, August 11, 1955

Lynn was pouring the breakfast orange juice when the phone sounded.

"Hi, Lynn. Meredith here. I'm glad it's you. Listen, I've got some news. Walsh called this morning. The SOB has decided to prosecute Lloyd. I thought once he reviewed the flimsy hearsay the charge is based on, he'd drop it like a hot skillet, but no. Which confirms what I learned about him. The scuttlebutt is Patrick Walsh has set his cap on being elected district attorney this November. Ergo, he wants to make a name for himself as being tough on crime. So, we gird up our loins and make Patrick Walsh rue the day he decided to go after us."

"Shit," Lynn said.

"Yeah, shit is right."

"Has a trial date been set?"

"No, that won't happen until after the arraignment, which Judge Tate scheduled two weeks from today—August 25. Then he'll let me know about the trial."

"So, Lloyd has to sit around on tenterhooks until the damn judge has made him wait until desperation sets in?"

"Not sure that's Tate's reasoning, but I understand where you're coming from, and I can't blame you for being angry. Listen, I contacted Dr. Sharon Castle, an eminent child psychologist, who has agreed to be an expert witness on Lloyd's behalf. Once the arraignment is out of the way, I'll have Dr. Castle contact you for an interview. She'll want to hear what you and Lloyd have to say, your reactions to this, your impressions of the Harris family. But her main value to us comes when she gets to the nitty-gritty about Walter and Allison. Sharon is smart and tough. She's not going to leave anything to chance."

"Will that little brat be allowed to testify?"

"The law's complicated on that score. As defendant, Lloyd has the right to confront his accuser. Allison is nine. If Walsh wants her testimony, the judge must query her to decide if she is competent. For example, does she know the difference between truth and fiction? If Judge Tate is convinced she does, he might allow her testimony to be heard.

"However, if I were Walsh, I wouldn't do it. From what you and Lloyd have told me, Allison and her sister liked Lloyd. He listened to them, taught them how to grow tomatoes . . . that sort of thing. Would Allison be willing, under oath, to falsely accuse a man who cared about her as a human being?"

"She might. Her father scares hell out of those kids."

"Since the Harrises didn't press charges against Lloyd for almost a week for some reason, no officer nor anyone from social services examined Allison the day she presented with the perfume oil on her. Police examined the swimsuit and found a stain on the outside of it. There was a tiny smear on the inside, but it was too small to be identified."

"Doesn't this prove Lloyd never touched her little bare ass?"

"In his statement to police, Walter declared he smelled the aroma of perfume on Allison while they were seated at the dinner table that evening. Regina concurred."

"Are you saying the cops just took Walter's word on this?"

"That's how I see it."

"Doesn't that strengthen Lloyd's position?"

"It's a very strong point in Lloyd's favor. Don't get your hopes pinned on this, though. We have a way to go before it's over. I'm being realistic with you."

Lynn's silence spoke loudly.

"Remember, Lynn, this is a marathon, not a sprint. Your responsibility is to make sure you and Lloyd stay strong, keep a positive outlook, and are ready to fight tooth and nail. My job is to build an ironclad defense. Okay?"

"Okay."

"If you two are available on Friday the twenty-sixth, I want to meet. Will one-thirty suit?"

Lynn checked the calendar. "We'll be there."

"Don't hesitate to call me if you or Lloyd have questions, or if you think of anything that may be helpful information for me. I don't want you guys to fret or worry about the legal process. I've done this before. Just remember one thing—I'm utterly and totally convinced Lloyd is innocent. I'll get back to you in the next couple of days. And one more thing—don't hide. Go about your regular routines, dining out, movies, shopping. Got it?"

"Yes. Thanks, Meredith. We have complete confidence in you."

CHAPTER 19

Friday, August 26, 1955

Regina's trembling finger fumbled the telephone dial. She pressed the disconnect bar and put the phone on its base. After a time—maybe a couple of minutes—she checked the number in the phone book and lifted the receiver. This time, the call connected. A man's voice came over the line. "Allegheny County Police Department."

Fear squeezed her throat. Her pulse raced. "I, uh . . . Sorry. I dialed the wrong number." Regina hung up.

• • •

"Sorry I kept you waiting, guys," Meredith said. "I didn't think the phone call would last that long." She led them into her office.

Lynn gazed at the décor—no frills, no lavish touches. Comfortable chairs, a small conference table, Meredith's ordinary looking desk. An easel holding a flip chart stood near the table. Her office afforded clients a view of the Point, the juncture of the Allegheny and Monongahela Rivers, and the demolition of old warehouses along their banks—the beginnings of Pittsburgh's controversial Renaissance Project. The steel frameworks of a few buildings had already been erected.

"Quite a mess down there," said Meredith. "Walking from here to the courthouse can be an adventure some days. Would you like some water? Coffee?"

"No, thanks. Eileen already asked us," said Lloyd.

At Meredith's invitation, Lloyd and Lynn sat at the table.

Meredith joined them and opened a leather-bound notebook. "As I mentioned on the phone, the arraignment went smoothly, no surprises, just the usual routine. Patrick Walsh met with me afterward to get down to the business of the discovery phase. I filed a demand that Walsh provide us with all the evidence he has against you so far. By law, he has two weeks to give us all of it."

"You mean the stuff they took from the house?"

"That's part of it. But he must fork over the names, addresses, and statements of witnesses *and* the physical evidence, which includes the things the police collected from your home and the swimsuit.

"Once Walsh certifies to me that I have all the evidence the law requires him to provide, I'll go over it with a fine-toothed comb. If in my judgment the evidence doesn't amount to the crime you're charged with, I'll file a motion to dismiss. I'll also make sure none of the evidence has been filed improperly or illegally. If it has, then we'll move to suppress that evidence. As I work through discovery, there may be other legal motions to consider."

Meredith turned a page and studied the typewritten content. She looked up, tapping the letter with her pencil eraser. "Walsh submitted the names and addresses of the kids who've been working with you. I need you to go over the list. Note which ones worked only a brief time and those who no longer have a hand in the remodeling project. Include any notes about them you think would be helpful."

"Notes?" Lloyd asked.

"You told me some of the kids showed an interest in literature, art, that sort of thing. Lynn said you provided time off for them to read. I need to know the names of those who took advantage of your generosity."

"What does that have to do with any of this?" asked Lynn.

Meredith studied her pencil, turning it along its hexagonal axis before she laid it on the desktop. She looked at Lloyd. "Is Nicole Palmer still working for you?"

"Nicky's one of my best helpers. eighteen, intelligent, reliable, picks up new techniques fast."

"Is she one of the kids you encouraged to read?"

"Yes. Nicky's very interested in literature . . . Shakespeare, Austen, Brontë, Fitzgerald—"

"Fitzgerald?" Meredith leaned forward. "F. Scott? Did you encourage her to read his novels?"

"I wouldn't say I *encouraged* her. But she indicated an interest in twentieth century novels, and I showed her the authors of that era I have in my library: James Baldwin, Steinbeck, Hemingway, Faulkner, Salinger, and Fitzgerald. Nicky's father forbids her to read novels. He believes many works of art and secular books are sinful. His attitude only whetted Nicky's appetite for—" He cocked his head to the side. "Where are you going with this?"

"As you know, both Walsh and I performed interviews to gather information on potential witnesses. On the day before Walsh interviewed Nicole, she asked her friend Donna Netzler if she had to tell Walsh that after reading *Tender Is the Night*, she masturbated and had an orgasm in your bathroom. When I interviewed Nicole, she informed me that she had, in fact, disclosed this to Walsh. Nicole didn't have to, but she did."

Lloyd surged from his chair and strode to the window, hands stuffed into his pockets. Five stories below, a wrecking ball smashed against a brick wall, which shuddered, then collapsed in a cloud of dust.

Lynn looked hard at Meredith. "Will the prosecutor call her to testify?"

"It's hard to say. Walsh has to take Nicole's favorable feelings toward Lloyd into account. They could make her a difficult witness for the prosecution. On the other side of it, Nicole admitted she was not working for you at that moment, but with your permission and encouragement, was instead lying on your bed reading a rather suggestive novel and subsequently masturbated to the extent of orgasm. Lloyd, were you aware of this outcome? I mean, did she tell you about it, or did you inadvertently witness her—"

He spun around. "No and no! How can you ask such a thing?"

"If Nicole testifies, Walsh will ask you the same thing, and may infer a lot more, Lloyd. This presents us with a potentially dangerous impression of your character."

The lawyer stood and went to the flip chart. With a black marker, she wrote,

Charge: sexual molestation of 9-year-old neighbor

Evidence: one-piece swimsuit with residue of perfume

Site: your home

Possible corollary: Nicole—admission of erotic stimulation

Site: your home

"You told me you afforded this opportunity to read to—Lloyd? Are you okay?"

He stared at the words on the chart, his right fist pressed over his mouth beneath his nose. "Yes," he answered in a flat voice, his eyes still on the chart.

"You offered all your kids the chance to take time off work to read, right? It wasn't a special favor to Nicole."

"What's that? Oh, yes. That was my standing offer to all the kids."

"And some of the other kids took advantage of this."

"Yes. Not all, of course, but Rudy Williams did some reading, mostly Langston Hughes. And David Elliott did last September after he got back from New Mexico."

"Were there others?"

"A few. Alex Tirakis, who majors in chemistry at Pitt, read a lot of my chemistry textbooks. Donna Netzler read *Of Mice and Men*. She told me it was her favorite book."

"Okay, that's good. Remember, I'd like an annotated list of all the kids who worked with you. Please indicate which of them would make good witnesses."

"We can have it for you by Monday," Lynn said.

"Great. Let's discuss your trial. As defendant and attorney, we have a choice as to the type of trial that would be best for you—a jury trial or a bench trial."

For the next several minutes, Meredith explained the differences between bench and jury trials, and their comparative advantages and drawbacks.

There was a discreet tap on the door, and Meredith's assistant entered bearing a tray of cheeses, grapes, crackers, and a pitcher of water. "Pardon my interruption," said the diminutive brunette, "but I figured you might need some refreshments."

"Thanks, Eileen. That's very thoughtful of you."

After placing the tray on the conference table, Eileen turned back toward the door.

"Oh, Eileen." Meredith held up a finger. "Will you pull Dr. Sharon Castle's file and make a carbon copy of her bona fides for Lloyd and Lynn, please?"

"Sure thing. I'll have that for you in a few minutes."

When the door had closed, Lloyd said, "I've decided I want a jury trial. Here's my thinking: I want people to know I'm innocent and to tell others why I've been acquitted. Perhaps some of the jurors' post trial comments will be made public in the papers and television. I want my friends and the community of Mount Lebanon to hear it from their peers. On the other hand, if it's just the judge who declares my innocence, I doubt if the results will be broadcast very far afield."

"That's what I want, too," said Lynn. "My reasons go somewhat beyond yours, honey. I want this to be a statement on behalf of *all* the men and women who have been falsely accused of crimes they didn't commit."

Lloyd nodded and held her hand. "Thanks, sweetheart." He

looked at Meredith. "As Admiral Farragut said, 'Damn the torpedoes! Full speed ahead!'"

"Good. Good!" Meredith said with a tight-lipped smile. "I'll notify Judge Tate and Prosecutor Walsh of our decision. Before we move on to other considerations, you have to decide whether you will testify."

"What do you think?" Lloyd asked.

"As your attorney, I decide the strategy and tactics. The decision to testify or not is strictly your call. Here are a couple of facts to think about: First, you are presumed innocent whether you testify or not. If you choose not to testify, that can't be held against you. That's your constitutional right, and the jury will be so instructed.

"If you decide to testify, you waive your right to remain silent. After you take the stand and testify, the prosecutor has the right to ask you any-and-all questions pertaining to the case and your testimony. Here's something to take into consideration. The evidence against you is flimsy and unbelievable. Walter Harris looks to be exactly who he is—a greedy little man who hasn't demonstrated any concern for his daughter. Ask yourself if it's worth the risk to testify in this situation."

"You're suggesting Lloyd's testimony may not be necessary," Lynn said.

"That's all it is—a suggestion."

"I'm not going to testify." Lloyd steepled his hands. "Just getting ready for this is stressful enough."

"I think you've made a good decision. One of the first things I want to do is schedule a time when I can come to your home—the alleged scene of the crime. I need to see for myself the layout of the rooms where Allison found and opened your perfumes, the room where you and the others were working that day, and so forth."

"Come whenever it's convenient for you," Lynn said.

Eileen entered and handed Meredith a file containing the information on Dr. Castle. "Thanks, Eileen." Meredith handed the file to Lloyd. "After you review this, I'd like you to meet Dr. Castle.

In my experience, Sharon is the top child psychologist in the eastern states. But I want you to see and hear her for yourself."

She gathered her notes. "I think we accomplished a lot today. As soon as you send me the list of kids who participated in the construction project, I'll set up interviews with as many as I can."

Lloyd and Lynn rose to leave. Meredith hugged them both. To Lloyd, she said, "Harris is after your life, everything you are, everything you believe in, everything you value. I said I'm going to fight him like a damn tiger, and I need you to be as fierce and committed to the fight as I am. Okay?"

"Okay," Lloyd said with more confidence than he'd had at the start of the meeting. "Thank you," he said, and he meant it.

CHAPTER 20

Thursday, September 1, 1955

The phone rang at 8:30 a.m., just as Lynn was making the coffee. Lloyd stood in the kitchen doorway.

"Hi, Sue. I was going to call you this morning. How's Brian feeling?" Lynn winced. "Ouch! There's nothing worse than a post-tonsillectomy throat. Has he been able to eat any of the ice cream we sent?" She sighed. "Well, give him a hug."

Lynn twisted the phone cord around her finger. "Listen, I've completed the feasibility interviews with the community leaders, and I'd like to schedule a meeting with you and the executive board to discuss them . . . What? You're not serious. Come on, Sue. We've been friends for years. You and Frank know Lloyd would never . . . Yes, I interviewed Mr. Hunt. He gave no indication that he had any reservations because of Lloyd. Matter of fact, he was welcoming and friendly."

Lynn listened for several minutes. Then she said, "Fine. I'll mail you the interview details and the final bill for my services . . . Sure, I'm angry. You've been my client for years and a friend for longer than that . . . A business decision? I thought there was more to our relationship than business. Tell Hunt to take a flying leap into the Allegheny."

Lynn hung up and gripped the top of a kitchen chair. Lloyd went to her and wrapped his arms around her. They didn't speak for some time.

"You know what really gets me? Sue assured me she and Frank know you're being falsely accused. Yet, she terminated our contract because one of her best customers said he would have to take his business elsewhere since Sue hired the wife of a . . . to hell with it. There are other fish in the river."

Lloyd patted Lynn on the fanny and went to the kitchen window. Last night's shower remained as sun-glistened water droplets on the grass, the roses, and the leaves of the holly hedge. A quiet beginning to a lovely late summer's day. A blue jay jeered and screeched.

He knew Marshall Hunt. More importantly, Marshall Hunt knew Lloyd. Until last January, they served together on the board of the Alice Neeley Children's Home. They had worked together on the Education and Literacy Committee.

A conversation the two had last year after a committee meeting came to him.

"Lloyd," Marshall had said, "you trust everyone. You say it's fundamental to your Jesuit ideology. I admire you as a man of principle and integrity. But not everyone is worthy of trust. Someday, your trust may be misplaced, and you may be hurt. Seriously hurt. Even these kids here at the home—not all of them are saints. Far from it. I think you need to develop an arm's-length attitude toward these kids. Most of them are grade-A manipulators. They don't care about anybody but themselves. I can't blame them. I've read their case histories. They'll do whatever it takes to survive, and I mean *whatever*. When you've been on this board for as long as I have, you'll see what I mean."

Obviously, Hunt thought his trust in Lloyd had been misplaced. He could deal with that, but Lynn didn't deserve to be treated this way.

"Honey, did you hear me?" Lynn asked. "You're going into analysis mode. Let it go. It's not the end of the world."

How do I let it go when the woman I love and prize above all other human beings has been hurt unjustifiably because she's married to me?

They ate breakfast in silence. Lloyd's recent spells of moodiness had begun to frighten Lynn. She recognized the signs of introspection, which at times had enabled her husband to concentrate on solving complex chemistry problems. But now, she feared the onset of depression.

"Do you want another cup of coffee?" she asked.

He shook his head.

"Okay. Rinse out your cup and come up to my craft room with me. I need your opinion on something."

Upstairs, Lynn put her hands on her hips as she glanced around the craft room. "I'm thinking of adding a fold-up worktable along this wall. When I need to measure fabric to re-cover furniture, the existing workspace isn't long enough, and it's barely wide enough to lay out the material. Doesn't have to be fancy, but I would want it to be out of my way when I finish a job."

Lloyd pulled out his measuring tape and made a quick calculation. "I have a piece of maple that may fill the bill. I've got a set of heavy-duty retracting spring hinges I'll use to close it."

• • •

A week went by, and Lloyd hadn't done anything on Lynn's requested project. She saw it as an ominous sign. When Lynn asked Lloyd to do something for her, he always had done so right away. She went to his workshop in the basement. On the floor was the rough maple slab—unmeasured, uncut, unsanded. The hinges and screws were on the workbench.

The signs suggested that either Lloyd was preoccupied or depressed. She remembered her visit with Adam, her younger brother, just weeks before he committed suicide. On the floor of his garage, the parts to his outboard engine had remained just where she'd seen them six months earlier. It was completely out of character for Adam, and she had voiced her alarm to their mother.

She took in the scene in Lloyd's workshop. *Am I jumping to conclusions? After all, Lloyd's been working for four years on the home addition. Maybe he just needs a break.* Lynn climbed the basement stairs, mulling over what action to take. When she got back to the kitchen, it dawned on her that in the days since the work on the addition had been completed, Lloyd had been in the new rooms—including the sunroom, his pride and joy—only once.

She found him in his study, paying bills. He looked up, waved a handful of papers, and gave her a satisfied smile. "These are the final payments for the materials we used for the addition. And guess what? We still have a balance of a buck-fifty in our savings account."

"A buck-fifty? Great! You can pay for lunch."

"You are an inexpensive date, kiddo." He stood, wrapping his arms around her waist. "I owe you an apology. While paying one of the bills to Barnes Lumber, I noticed the purchase of a good-sized piece of maple. I promised to make you a folding table for your craft room. I'm sorry, I—"

Lloyd didn't understand why Lynn had tears on her cheeks, but her kisses and laughter indicated his apology had been accepted.

"I have an idea, honey," Lynn said. "We have a two-thirty appointment this afternoon with Meredith. Bev mentioned a gallery on the South Side is having an exhibition of Edward Hopper prints. I think she said Preston Dickinson's and Charles Burchfield's works are also in the show." She tugged on his sleeve. "Let's get showered and dressed. The gallery opens today at eleven. We can view the exhibition, have a late lunch at Charlie Bly's, and jump across the Monongahela to Meredith's. What do you say?"

"Hopper and Burchfield? You're on."

Her tears flowed unabated.

"You okay, sweetheart?"

"Of course. You know I only cry when I'm happy."

• • •

At half past two, the MacDonalds arrived at Meredith Goldsmith's office. She'd asked Lynn and Lloyd to meet before the conference with Judge Tate and Prosecutor Patrick Walsh to set the trial date.

"Thanks for coming in on such short notice," Meredith said once they were seated in her office. "Walsh called me yesterday. He's offering a plea deal. Harris is willing to reduce the charge to simple sexual misconduct. You touched Allison through her clothing in the buttocks area without her consent. If you are convicted on this charge, you may be sentenced to one year in prison and a fine of $3,000. Additionally, Walsh gave notice that Harris intends to file a civil case claiming damages in the amount of $100,000 for the emotional pain and suffering you've caused them. As I've told you, under the present charge of sexual abuse, you face eight to ten years in prison and a fine of $10,000. After our session, you may want to go home and think about it. There's no need for an immediate answer."

Lynn and Lloyd exchanged looks.

"No deals!" Lloyd dismissed the offer with a swipe of his arm. "There's nothing to consider. I didn't do anything to her. I did not touch her. I did not *think* of touching her. Lynn and I have suffered enough for a lifetime over this. I'll never confess to something I haven't done. Furthermore," he pointed his finger, "I will never give that man a penny of our money. I'd rather die first."

For a moment, no one spoke. Then Lloyd resumed.

"I want to go to trial as soon as possible. I want my name cleared and my reputation restored. People I trusted as friends have given signs that they at least suspect I did it. Strangers at the lumberyard or the hardware store act like I'm a leper or a monster. Now Lynn has lost her top client and friend over this. What is wrong with these people?" He smacked the table with the flat of his hand.

Lynn covered his hand with hers. She caught Meredith's eye. "I agree. No deals. Walter can go to—"

Meredith nodded. She felt confident Lloyd would be acquitted, but that would not necessarily result in a sea change in the public's attitude. She recalled reading of ancient King Pyrrhus, who defeated the Roman army but suffered the staggering loss of his best officers and most of his soldiers. The court of public opinion could, and often did, cause staggering emotional, professional, and social losses to a defendant who received a verdict of not guilty in a legal court. Meredith had raised this possibility with Lloyd and Lynn MacDonald in her first meeting with them. She saw no reason to remind them.

After they left, Meredith took a call from Sharon Castle.

The psychologist summarized her meetings with the Harris family and her private session with Allison.

"First, I doubt the prosecution will have Allison testify in court. Not once did she say Mr. MacDonald touched her, nor did she say he said anything that made her uncomfortable. But she didn't say he didn't, either. I asked her how the perfume got on her butt and swimsuit, and she immediately began to cry and put her head down on the table. When I explained that it's always best to tell the truth, she mumbled an affirmative. But when I asked again if she had rubbed the perfume on herself, she wailed, sobbing to beat the band, coughing, gagging. It took her a long time to recover."

"Allison accidentally did it herself," Meredith said.

"Yes, I think so, but I'm not paid to make guesses. The girl presents with a deep fear of her father. If she doesn't say what he wants her to say or behave as he wants her to, there's hell to pay. Tragically, Allison is the one who pays. I'm really concerned about the unconscionable power Harris holds over her. There's no doubt this will result in severe psychological damage to her. To some extent, she's been damaged already."

"Thanks, Sharon," said Meredith, trying to maintain her objective attorney voice. "That's important information."

"Listen, what I'm about to say is inadmissible in court, but between us, Meredith, if Allison was sexually molested, Walter Harris did it. I'd bet my license on it."

CHAPTER 21

Tuesday, September 20, 1955

Lloyd woke before dawn. His pajama shirt was soaked in sweat. He'd dreamed of a large herd of goats dashing into a heavy sea. Lloyd seldom remembered dreams, and although he attempted to discern the meaning of those he did remember, he had no clue if his analyses were correct. The goats frightened him. Was the dream an omen of the outcome of his trial?

He rolled onto his left side. Lynn had already risen. Lloyd heard the shower. She hadn't slept well either. No surprise there. He switched on the bedside lamp, took off his wet pajama top, donned his robe and slippers, and parted the drapes. No lights were on in the Harrises' house. Lloyd let the drapes fall back into place.

Had it only been two months since Walter accused him? It seemed like two years. He tried to imagine what Allison was going through now that the day of the trial was here. Unlike Lynn, Lloyd wished her no ill will. She had been intimidated and manipulated by her father. This would affect her the rest of her life. *As it will affect me.*

Lloyd felt the roll of fat around his waist. He hadn't been getting enough exercise. His diet had gone off the tracks, too. When Lynn was at home, she made sure Lloyd ate healthy foods at regular times and restricted his alcohol consumption.

Lloyd didn't need a urine test to tell him his blood sugar was high. He was experiencing the diabetic's triple whammy of intense thirst, hunger, and weariness. He swallowed the contents of the ten-ounce glass of water from his nightstand in two gulps. It didn't relieve the dryness in his mouth.

While he waited his turn in the bathroom, Lloyd distilled his thoughts, condensing them until only beneficial assertions remained. Lynn emerged from the bathroom, her head swathed in a towel. "It's all yours," she said. "I laid out your suit, shirt, and tie. Your shoes could use a bit of polish."

"Anything else, Sergeant?"

She grinned. "Yes. No substitutes on the clothing. Last night, I buried that godawful tie you bought at the women's auxiliary rummage sale."

"Roger and out," he replied.

After soaping and shampooing, Lloyd stood under the hot water. He had wanted this day to come for weeks, but standing naked in the shower stripped Lloyd of confident optimism.

The fact that he was innocent of the charges guaranteed nothing. *Sure, an individual is innocent until proven guilty. That's fundamental to the rule of law. But that doesn't mean it always works out that way.* He lifted his face to the stream of water. On the positive side, he trusted Meredith's ability and judgment. He picked at a scab covering a gash on his forearm. *On the other hand, trials can be a crapshoot. He had to be realistic. The verdict might not be favorable.*

Lloyd turned off the water and pulled back the shower curtain. As he reached for a towel, a wave of dizziness hit him. He grabbed the towel bar with both hands until the feeling subsided. Shaky, naked, and wet, he made his way to the bedroom, holding on to the wall. He lifted a bunch of grapes from the bowl of fruit Lynn had put in the bedroom as a not-so-subtle reminder to keep his blood sugar in range. Soon after he ate the fruit the shaky feeling dissipated.

• • •

Thirty minutes before the trial, Lynn and Lloyd conferred with Meredith Goldsmith in a small room one floor below the courtroom. Meredith briefly went over details and asked if there were any questions. Neither had any.

"Okay, we're ready. Dr. Castle's on hand. You'll sit next to me, Lloyd. Eileen has a seat saved for you, Lynn—first row behind our table." She hugged Lloyd. "Listen, if you feel you need a break, let me know."

They exited the elevator and walked into the courtroom. Meredith led the way to the defense table. Lynn hugged Lloyd and went to her chair.

Lloyd had just settled in his chair. Then he stood along with everyone in the courtroom as the bailiff announced, "The Court of the Fifth District of Allegheny County is now in session, the Honorable Judge Frederick Tate presiding."

Judge Tate, a short, balding man Lloyd estimated to be in his sixties, entered and took his seat. He asked both attorneys if they were ready to begin the trial. They said they were. Three weeks before, Meredith and Prosecutor Walsh, along with Judge Tate, had selected the twelve individuals and four alternates who would serve on the jury. Judge Tate swore in the jurors.

Prosecutor Patrick Walsh made his opening statement, in which he outlined the evidence he would present during the trial.

"Your Honor and members of the jury, the defendant, Lloyd MacDonald, has been charged with the crime of sexual abuse of a child, Allison Harris, age nine. The evidence will show that on several occasions during the months of June and July, the defendant invited Allison and her sister to his home, ostensibly to teach them about gardening and chemistry.

"On the afternoon of Saturday, July 16, following a family outing at the Dormont Municipal Swimming Pool, Allison, who was still wearing her swimsuit, decided to visit the defendant to learn more about growing tomatoes from seed. Instead, to her utter horror, the defendant took her into his bedroom and rubbed perfumed oil on her bare buttocks. The innocent girl broke free, fled to her home, and told her parents of the horrible ordeal.

"Granted a search warrant, Mount Lebanon police officers confiscated a bottle of perfumed oil from the defendant's home. The evidence I present will prove that the defendant is guilty as charged."

When he had finished, Meredith stood and addressed the jurors.

"Good morning, ladies and gentlemen of the jury. My name is Meredith Goldsmith, and it is my privilege to represent Lloyd MacDonald in the case before you today. You have heard the prosecutor explain what he hopes will be proven, but he did not tell you all the facts.

"The prosecutor said my client inappropriately rubbed perfumed oil on Allison Harris. But in fact, no police officer or social services professional examined Allison Harris on the day this crime is alleged to have occurred. Police and social services were not negligent in this matter, ladies and gentlemen. The parents of Allison Harris did not notify authorities of their accusation against Mr. MacDonald until two days later. Most significantly, the prosecutor did not tell you that eleven days prior to this dubious incident, Allison Harris was discovered in Mr. MacDonald's home without permission, rummaging through his wife's cosmetics drawer. This was reported immediately to Mr. Walter Harris, Allison's father, who stated he would, and I quote, 'take care of it.'

"We will call as witnesses two men who worked alongside Mr. MacDonald for the entire afternoon when this questionable incident is said to have occurred. We will call as expert witness Dr. Sharon Castle, an eminent child psychologist who interviewed Allison Harris. We ask you to keep an open mind and listen to all the evidence and return a verdict of not guilty. Thank you."

"The prosecution may call its first witness," Judge Tate declared.

The spectators in court sat up expectantly. It reminded Lynn of a movie scene in which the crowd in the Roman Colosseum craned their necks to see the lions released upon the Christians.

The prosecutor called in succession the lead officer during Lloyd's arrest and the supervising officer who conducted the search of the MacDonalds' house and premises. Their testimony established the dates and times of the actions, but little else. In her questioning, Meredith drew an admission from the police officer who made the arrest that no one in the police department or the Allegheny County Social Services Agency had examined Allison Harris on the day of the alleged incident. He testified that the complaint was received Monday, July 18, two days after the incident.

"Did you examine the swimsuit worn by the alleged victim?"

"Yes."

"Please tell the court the date of this examination."

Sergeant Armstrong looked at his notes. "Wednesday, July 20."

"The alleged incident is said to have occurred Saturday, July 16, but the swimsuit was not examined until Wednesday the twentieth. Why the delay, Sergeant?"

"The swimsuit had been put in the clothes hamper for washing."

"The swimsuit was washed?"

Someone laughed.

"No, it was retrieved unwashed."

"You testified there were stains on the exterior of the swimsuit in the buttocks area. Were any stains found on the interior?"

"A faint smudge about the size of a grain of rice. Too small to be determinative."

Meredith studied his face. "No identifiable stains on the inside of the suit?"

"That's correct, Counselor."

"Please describe the size and shape of the exterior stains you examined."

Again, Armstrong referred to his notes. "We made a color slide of the swimsuit showing the stains, entered into evidence as Exhibit

C." A police officer switched on a projector. "You can see two parallel dark smudges. The one on the left measures five-eighths of one inch. The right stain measures three-eighths of one inch."

"What forensic test was used to determine the stains were from perfumed oil?"

"Olfactory."

Laughter from the gallery.

"In plain English, you smelled the stains. What further tests were done?"

"I decided none were needed. You could tell it was perfume right away."

"This garment, this orange swimsuit, lay in the family's dirty clothes hamper for four days, yet you determined the scent of perfume could only have come from the stains on the swimsuit?" Meredith turned toward the jury. "No further questions, Your Honor."

Meredith's only question for the Mount Lebanon officers who had searched the home of Lloyd and Lynn MacDonald was, "Can you declare, without a doubt, that the bottle of perfumed oil you appropriated from Mrs. MacDonald's cosmetics drawer is the very oil alleged to have been rubbed on Allison Harris?"

Both answered in the negative.

"That'll be all, Your Honor."

Prosecutor Walsh stood as Meredith resumed her seat. "The People call Walter Harris."

Walter, dressed in a fashionable business suit and a tie with a pattern that appeared like splotches of spaghetti sauce, swore to tell the truth. He declared he had been suspicious of Lloyd MacDonald's interest in his daughters from the beginning—even more so since Lloyd was supervising an extensive construction project at his home.

"He had some teenage girls working on his project," Walter said.

"Objection," Meredith called. "Irrelevant."

"Sustained," the judge agreed.

Walter testified that during dinner on July 16, he asked Allison if she was wearing perfume. He claimed both daughters understood his opposition to using perfume at their age. According to Walter, Allison immediately collapsed, wailing, and repeated her nickname for Lloyd MacDonald—Mr. Mac. Walter explained that he had immediately confronted the defendant and told him he was not to speak to his daughters or his wife. Two days later, he called the Mount Lebanon police and filed the charge of sexual molestation. He concluded his testimony with a recitation of the mental and emotional harm he and his family had endured daily since then.

"Does the defense wish to cross-examine?"

"Yes, Your Honor." Meredith reached the witness stand in swift strides. "Mr. Harris, you testified that you moved next door to Mr. and Mrs. MacDonald June 4 of this year. Is that correct?"

"Yes."

"Will you please tell the court what happened the next evening, Sunday, June 5."

Walter looked puzzled. "I don't recall."

"Allow me to refresh your memory," Meredith said. "Your daughter Carin was admitted to the local hospital to undergo an emergency appendectomy, and you and your wife, Regina, asked Lloyd and Lynn MacDonald to take Allison for the night."

"Now I remember."

"Mr. Harris, do you recall that on June 14, Mrs. Harris asked Mr. MacDonald to watch your daughters for the afternoon while she went to a doctor's appointment in Oakland?"

"Yes, I remember. I had scheduled a sales meeting that day and was unable to drive her."

"Mr. Harris, do you recall that on June 28, Mrs. Lynn MacDonald told you that Carin and Allison had been in their home the previous four days in a row without being invited?"

"I don't remember the date, but yes, I remember."

"She asked if you would consider limiting your daughters' visits to when they were invited, or occasions when you and Mrs. Harris had to be away and could not secure anyone to stay with them. Is this an accurate account of your discussion?"

"Yes." Walter fidgeted with his tie.

"Mrs. MacDonald's affidavit states you were visibly upset at her request. Were you upset?"

"I thought she was being a pushy—"

"A pushy what, Mr. Harris?"

"I misspoke. I apologize, Your Honor."

Meredith paused, making a show of searching her notes. "Mr. Harris, you testified today under oath that, quote, 'I was suspicious of his—Lloyd MacDonald's—interest in my daughters from the beginning.' The records demonstrate you were aware your daughters spent a lot of time at the MacDonalds'. Did you at any time share your suspicions of my client with Mrs. Harris?"

"I don't recall. I may have thought—"

"Yes or no, please."

Walter looked at Prosecutor Walsh, who did not look at him. "No. That is—"

"'No' is a complete sentence, Mr. Harris. No further questions, Your Honor.

"Mr. Walsh," the judge inquired, "do you wish to redirect?"

"No, Your Honor. The People rest their case."

"Is the defense ready with its case?"

"Yes, Your Honor," said Meredith.

She called character witnesses, including Jim Ellsworth and individuals who had worked on the construction project. They testified to Lloyd's impeccable character and his sincere passion for teaching new skills to interested youth. "He really cared about us," one of his previous workers said. "He encouraged me to read literature and to share what the play or novel was about."

The prosecutor had no questions for the character witnesses.

"I call Alex Tirakis," Meredith said.

Alex affirmed that on July 5, he saw a young girl—later identified as Allison Harris—going through Mrs. MacDonald's cosmetics drawer, and that she fled when he ordered her to get out of the house. Meredith then called Bruce MacDonald, who testified he told Walter Harris about the incident that same evening. Bruce claimed no one had given Allison permission to be in the bedroom or in any private areas of the home. He also affirmed that Walter had said he would "take care of it" when informed about the incident.

Prosecutor Walsh cross-examined Alex and Bruce but was unable to confuse them or make any points from their answers.

"I call Rudy Williams," Meredith said.

Rudy was sworn in and sat in the witness stand.

"Mr. Williams, may I call by your first name?" she asked.

"Yes, of course."

"Rudy, what is your relationship with my client and his family?"

"Mr. Mac—I mean, Mr. and Mrs. MacDonald's son, Bruce, is my close friend. He asked me if I wanted to earn some money working on the addition to their home. I've worked on various aspects of the project for two years."

"Did you work every day?"

"In the summer months, I did."

"Did you work by yourself or with others?"

"Mostly with other kids. I often worked as a team with Bruce and Nicky—I mean, Nicole Palmer."

"You worked on July 16 of this year?"

"Yes."

"Please tell the court who worked with you that day, what you worked on, and where in the house you did this job."

"I worked with Bruce and Mr. Mac—Mr. MacDonald. We spent all day measuring and cutting sheets of plywood in the sunroom on the third floor. Then we nailed up the plywood for the subflooring. It took all day, but we laid the whole floor."

"Who else worked that day?"

"Nobody. Just the three of us."

"And Mrs. MacDonald, was she in the house?"

"No. Bruce told me she was visiting a friend in West Virginia for the weekend."

"Did you see or hear anyone come into the house?"

"No, Ma'am. What with the noise of the table saw and the hammering, we couldn't hear ourselves talk sometimes."

"Mr. MacDonald worked alongside you and Bruce the entire day?"

"Yes. We knocked off for lunch and of course took time to go to the bathroom. Right after we started work in the morning, the head of Mr. MacDonald's hammer came loose, so he went down to the basement to put an extra wedge in it."

"What time did that happen?"

"We started at eight that morning. Couldn't have been more than twenty minutes later. He was back in about ten minutes."

"None of you went downstairs for water while you were working?"

"No. We had an ice chest of cold pop and a jug of water."

"Thank you, Rudy. I have no further questions, Your Honor."

The prosecutor questioned Rudy as to the time they finished work. Rudy said it was after four o'clock, but that the three of them then sat on the sunroom floor and emptied the ice chest of pop and three bottles of beer supplied by Bruce. When Rudy left the house, it was quarter to five. Mr. Mac had gone to phone his wife and Bruce was running water for a bath. Walsh landed no punches during his cross.

Meredith called Dr. Sharon Castle, a child psychologist, whom Judge Tate had approved as an expert witness. Meredith's question drew out Dr. Castle's curriculum vitae including her awards, professional affiliations, and lectureships during her ten years of experience in the field of psychology.

Dr. Castle's testimony supplied the *coup de grâce*. "On August 29, I interviewed Allison Harris in the presence of Mary Long, a licensed social worker for Allegheny County. We administered the Walters-Grimes Cognitive Assessment and Socialization Test, which confirmed Allison can distinguish truth from falsehood. Mrs. Long and

I explored in depth Allison's relationship with Mr. Lloyd MacDonald. At no point did she present indicators of fear or suspicion of Mr. MacDonald. Allison did not accuse him of any improper touching, nor did she imply any such actions through nonverbal body language. My professional evaluation of the child's responses is that at no time did Mr. MacDonald make any improper remarks or behavior toward Allison Harris."

"Thank you, Dr. Castle."

Walsh stood at his place to cross-examine Dr. Castle. He flourished a sheaf of papers. "Dr. Castle, there are a number of accredited cognitive assessment tests used by psychologists, but you seem to have an extraordinary preference for Walters-Grimes. My research reveals you have administered this test almost exclusively during your career. Are you familiar with the Michael Vincent Cognitive Assessment Examination?"

"Yes."

"The Gleischner-Lipinsky Instrument?

"Yes."

"Satterlind, Chamberino, and Forester Cognitive Behavior Quotient?"

"Yes."

"All duly accredited and sanctioned by the American Association of Credentialed Psychologists, are they not?"

"Yes, they are exceptionally well-regarded in the field of psychology."

"Yet, you have exclusively administered the Walters-Grimes Cognitive Assessment in this instance and all previous examinations. Your colleagues do not share your preference for Walters-Grimes. Doctors Richard Gleischner and Mary Ann Lipinsky declared in the March 1952 edition of the Journal of Psychological Testing, "Walters-Grimes Cognitive Assessment and Socialization Test is without merit in our field of study." Walsh flipped to the next page. "Dr. Michael Vincent said in his December 1949 Saturday Evening Post interview, 'My team has never used Walters-Grimes. It is irrelevant and the questions meaningless.'" Walsh paused and looked at the jurors. "Dr. Malcolm Satterlind of Satterlind, Chamberino, and Forester who led the development of the renowned Cognitive Behavior Quotient, said during his NBC television interview February 16, 1955, 'The Walters-Grimes Assessment Test cannot produce any meaningful results we can use.'"

Patrick Walsh walked and stood in front of the jurors. "Dr. Castle's peers in the field of psychological testing have unanimously and publicly dismissed the Walters-Grimes Cognitive Assessment and Socialization Test as being 'without merit,' 'irrelevant,' 'meaningless.' This expert witness based her findings and decisions in her examination of Allison Harris on a worthless test. Therefore, we maintain her assessment that Allison had no fear of the defendant, that she gave no indication that the defendant spread perfume on her body and touched her inappropriately is suspect and unreliable. No further questions, Your Honor."

"Attorney Goldsmith, do you wish to rebut?"

"Yes. Thank you, Your Honor." Meredith got right to the point. "Dr. Castle, do you wish to dispute the negative judgments of the Walters-Grimes test expressed by your colleagues?"

"No, I do not."

Meredith turned and looked at the jurors. "Please explain your answer to the court."

"The experts cited would have no use for Walters-Grimes because they are not child psychologists. The Gleischner-Lipinsky test is designed for individuals ages eighteen to twenty-two. Dr. Vincent and his team devised their test to measure the cognitive levels of the elderly, and Dr. Satterlind's Cognitive Behavior Quotient is administered to individuals afflicted with dementia, his special area of psychology. The Walters-Grimes assessment test focuses on children between the ages of five through ten. It is recognized by child psychologists as the definitive cognitive and socialization assessment for children in that age range."

"Thank you, Dr. Castle."

Walsh did not call Allison or Nicole Palmer to testify.

• • •

The trial lasted less than two hours, and the jury returned a verdict of not guilty in thirty-five minutes.

The foreman of the jury spoke privately with the MacDonalds as they were leaving the courthouse. "This trial never should have happened. Good luck to you, Mr. MacDonald."

Lloyd shook his hand and thanked him.

Meredith asked them to wait while she finished her post trial routine. When she reappeared, she rushed to them, a ball of energy, skin aglow, eyes dancing. "Come on, you two! I have reservations for a champagne lunch at LeMont's on Mount Washington. Sharon will join us. Her testimony was superb!" Meredith hustled them to a private elevator. "We'll go in my car just in case that Ford of yours won't make it up McArdle Roadway." She chuckled.

As he held open the car door for Lynn, Lloyd spotted Walter Harris and his wife walking toward a parking lot a block over. Harris looked like he was chewing out Regina. Lloyd pitied her and the two girls, especially Allie. Lloyd sat in the front seat. He couldn't shake the thought that Allie would carry the aftermath of this for the rest of her life. He prayed he was wrong.

• • •

As Meredith drove over the Monongahela River on the Liberty Bridge, Lloyd squinted against the September sunlight and inhaled from the depth of his lungs. *It's over,* he said to himself. *No more nasty stares and snide comments from folks who don't know the first thing about me.*

There had been casualties, though—Sue Hagberg, Lynn's longtime friend and client, and hardest of all, his close friend Dick Wyant. They'd worked together on some significant projects at Leblanc Tennant Chemical Corporation. Dick and his wife, Patty, had traveled to Scotland with Lynn and Lloyd. Three weeks earlier, Lloyd had phoned the Wyants to ask if they were available for dinner at LeMont's. Dick had replied that he and Patty didn't associate with pedophiles.

As if reading his thoughts, Lynn reached from the back seat and squeezed his shoulder.

At the restaurant, Lloyd stood under the entrance canopy to hold the door for Meredith and Lynn, then let two other women in. The second woman, stylishly dressed in a pale-green suit with a pencil skirt, addressed him, speaking just above a whisper. "You got away with it, MacDonald. I hope you rot in hell."

He continued holding the door, staring absently at the opposite wall, stunned by her words.

Lynn came to him. "What's going on, hon? Are you okay?"

"Daydreaming," said Lloyd.

The young woman at the reception podium led them to a window table with a marvelous panoramic view of the city and the junction of the three rivers. The woman in the green suit and her companion were sitting at a table in a far corner. Lloyd chose a chair with his back to them. His appetite had disappeared. Meredith was speaking, and after a moment, Lloyd realized she had addressed him.

"I apologize, Meredith. I wasn't listening. What were you saying?"

"Apology unnecessary but accepted." She smiled. "Lynn mentioned your favorite here is the Colossal Crab Hoelzel, which I took the liberty of ordering for you."

"Thank you, Meredith," Lloyd said with feigned enthusiasm.

Dr. Castle arrived, and Lloyd stood until she was seated. He thanked her for her testimony, adding that he was certain it had favorably impressed the jury and Judge Tate.

The waiter opened the champagne with a satisfying report and poured the bubbling wine into a flute for each of them. Uncharacteristically, Lloyd drained his in two swift swallows. The waiter refilled it. As he tipped the flute to his lips, he noticed Lynn watching him across the table. He set the glass on the linen tablecloth without drinking from it.

Meredith proposed a toast to Lloyd and Lynn. He drank the contents. When the attentive server had refilled his glass, Lloyd rose, a bit on the tipsy side, to toast Meredith. His three companions regarded him, Castle and Goldsmith with mild amusement, Lynn with a puzzled frown. Before resuming his chair, Lloyd turned and glanced toward the woman in the corner.

To hell with you, he thought. *I'm a free man.*

The Colossal Crab Hoelzel was placed before him, and Lloyd rediscovered his appetite. He placed the first morsel of lump crabmeat in his mouth, knowing he would pay a diabetic price for eating such rich food, but it was worth it.

CHAPTER 22

Saturday, September 24, 1955

The morning sun sparkled over the dewy grass and filtered through the yellowing leaves of the beech at the rear of the yard. Lynn, a coffee cup in one hand and a buttered croissant in the other, found Lloyd in the library, pajama-clad, staring into space.

"I thought you'd be in the sunroom watching the sunrise. What a lovely view through the sunlit trees. Were you there earlier?"

"No. I had some thinking to do and didn't want to be distracted."

"About what?"

"Oh, just some theological questions I've been mulling over."

Lynn raised an eyebrow. "Such as?"

"Does God send suffering to people to strengthen their faith," he said, "to enable them to be saints?"

Lynn blinked. *Not again.* "Well, if that's true, I'll have to address you as St. Lloyd. But my Methodist Sunday school teacher would say that's baloney." Lynn surveyed her husband. "Have you had anything to eat?"

"No, not yet. I wasn't hungry when I got up."

"Well, you're hungry now." She grabbed his arm and pulled him to his feet. "Have you checked your sugar?"

"I will."

"Yes, you will . . . *now*."

When Lloyd returned from the bathroom, Lynn led him into the kitchen and told him to sit. She gathered the paraphernalia and dropped the reagent into the urine sample.

She watched the color develop. "Seriously?"

Lynn went to the refrigerator and brought out a cantaloupe, cut it in half, scooped out the seeds, and produced a plate, knife, fork, and spoon. "Here you go. I'll have some toast and marmalade in a jiffy." As she busied herself with the breakfast preparations, she said, "Let's not waste this spectacular day. Let's put the canoe on the car and drive over to Indian Lake. I'll put together a picnic and you pick out a bottle of wine. Maybe we can have dinner at that nice Italian place in North Huntingdon on the way back. We haven't been in the canoe all summer. What do you say?"

"How soon do you want to go?"

"You need to shower, shave, and get dressed, so let's shoot for an hour."

"I don't shave on Saturdays, but let's make it two. I'll have to wash the canoe. It's been in the garage all summer and will be covered in spider webs and spider poop."

"I'm capable of scrubbing out the canoe, Captain Ahab. Just get yourself clean and into your canoe-paddling duds. That's your job."

Lynn washed tomatoes and cucumbers from the vegetable bin and packed them, along with olive oil, lemon juice, and a couple of Lloyd's favorite McIntosh apples. She made two ham-and-Swiss cheese sandwiches on rye, filled a large thermos with ice cubes and water, and placed the lunch in a large canvas boat bag.

Without missing a beat, she dragged the twelve-foot canoe out of the garage and turned the hose on it. Using a stiff bristle brush, Lynn attacked the tiny spider droppings dotting the aluminum surface. After a lot of scrubbing and swearing, Lynn decided the job was good enough for government work. She rinsed off the detergent and left the canoe to dry in the sun.

As she washed her hands at the kitchen sink, Lynn noticed Lloyd hadn't selected the wine. She chose a white Bordeaux and snuggled it in a bag of ice cubes.

She glanced at the kitchen clock, then climbed the rear stairs. Lloyd was sitting on their bed, clad only in undershorts, holding a faded T-shirt in his hands.

"Lloyd, are you okay?"

He looked at his wife and shook his head. "Kids around here will always wonder if I did actually molest Allison. But that's only part of it." He bent to slip on his moccasins, then straightened. "I don't trust kids anymore. Fact is, I don't really trust people. I wish it weren't so, but aside from a few close and reliable friends, I can't let down my guard anymore."

"You don't mean that, honey. This just isn't you. You could no more change your character or your outlook than . . . than a tiger could decide to become stripeless." Lynn moved to stand in front of him. "Listen, you're grieving. Let the grief process work, and then see if you still feel this way. As for now," she extended her hand and helped him up, "we're going to enjoy this day." She kissed his cheek. "We fought together before and during the trial, and we're sure as hell going to fight together now."

• • •

Indian Lake was busy with boaters and fishermen taking advantage of the warm, early fall day. Lynn and Lloyd loaded the canoe with their picnic trappings and pushed off into the choppy lake. They hugged the western shore, paddling for their favorite inlet, hoping it would be relatively uncrowded. Lynn paddled from the bow, while Lloyd paddled and steered from the stern.

Although there was a following breeze, Lynn began to feel they were having an unusual amount of difficulty making headway. She turned around. Lloyd was steering but not pulling his weight.

"Ahoy, the stern thwart! In case you've forgotten, canoes move better and faster if both crew members work the paddles."

"What? Oh, sorry. Wasn't thinking." Lloyd put his back into it, and the canoe responded.

Lynn kept her eyes on him for a few more seconds before resuming.

Within twenty minutes, they entered the inlet. There were only two canoes pulled out of the water and a small open boat with an outboard engine anchored near the bank. A man and woman were fishing.

They beached the canoe at a grassy meadow. Lloyd stuck the anchor into the soil, and they walked to a shade tree where they spread blankets and the bag of food and wine. Lynn lay back, propped on an elbow, and watched her husband. He sat gazing out at the water, chewing on a grass stem.

She brushed his arm with her leg. "Say, big guy, I've reconnoitered this spot and wish to report the canoeists and the couple fishing are unable to see us with naked eyes. Or binocular eyes, for that matter. Perhaps you'd like to ditch the grass and chew on me for a time?"

"Dessert first?" Lloyd laughed, turning to embrace her. "Now that's what I call a picnic." He met her open mouth with his. Lynn unzipped his fly and began to caress him. Lloyd kissed her neck, then her chest, unbuttoning her blouse as he moved lower. After some minutes, he rolled away. "Lynn, I'm sorry. It's not you. I can't seem to—"

She kissed his forehead. "It's okay, honey. Nothing to fret about." She sat up and buttoned her blouse. "Tell you what, while I set out the food, why don't you open the wine? The corkscrew's in the boat bag with the wine glasses."

Lloyd pulled the cork from the bottle, wondering if this stain on his life and attitude would permanently dampen his intimacy with Lynn.

Self-evaluation had always been an essential element of his character. Lloyd had realized from the moment the police arrested him that he was no longer himself. He was removed from himself—totally and irrevocably. It had not been a gradual change.

It had happened all at once after that first knock on the door back in July. He'd never forget it. *It's as if it happened yesterday.* He never thought it would happen, not to him, and now he wasn't the same person anymore, emotionally, mentally, or physically.

"Honey," Lynn eyed the bottle in his hands, "Will you pour us some wine?"

"Oh, sure. Where did you say the glasses were stowed?"

"I got them. Here you go. Rex, the nice man at Grant's Wines, recommended this Bordeaux a couple weeks ago. He knows we don't like fruity wines."

Lloyd held his glass up to the sun and studied the color of the wine, then threw the contents of his glass into the grass. "Damn it! Can't I do anything right? There was a hunk of cork in my glass. Check yours, Lynn."

"Sweetheart," she said, her calm voice belying her alarm. "Remember, *don't throw out the wine with the cork.* Nobody ever died from swallowing a piece of cork. Pour yourself another glass while I dress and toss the tomatoes and cucumbers."

Lloyd watched a sloop with red sails rigged fore and aft move across the cove entrance on a starboard tack. He wondered if the two persons on board knew of the sandbar just south of the mouth of the inlet.

That's the way life is, he mused. *You go sailing along, peacefully minding your own business, and without warning, you run aground or strike a reef, and your boat sinks with you in it.* He drank the wine, not really tasting it, then toyed with the salad and ate only a few bites of his sandwich.

Lynn dug out the apples. "How about a McIntosh? First ones of the season from Baker's farm."

"I think I'll save it for later." Then he added, "They look ripe. Apples fresh from the tree beat supermarket fruit every time."

Lynn knew better than to insist he eat. "I saw that sailboat with the red sails. Too bad it's not time for the sun to set. You could sing

'Red Sails in the Sunset' to me." She grinned. "You had a sailboat one time. I remember you said you sold it, but I don't think you told me why."

"I bought a centerboard daysailer from a college friend. I knew nothing about sailing—and I mean *nothing.* He gave me a brief course as we stood on the dock. I climbed in and sat on the stern thwart, and he cast off the lines. I hauled up the mainsail, and after banging into a couple of other boats and narrowly avoiding the rock jetty, I was sailing. I was really proud of myself."

Lloyd shook his head. "My friend didn't include tacking in my instruction course. The other shore of the small lake loomed. I had stowed a copy of *Sailing* magazine in the map drawer and began paging through it to find out how to change direction. I had no luck, so I just ran the boat aground."

He chuckled. "During that entire summer, I never sailed home. It was either swim while pushing the boat or have a friendly and highly amused fisherman tow me in. The only good thing about my career as a sailor was the profit I made when I sold the boat in September."

"Did you name your boat?"

"Yes, but not till the day I sold it."

"And the name of this vessel was?"

Lloyd smiled. "The Pequod."

"Herman Melville and Moby Dick would be honored," Lynn joked.

They erupted in boisterous laughter. When the laughing died down, one or the other would say "The Pequod," and they broke down giggling and guffawing again.

The sun touched the rim of the hill behind them, and the breeze began to kick up. Lloyd looked at the sky. "We'd better think about heading back. Looks like we'll be paddling into the wind."

"Okay, Skipper," said Lynn. "There's a smidgeon of grape left. Let's polish it off. Without sounding too much like a noodge, may I tempt you to eat the rest of your sandwich, or maybe the apple? I don't want to have to do all the paddling on the return to the ramp."

"You *are* a noodge, but a well-meaning noodge. We're still planning to dine at Piccolo Forno?"

Lynn nodded.

"That settles it. I'll just have the apple, no sandwich, so I can save room for dessert."

CHAPTER 23

Tuesday, October 19, 1955

While Lynn MacDonald was brushing her hair in the bathroom, a heavy truck engine rumbled outside followed by an explosive report of air brakes. She looked out the window. A large moving van stood before the Harrises' house. The crew opened the side doors and attached a ramp.

"Thank you, Lord," Lynn whispered.

There had been no *For Sale* sign on their lawn, but Bev Ellsworth, fount of all neighborhood goings-on, told her Walter had lost his job with Dornhoefer Motors. Bev hinted he'd pitched *his* personal styling and body features instead of the Cadillac Eldorado to a married woman prospective customer. Unpersuaded and mad as a hornet, the woman had driven to the Hudson Motor Car dealership and bought a 1955 Hornet. Dornhoefer also was mad as a hornet. He kept the Eldorado but unleashed Walter.

The interval since Lloyd's trial had been a backbreaker for Lynn and her husband. Living next door to the man who'd maliciously and baselessly accused Lloyd had frayed her nerves and thrown Lloyd into a downward spiral, emotionally and physically. Each accidental or unavoidable sighting of the Harrises, however brief, was god-awful.

Lynn viewed the arrival of the moving van as divine intervention. Without the constant physical presence of that loathsome man, his subservient mouse wife, and their damaged daughters, maybe Lloyd would begin to recover from his increasingly frequent bouts of depression.

Using the teeth of her comb, Lynn pulled out some entangled strands of hair from her hairbrush. "Damn it. Now my hair's falling out." She cursed the day in June when she had welcomed Regina Harris as neighbor. She threw the brush into the drawer and slammed it shut.

The bathroom mirror revealed the face of a tense, angry, worried woman. Lynn studied her reflection. She admitted there were times when her fear for Lloyd's mental state boiled over into anger toward him. *Why can't he snap out of it?* He hadn't left the house since their picnic at Indian Lake. He never set foot in the sunroom. And he wasn't taking care of himself. His sugar count was too high, and his poor eating habits only made it more dangerous.

His depression deepened when his son returned to Ohio State for fall semester. Lloyd lost interest in dining at their favorite restaurants or going to the theater or to the Pittsburgh Symphony Orchestra. He no longer read literature.

Lynn had suggested he see a psychologist. He'd turned on her, asking if she thought he was mentally ill. *Does she secretly suspect that I assaulted Allison, and Nicky Palmer as well?*

Lynn decided to ask a professional for advice. She called Dr. Sharon Castle, who insisted Lynn meet her that afternoon in her office to discuss the situation.

• • •

"I appreciate your taking the time to see me about this, Dr. Castle."

"Please, call me Sharon, Lynn. Let's sit in the comfortable chairs. Tell me what's happening with you and Lloyd."

Lynn spilled it all. Lloyd's despondent nature, his lack of interest in his passions, the decline in his health, and most of all, her fear that he wouldn't be able to recover. Dr. Castle told her that more than a third of individuals wrongly accused of sexual misconduct who were subsequently exonerated suffered long-lasting trauma. As she listened, Lynn felt overwhelmed.

"Lloyd is a sensitive, trusting, extremely intelligent man," Sharon said. "A man who has always enjoyed an impeccable reputation, socially and professionally. Despite the not guilty verdict, he believes his reputation has been tainted, or even lost, because of this."

"*Lost?* You mean for the rest of his life?"

"I can't predict Lloyd's future, but studies have shown that those absolved of an unwarranted charge of sexual misconduct sometimes have difficult and at times lengthy recoveries, especially those with trusting, caring natures."

"But you're speaking of people who couldn't or wouldn't go to psychologists or trauma counselors, right?"

Sharon touched Lynn's hand. "Lynn, there are no guarantees in these cases. Professional help is the best course of action, for sure. Lloyd's attitude is of paramount importance to his recovery. He has to want to be well. He must do the work. But if he doesn't have confidence and trust in the psychologist, he may as well consult the milkman."

Lynn mashed her cigarette in the ashtray, and with unsteady fingers, lit another. She was unsure if Lloyd's present state of mind indicated a readiness to be well. *Goddamn you, Walter Harris.* With effort, she collected herself.

"Okay, Sharon. Here's how I see this. Unless this situation turns around, I'm going to lose my marriage, or Lloyd. All his life, Lloyd's been a man who will not give up. He's always been a fighter who never backs away from challenges or problems. Right now, I don't recognize him. As I said on the phone, he's disinterested in socializing at any level, has neglected his health big time, and he's withdrawn from me. This has to be his decision, but I want to help him get there. I know this isn't your area of psychology. Can you refer us to someone you know, someone you believe to be the best?"

Without hesitation Sharon said, "Dr. John Melnick. Melnick is an expert in counseling people who have been falsely accused and wrongfully indicted on sexual misconduct charges." She handed Lynn a business card. "Contact him at this number and tell him I referred you."

Lynn studied the card. "*Dr. Melnick.* Didn't I read something about him in the paper a while ago?"

"John was the psychologist who counseled the defendants falsely accused of sexually molesting preschoolers at the Mother Goose Daycare Center out in Ross Township. All the defendants were acquitted of all charges. Three of the six women made a full return to normal life."

"What about the other three? What happened to them?"

"That's confidential patient-doctor information. They may be in continuing consultations with Dr. Melnick."

"He's the expert, yet only half of the Mother Goose defendants made it back to a normal life?"

Sharon looked steadily at Lynn but said nothing.

With calculated slowness, Lynn placed the card on the end table. "Thank you, Dr. Castle." She stood.

"Lynn, this isn't a do-it-yourself project. I believe Dr. Melnick can help you and Lloyd. Give it your earnest consideration. Discuss it with Lloyd. If you decide to contact Dr. Melnick, call me." She watched Lynn exit her office and close the door behind her.

Lynn stepped into the elevator, a milk train that stopped at every floor to load a passenger or three, all likely homeward bound after work. A burly man who'd apparently bathed in cologne stepped on her foot. She barely felt it. The battle for Lloyd's return to himself superseded everything. She would not depend on the Dr. Melnicks of the world—not with a 50 percent success rate. She knew her husband better than any professional. What's more, she loved him.

We need to get away, she concluded. They'd been chained to the house for four years. Their last trip outside of the States was to

Scotland eight years earlier. Lynn had a sudden inspiration. During a dinner party last spring at Jim and Bev's, Bev had raved about the trip they'd made to the Greek islands. The more Lynn thought about a Greek getaway, the more she liked the idea.

Lynn called Bev from a pay phone in the lobby. Her friend agreed that Lloyd and Lynn needed time away and invited Lynn to have coffee with her the next day.

"Corfu is the perfect destination for you," Bev said. "You may not want to come back. I've got tons of stuff about all the Ionian Islands but wait till I show you our pictures from Corfu. Lloyd will love St. Spyridon Church and the Achilleion. The best thing is that the tourists haven't discovered it yet." Bev changed the topic. "You guys must be over-the-top crazy happy they're moving. Cissy, on the other hand, isn't. Allison and Cissy got to be friends."

"I saw them hanging out a few times. Cissy would've been a good influence on Allison." Lynn checked her watch. "Listen, Bev, I'm sorry to cut this short, but I'm in Oakland and I need to get home. What time tomorrow?"

"Eleven. Okay?"

"Sure. I'll bring some of your favorite lemon bars. Thanks, Bev. You're just what the doctor ordered."

• • •

Lloyd sat in the library, a cut crystal glass of scotch on the end table, a cigar cradled between his thumb and fingers. He welcomed Lynn with an announcement.

"Darling." He nodded gravely. "The Royal Mail Ship Walter Harris left port on her maiden voyage twenty-one minutes and thirteen seconds ago. I'm sorry you weren't here to lift a one-finger salute to the ship's namesake and shout '*bon débarras*' to the passengers. From my vantage point in the sunroom, I observed the crew loading the passengers' luggage and personal belongings. When the stevedores removed the gangplank, I felt like shouting for joy, so I did."

Lloyd sipped his scotch. His eyes crinkled with a broad smile.

"Okay, so it was a moving van rolling away with the Harrises' furniture."

Lynn plunked herself on Lloyd's lap, snuggling against his chest. She lifted her left arm in a fist salute. "*Bon débarras,* Walter, you no-good bastard! *Bon débarras,* Regina! *Bon débarras,* Allison and Carin!"

Lloyd placed the cigar in the ashtray. "I deem this an event that demands celebration, my little chickadee. Therefore, I proclaim this nineteenth day of October 1955, to be *Bon Débarras* Harris Day. The festivities shall commence at a time to be determined by the reservation maître d' at Pescado's and will conclude in our boudoir at a time mutually agreeable to both parties."

Lynn kissed him. "The meal will only be the appetizer, my good man. I will handle the reservation while you take whatever actions you deem necessary to make yourself even more appealing than you already are."

• • •

Dusk was deepening when they left the house by the back door, chattering happily as they headed for the garage.

Lloyd saw it first.

Stapled to the door of the carriage house was the orange maillot.

CHAPTER 24

Friday, December 2, 1955

David Elliott picked up his mail after morning classes at Gettysburg Lutheran Seminary. A large wastebasket had been placed beneath the rows of mailboxes. He tossed a flyer advertising the sale of clerical stoles, robes, and collar shirts. As a first-year student, he would not be in the market for such trappings for three years. Not even then if he couldn't cut the mustard in his courses. Monday, the first day back after Thanksgiving break, Dr. Reinberger surprised his New Testament class with a pop exam on the Letter to the Hebrews. Reinberger's margin notes convinced David that he had not done well. One of the guys complained about the unexpected, unannounced test. Dr. Reinberger reminded the class that, as pastors, the unexpected would be a way of life. "Get used to it," he had advised.

David thumbed through the rest of his mail, which included a letter from Bruce MacDonald. David's guilt machine started. He had intended to visit Mr. Mac over Thanksgiving but hadn't. No excuse. He had phoned Mr. Mac from Gettysburg after the jury acquitted him in late September. They had a long conversation, covering a range of topics. Lloyd sounded less cheerful than David had expected, but he'd chalked it up to understandable weariness and emotional letdown after the ordeal.

He opened and read Judy's letter as he walked through the slushy remains of yesterday's snow to his dorm room. They'd shared a loving goodbye Sunday morning before David started back to G-burg from Mount Lebanon. Her letter didn't include any new info about family and friends, but a love letter shouldn't be newsy.

"Hey, Dave!" his roomie, Barry, called from the steps of the Baughman building. "Are you heading to the room?"

"Yeah." David stopped. Barry jumped a puddle. "Where were you assigned for your fieldwork?"

"First Lutheran, Baltimore."

David snorted. "You got assigned to your hometown? How'd you pull that off? Home cooking every weekend, Saturdays with Audrey. Man, you continue to impress me."

"First Lutheran has a strong social services outreach. I mentioned to the director that I want to focus my future ministry in social services. He practically jumped across the desk to get my signature." Barry laughed. "How about you?"

"After telling the director about my experiences in Las Cruces doing a door-to-door feasibility study for the Board of Home Missions, he assigned me to a mission congregation in Slater's Gap." The roommates climbed the steps to their dormitory.

"Slater's Gap sounds cosmopolitan. I see it as a metropolitan hub," Barry ribbed.

"I heard it makes Baltimore look like a one-dog town," David said. "I'm heading there tomorrow to meet the pastor and his family. Gene served there last year. He says the pastor will give me lots of practical experience, and apparently his wife is a fantastic cook."

Barry retrieved a pad of notepaper from his desk. "I'm heading to the library after chow. How about you?"

"I want to read this letter first. Save some food for your starving roomie."

• • •

David stood by his desk and opened the letter from Bruce MacDonald. After reading the first sentence he sat, holding it with both hands.

Saturday, November 26, 1955

Dave,

I know you and Dad have a close relationship, so I'm sorry to be the bearer of bad news about him. Since October, he has gone steadily downhill as far as his health is concerned. I ended up staying home after Thanksgiving to help Mom take care of him.

In a nutshell, Dad has changed. His personality is radically different from who he was before this damn Harris thing. He doesn't trust people, if you can believe that, and he's apparently lost interest in literature and philosophy. His eating habits have become life-threatening despite Mom's efforts. He consumes food that would give you and me diabetes. Dad slops around the house everyday wearing the same T-shirt, shorts, and flip-flops, drinking from a quart of orange pop. When Mom and I try to reason with him, he flies off the handle.

In October, Mom consulted with Dr. Castle, the psychologist who testified at Dad's trial. She recommended a psychologist, but Mom wasn't convinced. She decided no one knows Dad like she does and instead began to make plans for the two of them to get away for a while. The Harrises moved that same day, and Mom said Dad was his former confident, fun-loving self until that evening.

Turns out, before the Harrises departed, that evil son of a bitch Walter nailed Allison's swimsuit to the carriage house as a parting shot. Dad fell apart. Since then, Mom has repeatedly begged Dad to see a psychologist, but his response is always, 'What's the use?' And that's where things stand right now. Honestly, unless Dad pulls out of this, I doubt if he'll live to see the new year.

If you have an opportunity to stop over when you're home on Christmas break, I'd really appreciate it. I know Dad will want to hear how things are going with you.

—Bruce

CHAPTER 25

Friday, December 23, 1955

David stepped off the Greyhound. He glimpsed his dad standing at the window of the waiting room. They hugged when David stepped inside and kissed his dad's cheek.

"How's it going, Dad? Doing okay?"

Harold Elliott looked beat. *Still being worked like a rented mule,* David mused. At least he had quit the cigarettes.

"I'm fine. How was the trip?"

"From G-burg to the turnpike, the road was snow covered. I'm glad I didn't have to drive over Mount Tuscarora. It's good to be home, even though it's only been a month. Hang on a second." Outside, he hefted his suitcase then rejoined his dad to walk to the car.

During the short ride home, David quizzed his father about his health. Was the medicine helping him relax? Had his plan to delegate more responsibility to his assistant worked out?

"Yes to the medicine, and a firm maybe to delegating. I'm having more difficulty with it than he is," he admitted with a chuckle. "You're a bigger worrywart than your mother. Save some worry for Lloyd MacDonald. He's not doing well."

"Yeah, Bruce wrote me a grim letter about his dad."

"Your mother tries to call Lynn once a week. Sounds like Lloyd has thrown in the towel."

That evening, after dinner, David called the MacDonalds.

Lynn sounded relieved to hear from him. "Can you come over now, Dave? I know you just got home, but—"

"Sure, Mrs. Mac. Thanks for getting me out of scrubbing the pans."

• • •

Nothing in Bruce's letter could have prepared David. Lloyd seemed to have aged twenty years since David had last seen him. Open sores dotted his forearms and lower legs. He had lost a considerable amount of weight. A large bottle of water sat on the floor beside his easy chair.

"Your Christmas tree's a stunner, Mr. Mac. Having it in the sunroom window gives neighbors and passersby a beautiful view."

"Lynn's talent for holiday decorating is unsurpassed."

"I bet you and Bruce had a hand in the lighting. You must have put a dozen strings of white lights on to get such a dazzling effect. I've never seen a Christmas tree with only white lights. I think I like the effect better than multicolored lights. How about you?"

"I haven't seen it yet. I don't go up to the sunroom."

His words surprised David, who maintained his cheerful expression.

"Bruce gave me a tour of the addition. You did a fantastic—"

"Excuse me, David." Lloyd struggled to his feet. "Got to take a pee."

When he returned and dropped back into his chair, Lloyd said, "It seems like all I do anymore is drink water and pee." He raked at a sore on his arm. "How are your seminary studies? Difficult, I imagine."

"Yes, particularly Systematic Theology. Lots of unfamiliar terms and Biblical concepts I've never heard—"

"David, do you think God sends us suffering to strengthen our faith?" Lloyd leaned forward in his chair. "To enable us to be great saints?"

"Gosh, I've never thought—"

"Ignatius of Loyola, who founded the Jesuits in the sixteenth century, believed it. I was educated by Jesuits who believed it, and after thorough analysis, I came to believe it. The question of why innocent people suffer has always—"

Lynn swept into the library before Lloyd could finish his thought. "Honey, why don't you tell Dave about Rudy Williams deciding to study engineering at Carnegie Tech? Rudy credits Lloyd with inspiring him to go for a degree in engineering," she said to David. "He says Lloyd's encouragement to follow his passion gave him confidence that engineering was the right fit for him."

"Mr. Mac has a way of inspiring people." David turned a grateful look at Lloyd. "Without your counseling, I wouldn't have been fit to return to college. I'll never be able to thank you enough."

"Sorry." Lloyd labored to get up. "Nature calls. Again."

As soon as Lloyd was out of earshot, Lynn's face drooped with despair. "He's given up," she said. "He refuses to see a psychologist. God, why did I think the way to restore his health was a trip to the Greek islands? I kick myself every day for not contacting Dr. Melnick in October as Dr. Castle urged me to do. I can't get him to take care of his diabetes. I can't get him to read the literature he used to love." She shook her head. "I asked Nicky to round up some of the other kids who worked for Lloyd. She called this morning and told me she and three kids will be here tomorrow afternoon—Alex, Rudy, Donna, and Bruce, of course. They're going to hide in the sunroom, and Nicky's going to work her magic to persuade Lloyd to take her up to see the Christmas tree. If anyone can get Lloyd to go up there, it's Nicky." Lynn's eyes reflected single-minded resolve. "I'm not giving up, Dave. I'll do whatever it takes to save him."

David regretted he'd agreed to help with Christmas Eve worship services tomorrow at Mount Lebanon Lutheran. The pastor had scheduled a rehearsal in the afternoon. David wouldn't be able to join them in the MacDonalds' sunroom. He opened his mouth to say as much, but a phone rang somewhere in the house, and Lynn excused herself.

Lloyd entered a moment later and walked to the bookshelves. "Let's see, Ignatius of Loyola's writings on prayer should be . . . oh, actually, I have it in the bedroom."

"That's okay, Mr. Mac. I'll see it the next time I come by. Listen, if you have a few minutes, I'd like to talk with you about something else."

"Of course, David." Lloyd bent to turn on the gas fireplace. "It's chilly this afternoon. Ah, that's better already. Why don't you sit in the leather chair?"

Outside, the darkening sky began to spit snow. Lloyd stared at the blue-orange flames dancing in the fireplace.

"You're a good person," David began. "To me, you were a lifesaver. You're an outstanding chemist and well versed in the classics of art, literature, philosophy, theology, and you love to share these with people like me. You taught a bunch of kids the fine points of construction. You've been a positive influence on—"

"David," Lloyd broke in, "in addition to being an exceptional literary critic, my father, Angus MacDonald, loved gardening. He had a natural ability to match appropriate soils to particular varieties of legumes and root vegetables. Our family always had abundant supplies of the vegetables and fruits he grew." He smiled wistfully. "As a boy, I loved working with him—planting, weeding, watering, hoeing, picking. From time to time, he shared gems of gardening wisdom. One of his axioms was, 'Don't waste water or fertilizer on dying or dead plants.'"

David stared. A terrible, heavy dread pinned him to the leather chair. He couldn't find the words to form an appropriate reply. Mr. Mac wrenched himself to his feet. He moved to the doorway, then turned back toward David.

"Thank you, David. Take care of yourself." Then he was gone.

David had no idea how long he sat there, staring but not seeing anything, but at some point, Bruce appeared crouched in front of him.

"Are you okay?" he asked, searching David's face.

"My God, Bruce."

"C'mon, pal. You need some scotch."

David didn't protest.

CHAPTER 26

Wednesday, January 11, 1956

The phone call cut short their game of hearts. David hung up the hall phone. He put his forehead against the cool surface of the wall. The news of Lloyd MacDonald's death hit him hard, but he wasn't surprised. When David last saw Mr. Mac just before Christmas, it was obvious he had decided not to live. *But why? Why would a man of his intelligence just give up?* Lloyd had completed the construction of his dream house. He had been acquitted of a felony. He was blessed with a loving wife and son.

• • •

David and his parents attended the funeral. Most of the kids who worked for Mr. Mac were there as well. Nicky Palmer slid into the pew behind Lynn and Bruce just as the opening hymn concluded. David saw her touch Bruce on the shoulder.

Lloyd's funeral was a wonderful celebration of his life—his accomplishments as a chemist, his love of literature and the arts, his unfailing joy in helping youth and children, his willingness to teach and share ideas, his ability to understand what made young people tick.

The priest invited remarks from the family and friends. David spoke first.

"A little while back, I was suffering from shell shock. I wasn't worth a dime as one of Mr. Mac's workers, but he didn't care. For hours, over a period of weeks, he listened as I disclosed my fears and terrors. He held me in his arms when I cried and when I relived in flashbacks the events that scared me out of my mind. Mr. Mac's wise and compassionate care enabled me to return to a more normal life. I'll never forget him.

"Mr. Mac had this rare gift to perceive the inner reality of each of us, our hidden potential. And then he inspired us to grab our potential and let it fly. Mr. Mac built a great addition to his home, but he also built us."

Rudy Williams concluded his eulogy by singing the first verse of "Amazing Grace." All of Mr. Mac's kids knew the story of Rudy dancing in a paint pan, but none knew he had a beautiful voice.

Bruce stood and walked up the steps to the lectern. He took a sheet of paper from his suit coat. He read only a sentence before he began to sob. Nicky rose, went to his side, and took his hand in both of hers. Bruce bowed his head and started over. He stumbled over tears and painful silences, but he finished his tribute to his father. Still holding hands, Bruce and Nicky returned to the pews. Bruce took her arm and directed her to sit between him and his mother.

Lynn invited everyone to their home for a buffet luncheon—an appropriate continuation of the celebration of Lloyd MacDonald.

The atmosphere at the luncheon was festive. Friends in the neighborhood had provided plenty of food and drink. People gathered in small groups, talking animatedly, laughing mostly, probably telling their favorite Lloyd MacDonald tales.

David's mother stood outside one of the circles and pointed to her watch. David excused himself and went to her. "Give me a few minutes. I want to find Bruce and see if he's doing all right. None of the kids have seen him."

David found him sitting in the sunroom, watching the wind-whipped January snow fly.

"Hey, man. Can I come in?" Bruce waved him to a comfortable-looking chair. "Mother needs to get home, but I couldn't leave without seeing you. I'm heading back to seminary tomorrow morning."

"Did you ever hear where Walt Harris moved to?" Bruce asked.

"No."

"I heard they moved somewhere down near Little Washington. If you hear where, I want to know. Rudy's on this, too."

"Why do you care where he lives? He and his screwy family are gone."

"No, Dave. He's not gone. But he will be when I find him."

"Bruce, let it go. Your Dad would never seek revenge, and he'd be horrified to hear you say this."

"Yeah, well, Dad can't hear me. He's not here anymore, is he?" Bruce snapped, his voice climbing. "And why the hell isn't he? I'll never see or talk with him ever again. I'll never hear him laugh or have a drink with him. Who's responsible for that loss? *Harris,* that's who. I don't care how long it takes. One day, I'll find him, and that day will be Walter Harris's last."

"Bruce, listen—"

"I'm done listening!" he yelled. "All I need from you is where that piece of filth lives. Other than that, just keep your mouth shut. Neither you nor anyone else can talk me out of this."

He put his hands over his eyes and let out a terrible wail. David froze as Bruce broke down, bawling, howling. David went to him and touched his shoulder. Bruce brushed his hand away.

"*Get out!* Leave me alone!"

David would not see Bruce again for seven years.

CHAPTER 27

Monday, October 14, 1963

David Elliott had married Judy in 1958. A bittersweet year—the year of his ordination as a Lutheran minister, the year his father died. The year David accepted a call to serve as the pastor of Grace Lutheran Church in Ellerton, Pennsylvania, a rapidly growing community south of Pittsburgh. The expansion of industrial and commercial giants like Westinghouse, U.S. Steel, Alcoa, and Pittsburgh Plate Glass brought an influx of middle- and upper-management personnel to the Pittsburgh area. Ellerton, like similar communities in southwest Pennsylvania, was experiencing social and economic changes. But not all the transformations were smooth.

Pastor Elliott had just arrived home from a stormy church council meeting on an equally stormy night when his mother phoned. He assumed she was calling to tell them his sister, Jean, had had her baby. Instead, she told David that Bruce MacDonald had been arrested that afternoon by the Allegheny County Police Department and charged with first-degree murder. And not just any murder. Bruce had been accused of committing the brutal execution-style murder of Walter Harris eighteen days before. She had no further details.

Mother and son caught up on family news for a few minutes.

She liked her new supervisor at the insurance agency where she had worked as office manager since her husband's death in early 1958. Nothing to report on David's very pregnant sister. He assured his mother that both Judy and he were doing well. Affected by Bruce's situation, neither he nor his mother were inclined to chat.

After hanging up, David joined Judy on the sofa.

"How's your mother?" she asked.

David related the family stuff, then told her what happened to Bruce. "I'll never forget what Bruce said the night of his dad's funeral. He swore he'd kill Walter Harris, even if it took the rest of his life." David looked at Judy. "Still, that was seven years ago. A person can change a lot in seven years. Would Bruce carry that venom within him this long?"

"I don't know him as well as you, but I don't believe Bruce could kill anyone. What he said to you the night of his dad's funeral were the angry words of a grieving son."

"Yeah, I agree." David rubbed his aching shoulder. Rainy weather always brought an arthritic reminder of the fracture years ago. "Bruce is a lot like Lloyd. He has a strong moral character. He's intelligent and curious, always willing to help people, especially young kids."

Judy pursed her lips. "I guess there have been murderers who had similar qualities, especially the strong moral character bit."

David admitted that was true. But they both felt it unlikely Bruce had committed murder to avenge his father.

"Did she say why the police think he did it?"

He shook his head. "She heard it on KDKA. She said it was a news bulletin, no details. I'll call Lynn tomorrow. She'll know more about it."

"My heart goes out to Lynn. I can't imagine what she's feeling. Doesn't she have a sister?"

"Lynn's older sister in Chicago lives in a nursing home. I don't think she has any other family. As soon as the news about Bruce hits the paper, I'm sure the Ellsworths and Marberrys will be there to support her."

• • •

The next morning in the church office, Jan Henry the church secretary and David met briefly to discuss the next issue of the monthly congregational newsletter. Jan reminded him that she hadn't received any copy for the *Pastor's Page.*

"Oops. I think I have that on my desk," he said.

"On your desk? I think it would be quicker for you to write a new piece than to hunt for it in your paper stacks," she teased.

A few minutes before noon, he phoned Lynn MacDonald. The information she relayed about Bruce wasn't encouraging.

Apparently, a witness who said she knew Bruce had come forward after the news broke about Harris' murder. The witness told a Mount Lebanon police lieutenant that she had been at The Hot Corner Bar on Forbes Avenue on Friday, May 10, and heard Bruce say he was going to kill Walter Harris for what the man had done to his dad.

"What do you know about this woman?"

Lynn sighed. "All I know about her is what I read in the papers. She's twenty-one. Bruce says he doesn't know her."

"Was Bruce in the bar that night?"

"Unfortunately, yes. He said he stopped in after a sales meeting at Periplaneta Pharmaceuticals to have a beer with Rudy. According to the story in the *Post-Gazette*, the woman swears she wasn't drunk. She's a student at Carlow College, majoring in social studies, and has no criminal record."

Lynn went on to tell him Meredith Goldsmith, the criminal defense attorney who had successfully defended Lloyd in 1955, was representing Bruce. Bruce was being held in Allegheny County Jail, awaiting a decision on whether he would be released on bail. A trial date had not been set.

Afterward, David sat at his desk reflecting on the weariness and dismay in Lynn's voice. No wonder. She had experienced the wrongful arrest and trial of her husband and his inexorable decline into death. Now her only son had been arrested on a charge of first-degree murder.

How much heartbreak could she take before she broke?

CHAPTER 28

Wednesday, October 16, 1963

David had some hospital calls to make in Pittsburgh. After the final visit, he went to see Bruce at the county jail. Bruce shuffled into the small visitation room shackled in chains and handcuffs. The guard had told him the prisoner would be restrained, but still, it shook David.

"Fifteen minutes, Father," the guard said.

David dismissed the temptation to tell him he wouldn't be a father until his wife gave birth to their first child.

Bruce and David managed to shake hands despite the handcuffs. Bruce looked haggard, his complexion ashen, his normally bright eyes faded.

"How's Mom?" Bruce asked.

"She seems to be doing okay, considering. Of course, she's worried about you. Wants me to report back to her. Are you getting enough sleep? Is the food all right? Are you depressed? Do you think it's hopeless?"

"She's remembering Dad."

"Yeah. It would be hard not to. Your mom is strong and feisty. She just needs assurance that you're still feisty, too. I'll tell her you are."

"I am most of the time. Nicky's phone calls help. She's been good for me. She worshiped Dad. She said she's going to call Mom, see if they can arrange to get together. I know she'll do Mom a lot of good."

David weighed his friend's situation. Since his arrest, significant events had come together to make things worse for Bruce. The story unfolded every evening in the paper and local TV newscasts. So far, the police had stitched together a timeline and placed Bruce at the center.

On Thursday evening, September 26, 1963, Walter Harris failed to return from a short trip to the Ormsby Post Office. Regina Harris and her daughter Carin, fifteen, found his car in front of the post office. The driver's door was open. Together, they searched the neighborhood without success.

Friday, September 27, Regina telephoned the Washington County sheriff and reported Walter Harris missing. The sheriff sent a missing person bulletin to surrounding counties.

Saturday, September 28, the murdered body of an unidentified male was discovered in Chartiers Creek County Park.

Monday, September 30, the Allegheny County Police Department notified the Washington County Sheriff's Department that they were in possession of the remains of an unidentified man who fit the description of Walter Harris.

Tuesday, October 1, Regina Harris, accompanied by daughters Allison and Carin, drove to the Allegheny County morgue, where Mrs. Harris identified the corpse as her husband.

Wednesday, October 9, Allegheny County police detectives questioned Bruce MacDonald, whose name was etched on the blade of the murder weapon, and investigated his alibi that he was in Sewickley, Pennsylvania, the night of the murder.

Monday, October 14, based on the knife and witness testimonies, the Allegheny County district attorney charged Bruce MacDonald with premeditated murder and remanded him without bail.

"Do you feel like talking about this?" David asked.

"It's all pretty damning stuff," Bruce replied. "The cops showed me the knife. It's mine, all right. But I haven't seen it for years, not since I worked on our house. One day—I don't recall when—I noticed it wasn't in its sheath. I looked for it everywhere and asked the other kids if they'd seen it. I figured it must have been thrown out in one of the hundreds of boxes of scrap we got rid of during that project. How in hell it was the weapon that killed that son of a bitch, I've not the faintest idea." Bruce looked at the floor for a long moment, then his head came up, and he laughed. A bitter laugh. "From the day that bastard accused my dad of molesting his little snoop of a daughter, I swore someday I'd kill him. And now somebody else did, and I'm the sucker left holding the bag. Pretty ironic, huh, Dave?"

"Is there any way to revoke the no bail order?"

"From what Meredith told Mom and me, there are very few options. She's going to request bail be granted at the next hearing, which is two weeks from now. If the judge denies her request, she'll take it to a higher court—whatever that is. This whole mess is screwy." Bruce leaned forward. "Listen, Dave, if I had killed him, I wouldn't have bothered with some voodoo execution. I used to think about how I'd do it—shoot him, maybe strangle him, hang him from a tree. Hell, with some of the pharmaceuticals I sell now, I could have poisoned him." He shook his head and sat without speaking. "Did you read the *manifesto* they found with him?"

"No. There's been nothing in the news about a manifesto. What are you talking about?"

"Meredith showed me a copy. It's some mumbo jumbo about Harris having to pay for his sins with his blood, or something to that effect. Sounded nuts to me."

The guard hammered on the door and shouted that David's visit was over. He offered to pray with Bruce before he went, but he declined.

"I don't like foxhole religion. Hey, man, it was enough that you were here with me. But you can keep me in *your* prayers, okay?"

CHAPTER 29

Monday, October 21, 1963

The Stewardship Committee had wrapped up its monthly meeting. David walked out of the room, exchanging "so longs" with committee members.

Lieutenant Jim Jakubowski stood in the hallway. The detective, his wife, and son were among the first group of new members David had welcomed to Grace Lutheran Church six years ago.

"Hi, Pastor Elliott. Could I talk with you for a few minutes?"

"Sure. Let's go to my office."

As usual, David's desk was piled with papers, folders, and a book lying open, face-down. Luckily, he had cleared the chair earlier that day, so Jake had a place to sit. He didn't miss Jake's quick look at the desk disguised as an exploding office warehouse.

"My wife says I have a *piling* system—not a *filing* system," David said. "At least I know what stuff is in what pile." Jakubowski looked skeptical. "Well, most times."

Jake got right to the point, pulling a paper from his briefcase. He held it for a fraction of a second before handing it to David. "I'd appreciate it if this conversation stayed between us, Pastor. If my supervisor found out I showed this to you, my ass—geez, excuse me,

Pastor. What I mean to say is that it could end my career."

"Of course, Jake. Count on it." David read the words on the paper, then read them again. "What is this? It's kind of . . . terrifying."

"It's a copy of the message we found at the Walter Harris murder site. We haven't released it to the papers or TV stations on the off chance the killer or somebody who had a hand in the murder uses some words or a sentence from it."

"Do you know I'm a friend of Bruce MacDonald?"

"Yes, I do. That's part of the reason I decided to show this to you."

"You haven't asked for my opinion, but Bruce didn't write this. On a philosophical and theological spectrum, he's at the extreme opposite end from religious cultism. I doubt Bruce knows the word *atonement* or its definition."

"My partner, Sergeant Eggleston, and I dug into Bruce MacDonald's background. I've concluded he didn't write this either. His apparent motive for allegedly killing Harris was revenge, not sexual misdeeds, which the manifesto focuses on. Eggleston is less convinced than I am, but that's okay. I need him to be skeptical sometimes. Now, don't get me wrong, Pastor, I'm not saying MacDonald didn't do this. But he didn't write that notice. Which means if Bruce MacDonald did kill Harris, someone else was involved from beginning to end. So more to the point, I figured you studied Hebrew and Greek in seminary, and I was wondering, are these words"—he pointed to the capitalized words at the beginning and end of the message NAQAM MALAKHIM— "Greek or Hebrew?"

"Well, I must confess, Hebrew and Greek were elective courses in seminary, and I decided not to take them. But I'm pretty sure they're not Greek." He went to the closet and pulled out a box. "I think there's a Hebrew-English dictionary somewhere among these old seminary texts." After a bit of rummaging, it came to hand.

He blew off the dust and took the book to the desk. "Let's see. Malakhim—yeah, here it is. I'll be darned. *Malakhim* means angels or messengers. And *Malachi* is one of the minor prophets; in this case, minor means fewer words than a book of a major prophet. *Malakh,* the Hebrew word for Angel, is the root of his name. Interesting, huh?"

Jakubowski's expression mimicked one David had noticed on some of his confirmation class students.

"Okay, let's see about Naqam." David waded through about a half page of Biblical references and scholarly footnotes. "Yeah. Here we go. *Naqam* is a verb that means to *avenge.* So, when you put the two words together as they are in this notice, a basic translation to English is *the Avenging Angels.*"

Jakubowski scribbled in his notebook. "Malakhim is the plural form for angel? Do I have that right?"

"Right, according to the dictionary."

The detective leaned back, peering off into the distance, a chess player thinking two moves ahead. "You've helped a lot, Pastor. Let me know if I can do anything for you." He held up a finger. "But I don't fix parking or traffic tickets." He smiled.

"There is something you can do, Jake. I'd like you to be in church when I preach the sermon about Malachi."

"Sure, that'll be interesting after what we found out tonight. What Sunday will that be?"

"I don't know, but if you come to church with your wife and son every Sunday, you won't miss it."

Jakubowski gave David a strange look, then realized his chain had been pulled. They laughed.

David believed the detective's investigation of the Harris murder would be thorough and fair. Lieutenant Jakubowski had no interest in running a railroad.

CHAPTER 30

Monday, October 28, 1963

The kitchen phone rang. David downed the last of his coffee and picked up the receiver. He regretted this immediately. A member of his congregation was calling to report that someone had left the water running in the women's room. "Water costs money. No wonder the utilities bills climb higher and higher," she groused.

David interrupted the diatribe. "Did you turn off the faucet?"

"No. I'm not the janitor."

"I appoint you janitor of the day. Now turn off the blasted water!" He banged the phone on its cradle.

Judy covered her mouth, smothering a laugh.

"That's it," he said. "We need to get away from all this crap. I'm taking the day off."

"Let's see the fall flower show at Phipps Conservatory," Judy proposed.

• • •

The weather thought it was July, not October. They didn't complain. The outdoor gardens dazzled. Chrysanthemums, pansies, ornamental grasses, asters. They bought three pots of mums to display on their front steps and later plant below the living room window.

That evening, Lynn MacDonald called with good news. Meredith Goldsmith's appeal succeeded. The court released Bruce on bail and ordered him under house arrest.

"Are visitors permitted?" Judy asked.

"There's nothing in the court order that specifies no visitors, so I take that as a yes. He can't leave the house except for church or medical reasons," Lynn said. "The court refused to allow him to go to work. He'll likely lose his job. I know how it goes. Company image takes precedence."

After Judy hung up the phone, she sat on David's lap. She kissed him, then said, "What are we going to do about Bruce?"

"Do? What do you mean?"

"We can't just sit around and hope things turn out fine for him."

"There's a sinister aspect to this murder you don't know about. Jake told me the details last week and asked me to keep them to myself."

"All right, then. If you think it's something only men can handle."

"That's not it and you know it." He pinched her nose. "I made a promise to Jake."

"I won't tell him you told me."

He slid her a sidelong glance. "That eases my mind."

"Besides, two heads are better than one. You've said this to me a lot of times."

"I distinctly remember saying two *sets of eyes* are better than one."

"Means the same thing."

They seesawed back and forth.

"You're so stubborn, David. You need me on this. Your pastoral responsibilities require time and energy—especially when appointing janitors. We're a good team. We feed off each other like Daphnis and Chloe."

"Daphnis and Chloe?"

"Well, okay, Nick and Nora Charles."

David surrendered. He summarized the message of the manifesto Jakubowski and his partner found with Harris' body.

"How does this tie in with Bruce? Why would the police believe he had any connection to those cuckoo birds?" Judy asked.

"I don't think Jake necessarily believes Bruce was involved with Naqam Malakhim. In fact, he told me he's sure Bruce didn't write the manifesto. But—" David raised his index finger. "Bruce's knife was the murder weapon. That's the key evidence against him. Jake's going to turn over every rock to solve the murder. But really, what difference does it make whether Bruce was a member of the cult? He had a motive to kill Harris, and he made no bones about his determination to do it."

"We need to find more information about this wacky Naqam Malakhim business."

David kissed Judy on her nose. "Why don't we discuss this up in bed?" He nuzzled her neck.

"Later, gator," she said. "Work before play. I've been mulling over an idea or three."

"Really? What a surprise."

She slapped him lightly on the arm. "Don't be sarcastic. I wondered why the Harris family moved to Ormsby. Granted, they needed to get out of Mount Lebanon after the jury declared Lloyd MacDonald innocent, but why Ormsby? So, I did a little research on Ormsby. There's a car dealership in Canonsburg, which is only seven miles from Ormsby, but I didn't find any indication they had hired Walter. If you don't need the car tomorrow, I'll go to the library and dig deeper into the community of Ormsby. What are the attractions? What's the school system like and the current business situation?"

"I have a meeting tomorrow morning with area clergy to discuss a proposal to convert the vacant warehouse on Merchant Street into a youth center. It'll probably take up most of the day. You can use the car if you'll drop me off at St. Ann's. I'm sure one of the guys will give me a ride home."

"Thanks, hon. You're a sweetheart."

"Yes, I am. Have you just figured that out?"

Judy stuck out her tongue. "How about giving a summary of this proclamation Jake had you read?"

"Naqam Malakhim appears to be a cult that observes some bizarre idea that they are God's appointed agents to punish sinners. The notice begins, *'We have warned you.'* From what's written, it's obvious Walter Harris had been warned, maybe more than once over a period of time, to stop committing fornication and sexual misconduct. When he didn't repent, they swooped in and made sure he'd never sin again."

"So, whoever wrote the manifesto believed Walter had a sexual relationship with a woman or women for an extended time." Judy rubbed her chin.

"Maybe the affair began with a woman in Mount Lebanon and continued after Walter moved."

"That would be an unusually long-lasting affair. The Harrises left Mount Lebanon in '55, right?"

"Right, Jude. Which says to me Harris and this unknown woman had deeper feelings for one another than just sexual attraction. If Walter were just chasing skirts, he could have just found someone in Ormsby or Little Washington."

"That's a good point. Think of all the gas he would have saved."

He grinned. "You're bad."

"Look at this from the woman's point of view. If she were only interested in a fling, she could have found something on the side in Mount Lebanon or close by."

"Found something on the side?"

"Don't raise your eyebrows at me, Pastor. That expression's been around since I was a sophomore in high school. I overheard Mother tell Dad one of our neighbors was getting 'something on the side.'"

"Well, was she?"

"*He.* And how would I know? I asked Mother what that meant, and she threw a fit about eavesdropping."

"Okay, back to business. We don't know if Walter was a member of that bunch of mixed-up nuts, but the sentence that declares *we have warned you* at least indicates they knew Walter and some damaging personal details of his character. Apparently, Walter violated the cult's creed against sexual misconduct, so they decreed he had to be sacrificed, whether he was a member or not."

Judy studied her husband, cracking the beginning of a smile. "Okay, David. I know the sign. You're rubbing your earlobe. Something's eating you. What are you trying to figure out?"

"Two things, actually. One, why did this Naqam bunch want the police to suspect Bruce? Two, how did they get hold of his knife? Bruce said he must have lost it sometime during the construction of the addition."

"Do you think one of the guys working there saw it lying around and stole it?"

He shook his head. "No. I got to know most of the kids on Mr. Mac's crew. They liked Bruce. Besides, why would you steal something with the owner's name engraved on it?"

"Why does anyone steal anything, for that matter? You told me when you were ten, you and another kid stole cherries from a neighbor's tree even though they had given your parents a whole peck basket of them." Judy poked him in the side and grinned. "You worked for Mr. Mac soon after we got back from New Mexico. Do you remember seeing Bruce with the knife then?"

"I wasn't paying much attention to anything during that time. In my mental state, I was about as useful as a chocolate coffee pot." David held Judy close.

They sat in silence for several minutes.

"We've come a long way, babe," he said and squeezed her a little tighter.

"God used some very special people to heal us, David. We are blessed." Judy leaned away to look at her watch. "It's getting late. Let's head upstairs."

"Does that mean work is over and now it's play?"

"Why don't you find out for yourself?"

CHAPTER 31

Tuesday, October 29, 1963

The clergy meeting was productive, somewhat to David's surprise. By four o'clock, when the meeting adjourned, six ministers had volunteered to serve on the Fund Development Committee and the Bids Procurement Committee. David bummed a ride home with the pastor of the Presbyterian church. They agreed that the group had taken an important first step toward having a youth center in Ellerton.

His colleague dropped David off at the parking area at the rear of the parsonage. The Cape Cod bungalow was built in the 1940s. In 1957, Grace Lutheran Church had purchased it. They had enlarged the kitchen and added a small deck outside the den. David and Judy loved the place.

The weather had turned toward winter. David picked up an armload of firewood from the stack piled against the wall of the attached garage. After depositing the wood beside the living room fireplace, he joined Judy in the kitchen, where she was chopping carrots. David hugged her, and she rewarded him with a kiss and a piece of carrot. After he had changed into more comfortable clothes, they recapped the day's activities. Judy led off with her Ormsby research.

"The Ormsby Chamber of Commerce information was outdated.

The most recent edition of the Ormsby Business Index was 1958. So that was a bust. I loaded a microfilm of the history of Washington County, and doggone, up came a sensational story.

"In 1877, the Scofield family was murdered in their farmhouse outside of Ormsby—mother, father, twelve-year-old daughter, and eight-year-old son. The constable concluded all four had been killed with a hatchet or an axe, but no weapon was ever found. The Scofields had joined some weird religious group named Avardian. Mrs. Scofield—Prudence—was drummed out of Avardian because she was seen in public without a bonnet and, God forbid, with her hair unpinned. The Council of the Avardian Priesthood summoned her to a hearing, and the three so-called priests publicly declared Prudence 'unchaste' and a 'slattern.' They banished her from the group."

"Sounds to me like she got a *Get Out of Jail Free* card."

"Right. Anyway, the Council's action angered her husband. He and his family left the assembly. But not before he took on the three priesthood guys, 'beating them sorely,' according to the account."

"So, members of Avardian slaughtered the Scofields?"

"The Scofield killings were never solved. My impression is that the Ormsby community supported Avardian and its members. For example, the constable stated the Avardians were 'God fearing, peaceful citizens.'"

"Where are you going with this? What does this have to do with the Harrises' move to Ormsby?"

"Maybe nothing, but that notice found with Walter's body shows Naqam cult members were at least bystanders while he was being killed. In 1877, the Scofield family was probably murdered by members of Avardian—a freaky bunch of religious nuts. Walter Harris was probably executed by Naqam Malakhim—another bunch of freaky religious nuts. The link is Ormsby, Pennsylvania."

"You're thinking somebody in Ormsby may be a descendant of the Avardians and resurfaced as Naqam Malakhim?"

"I suppose it's a possibility. But I've been wondering about the atmosphere. The mood of the people in the town today. Would they be okay having members of a cult living in Ormsby?"

"Did the article mention the origin of the name Avardian?"

"No. I felt the reporter took for granted that the whole town knew the name—like how everybody in Pittsburgh knows the name Pirates. What puzzles me," Judy went on, "is if this cult is based or located in Ormsby, why bring Walter to Chartiers Creek County Park to kill him? That's what, twenty-five miles? It makes me wonder if these crazies meet around here someplace."

• • •

When the supper dishes had been washed, dried, and put away, they sat at the kitchen table and talked until nearly midnight.

"Jude, I keep thinking. What's the connection between this cult and Bruce? If Walter is—*was*—a member of Naqam, it's no surprise that his fellow cult members took him out because he was messing around with another woman. Maybe she was a member of the cult. But why pin this on Bruce?"

"That *is* odd, given the fact that they signed the name of the cult on the note found with Walter's corpse. Before getting into that, though, you said the cult killed Walter because he was possibly messing around with another member of the cult. If his lover was a Naqam member, why didn't they kill her, too?" Judy answered her own question. "Because she wasn't a Naqam. No way would they have given a woman a pass on fornication or adultery."

"Hold on. We don't know enough about the Naqams to determine how they would deal with a female fornicator."

"That's true. We don't *know* Walter was a cult member. We're making an educated guess. We don't know if the Naqams would kill a woman for adultery, but I wouldn't bet against it. Look what the Avardians did to Prudence Scofield for not wearing her bonnet or using hairpins."

"Let's go back to why the Naqams took responsibility for killing Walter, then put Bruce in the crosshairs."

"Wait a second." Judy grabbed David's arm. "We assumed the Naqams threw a fastball with their manifesto. They threw a curve, and we whiffed."

"What?"

"They didn't take responsibility for the killing. Naqam judged Walter. They declared him guilty and sentenced him to death. Someone else may have executed him. Probably a Naqam hit man. Do cults hire hit men?"

"I don't know," David said. "Pretty shrewd insight about Naqam acting as Harris' judges, babe. Gives a new slant to this. Here's a thought. One of the Naqams was in that bar and overheard Bruce say he was going to kill Walter."

"But how did they get his knife? Bruce told you he hadn't seen it for years. He claims he never carried it except when he worked on the house." She jumped up, opened the junk drawer, and came back with a sheet of notepaper and a pencil. "I think better when I make a list. Let's write down the possible ways the cult members could have gotten hold of Bruce's knife."

When their ideas ran dry, they reviewed the list:

1. Bruce loaned his knife to someone and doesn't remember doing so.
2. Bruce put it down in a room under construction, forgot it, and a person working for a contractor—maybe a cult member—stole it.
3. The knife was accidentally thrown out with the trash and found by a trash hauler at the dump, who sold it to a Naqam member.
4. One of the Harris girls found it and showed it to their mother, who said she would return it but didn't. Regina's brothers, possibly members of Naqam, murdered Walter to avenge their sister. They dropped the knife at the scene unintentionally.

5. Bruce murdered Walter and made up the cult, but he carelessly left his knife under the body.

"What do you think, David?"

"I think they all sound contrived. Unrealistic."

"I agree. Either the killer intended to frame Bruce, or he used Bruce's knife because it's what he had." Judy looked at him. "Can you come up with any other scenario?"

He tried to recall something he had seen or read in the run-up to the murder, something significant. No use. The more he concentrated, the further it receded.

"Where'd you go?"

"Sorry." He rubbed his forehead. "We're getting nowhere with the knife puzzle. What do we know about Naqam?"

"Not much. Okay, speculation aside, do we agree Naqam Malakhim is an actual cult?"

"I think we can accept the facts detailed in the manifesto. *We* warned you, not *I* warned you. The note points to a group. And the Hebrew words in the name lend credence to the possibility it's a religious cult."

Judy bit her bottom lip. "I keep asking myself, why did the Harrises move to Ormsby of all places? Did Walter or another member of the family have a connection to some influential person in the town? Did Walter assume that car dealership owners in this area would spread the word of his antics at Dornhoefer and blackball him? Did a manufacturing firm in or near Ormsby offer him a sales position?"

"You raise some interesting questions, sweetheart."

"We need some interesting *answers*. There are too many interesting questions floating around."

David looked at his watch—fifteen minutes before midnight. They agreed to call it a night.

CHAPTER 32

Wednesday, October 30, 1963

Sergeant Eggleston parked the patrol car in a spot near the entrance to The Whitfield. Lieutenant Jakubowski exited the passenger door, and the two men walked inside. They identified themselves to the woman at the desk as law officers, and rode the elevator to Nicole Palmer's fourth-floor apartment. Eggleston knocked. Nicole, who'd been expecting them, invited them in to her two-bedroom apartment. Jakubowski took in the surroundings—beige paint, department store variety Danish modern furniture. After introductions, Nicole sat in an armchair and the detectives took seats on the couch.

"Thank you for agreeing to meet with us this evening, Miss Palmer," Jakubowski said. "As you know, Mr. Bruce MacDonald gave your name as a witness to his whereabouts the night of Thursday, September 26, 1963. We have Mr. MacDonald's statement of the events he experienced that night. Sergeant Eggleston will read it for you. If you have any questions or would like any or all the statement to be repeated, please feel free to ask."

Eggleston read in a mechanical voice. Nicole already knew the words of Bruce's alibi from memory. Half listening, she studied

Eggleston's face. *Where have I seen him before? On a bus or streetcar? In a store? A restaurant during lunch hour? Wait. No, it couldn't—*

Eggleston turned toward Jakubowski, his face in profile. *My gosh. It is him.*

Suddenly, Nicole heard the silence. Sergeant Eggleston and Lieutenant Jakubowski were looking at her, waiting for a response.

"Miss Palmer, does Mr. MacDonald's statement correlate with what he told you on the phone and again in person later that night?" Jakubowski asked.

"Yes, sir, in all respects."

"Do you know a woman by the name of Melinda Baker?"

"No, sir. I do not."

"So, Mr. MacDonald drove from Mount Lebanon to an apartment building in Sewickley after being invited to a surprise party in your honor by Melinda Baker. He doesn't know her, but he assumed she worked with you?"

"There are a number of my colleagues Bruce—Mr. MacDonald—doesn't know by name."

"What time did Mr. MacDonald call that night?" Eggleston asked.

"Seventeen minutes after midnight. When the phone rang, I looked at the clock."

"Please tell us what you and Mr. MacDonald said to each other during that call."

"Bruce asked me what was going on. Had I been promoted or had Melinda Baker screwed up the date or given him the wrong address. He was mad. I asked him to come here so we could try to figure out who had tricked him and why. Unfortunately, he threw away the typewritten invitation on his way here that night. We talked for a little more than an hour after he arrived. He gave me the gift he'd bought for the party, then left."

Jakubowski raised an eyebrow. "A gift? What gift? MacDonald didn't mention that."

Nicole's heart leaped. *Please let Bruce still have the cash receipt.*

"He gave me a tin of mixed nuts to honor my promotion. He had the clerk at Mabel's Confectionery Shoppe on Washington Road gift wrap it."

Jakubowski jotted in his notepad.

Eggleston handed Bruce's statement to Nicole. He instructed her to read it, and if satisfied, to sign and date it.

"Miss Palmer, do you still have the tin of nuts?" Jakubowski inquired.

"No, they were gone the very next evening. I'm a nut for nuts." Her silliness seemed to surprise Jakubowski and Eggleston. She didn't care. When they checked with Mabel's employee, Bruce's alibi would prove to be the truth.

Nicole called Bruce before the detectives got to the elevator.

CHAPTER 33

Monday, November 4, 1963

The sun was a dim flashlight shining through the dirty window of clouds. Before David exited his car, he checked the names of the family on the visitation card. He walked to the front door of an attractive brick home in a new development a few blocks from the church. The Whittaker family had visited Grace Church the day before. Mel Whittaker had been transferred to the Pittsburgh area from Chicago. After the worship service, Sally Whittaker told David they were "church shopping."

David pressed the doorbell. In a flash, a large red setter charged around the corner of the house and buried his wet nose in David's crotch. He pushed the dog away, but it bounded back, tongue lolling, jumping from side to side. Sally Whittaker took in the spectacle, then recovered her composure while David attempted to restore his dignity.

She opened the screen door. The dog shot between them and into the house. Sally looked disconcerted as it raced from one room to the other, jumping onto David's lap, then onto hers. David hoped Mrs. Whitaker disciplined her teenage son and daughter better than her hyper dog. Sally and David tried to have a conversation, but the canine cannonball would have none of it. The setter dashed into the kitchen, toenails scrabbling and skidding on the hardwood floor followed by a thudding collision with what sounded like wooden chairs.

Sally jumped up from her chair, narrowly avoiding a collision with the wild-eyed pet, who thundered past her, galloped up the stairs, then back down.

"Pastor," she said, her tone as chilled as the Arctic Circle, "I must ask you to take your dog outside before he damages our furniture."

"My dog? I thought it was your dog!"

The two laughed helplessly. It took both of them to corral the clamorous canine and drag him outside. When David left Sally Whittaker a half hour later, they were still laughing. Thankfully, there was no sign of the red dog as he walked to the car. *Ho hum,* he mused. *Just another uneventful afternoon in the life of a suburban minister.*

• • •

That evening, while David dried the supper dishes, the phone buzzed. He tucked the receiver between his ear and shoulder as he wiped his hands with the dish towel.

"Hello, Pastor Elliott? This is Nicole, uh, Nicky Palmer. I don't know if you remember me, but when I was in high school, I worked—"

"Of course I remember you, Nicole. Please, call me Dave. How are you?

"Pastor—Dave—I have to talk to you. It's very important. It's about Bruce."

Although Bruce had never said anything to him, David heard that not long after Lloyd MacDonald died, Bruce and Nicky Palmer developed a close relationship, and during David's visit with Bruce at the jail, Bruce mentioned Nicky had called him. David opened his scheduler.

"Nicole, if you live in the Pittsburgh area, and you're available, I could see you at ten o'clock tomorrow morning here at the church. The address is—"

"Yes, I rent an apartment in Carnegie. But I can't come to your church. I understand this is coming at you out of the blue, but could you meet me this evening? Please, Dave, I don't know who else to talk to about this. I'm calling from a pay phone because my phone may have been tapped. And I can't come to your church. It's too risky."

David gave Judy a look and held the phone away from his ear so she could listen in. "Nicole, listen, you're frightened. If someone is threatening you, call the Carnegie Police Department and tell—"

"Dave," she said, "you need to hear what's been happening to me, the weird messages and threats I've received. It all has a bearing on Bruce's case. Some totally freakish people who belong to a religious sect have warned me to stop my efforts to vindicate him."

"What's the name of this sect?"

"The Eye of Naqam."

"The Eye of Naqam?"

"Yes. I guess that's how it's pronounced." Nicole was silent for a few seconds.

David heard faint background sounds.

"I have to go," she said. "I'll be at the Green Lantern on Howard Drive in Upper St. Clair at six-thirty, and I'll wait an hour for you. Please. I'm begging you."

When the call ended, Judy looked at him with wide eyes. "My gosh! The Eye of Naqam! What are you going to do?"

He looked at his watch. Five minutes till six. "When Nicky worked for Lloyd MacDonald, she was in high school, sixteen or seventeen, I think. Her father was minister of a fundamentalist church, and from what I heard, he ruled Nicky like a fanatical tyrant. I got the impression she was the most talented and reliable person who worked for Mr. Mac. If Nicky said she'd do something, she did it. If she said she would be at work at this or that hour, Nicky honored her promise. I have no doubt she's telling the truth now."

"So, you're going to meet her tonight?"

"Yeah, I am. Want to come with me?"

Judy grinned. "Just try to stop me."

Neither said much during the fifteen-minute drive from Ellerton to Upper St. Clair. The Green Lantern was a hole-in-the-wall bar in a row of commercial businesses, including a barber shop, a local hardware store, and a corner grocery. During Easter break his sophomore year, David had a couple beers in the Green Lantern with a buddy. He thought it was a strange place for a young woman to choose to meet. David and Judy stood under the green light fixture above the door, which cast a bilious hue on all who entered.

"Boy, David, Nicole must be desperate to choose this place."

He remembered the place as dark and smoky. It hadn't changed in ten years. Neither had the canned country and western music, but David thought all C&W songs sounded alike. They paused to let their eyes adjust to the dimness. The scent of the never-wiped bar to their left slapped them in the nose. The bartender, a short balding man, glanced at them. An older man sat at the bar, drinking a bottle of beer and smoking a cigarette. A silhouetted figure rose from a table in the back. David and Judy steered past the Green Lantern regular.

Nicole hurried to them. She hugged David. "Thank you, Dave. I was afraid you wouldn't come."

"Nicole, this is Judy, my wife. She knows some of what you told me."

Nicole took Judy's hand in both of hers. "Thank you, Judy."

Even in the dim light, Nicole Palmer's beauty was dazzling. She gestured toward a table against the back wall.

The bartender arrived before they sat. "What'll it be, folks?"

They ordered Cokes.

After he moved off, David asked, "What's going on, Nicole?"

"Right after Mr. Mac died, Bruce and I started seeing each other. But eventually, we realized we were just depending on one another to handle our grief. Bruce and I agreed to end it, but we still deeply care for each other."

Nicole took a folded paper from her pocket and gave it to David. "Here's my phone number. They—" The bartender walked to the table with their drinks. Nicole handed him money. "Keep the change."

When he was gone, Nicole bent closer over the tabletop and spoke in a hushed voice, describing details of the ruse that caused Bruce's wild goose chase to Sewickley the night Walter Harris was murdered. She recounted their attempt to figure out who would play such a trick on him and why. "We learned why soon enough," Nicole said.

"After he was arrested, I decided to find out what I could about all this. The Harrises were members of my father's church, but I didn't interact with any of them. Of course, I saw Allison and Carin at Mr. Mac's. I thought Walter was a lecherous creep. Regina was just there. I thought it was a weird coincidence when I heard he'd been murdered. Bruce told me about the manifesto and a few details about the murder itself. What Bruce described reminded me of a remark my father once made about blood-atonement killings.

"I've wondered what father thinks about the murder, but after my mother divorced him, I've had no contact with him. When my parents separated, the ruling council at Sola Scriptura insisted Father resign immediately. A divorced man as minister of their little fiefdom would never do. Mother told me he was so mad he just about had a stroke."

"What did your father say about blood-atonement killings?" David asked.

"I had just come home from school one day and heard Father and Mother discussing a murder reported in the paper. Father said the family of the victim ought to adopt blood atonement like the Mormons once used to take care of those kinds of fiends—or something like that. He said blood-atonement executions by religious bodies would save taxpayers a lot of money."

Judy gaped. "Your father believed religious groups should take the law into their own hands?"

"I can't say he believed it. That's just what he said. Anyhow, something Bruce mentioned about Walter Harris' killing recalled a drawing I came across when I was in junior high. Sometimes I snuck into father's office and paged through some of his books. One time,

I was poking through the pages of a book on cults and there was this awful drawing of cult members cutting the throat of a man who had disobeyed the beliefs of the cult. As shocking as the scene was, I couldn't stop staring at it. The drawing mesmerized me. Before I shut the book, I memorized every detail of the picture. The caption below the drawing said, *Blood Atonement at Wapakonee Oxbow, Chartiers Creek.*"

David almost knocked over his glass. "Chartiers Creek? Are you sure?"

Nicole nodded. "When I read Walter had been killed in Chartiers Creek Park, the details of the drawing came back to me. Once I put together the illustration and the information Bruce told me, I realized Walter was the victim of a blood-atonement execution."

"Was there a date on the caption?" Judy asked.

"No. The figures in the drawing wore old-fashioned clothes, though. The one who wielded the knife—actually, it looked more like a dagger—wore a derby hat. The guy restraining the victim had on a long coat and vest."

"Was the name of the cult mentioned?"

"I didn't read the text. I got scared that father would come in. I put back the book and got out of there." She lifted her glass but set it down without drinking. "One Saturday last month, I stopped in at the Sola Scriptura church office. I asked the secretary if I could research a topic in the church library. She and Father had been as thick as hornets at an ice cream social. She knew who I was, but she insisted I tell her the topic. When I said blood atonement, she gave me the squinty-eye and told me they had no reference materials on that subject. 'Mind if I have a look?' I asked, at which she got huffy, so I left.

"Not long after that exchange, I realized they've been monitoring me, watching when I leave my apartment at The Whitfield and when I return. My phone rings, and when I answer, there's someone on the line for a few seconds, then they hang up.

"I reported this to the Carnegie police. They basically said since no crime had been committed, they had no grounds to interfere. They advised me to change my phone number. I was mad. I said, 'I thought your job was to prevent crime from happening.' I told them this could be connected to the Harris murder. 'In that case,' the cop on the line said, 'call the Allegheny County police.' I didn't, though. They'd figure I made up the story to help Bruce."

"Wait," David said. "Who are *they*? Are you talking about this Eye of Naqam you mentioned on the phone?"

"Yes. Members of Naqam Malakhim." Nicole took a sip of Coke.

"How can you be so sure there's a connection between the hang-up calls and this cult? Maybe your father's keeping tabs on you for some reason."

Nicole poked around in her purse and pulled out a folded paper. "This is a handwritten copy of the message I found pushed under the door of my apartment the night after Bruce called me from jail." She unfolded it and placed it on the table.

At the top, in the center, Nicole had drawn a quarter-sized blue eye. Below the illustration, the text read:

We command you upon the threat of death to cease all efforts to exonerate he who is our trusted servant and agent of the will of Naqam Malakhim. His righteous act in shedding the blood of Harris the Transgressor hath avenged the suffering and death of his father. His execution at the bar of justice is necessary for him to appease God and win eternal life. You cannot evade us. The Eye of Naqam Malakhim is in every place, keeping watch on the evil and the good. The Eye of Naqam Malakhim sleepeth not.

Judy frowned and shook her head.

"What a pile of pseudo-theological garbage," David said. "They used the same Hebrew name, and the writing style resembles the sentences in the manifesto. Did you give this to Jake and his partner?"

"Yes. I mailed it to the homicide department of Allegheny County Police Department right away. I haven't received a reply or a phone call about it yet. I intended to ask about it the night Detective

Jakubowski and his partner interviewed me about Bruce's alibi, but I got distracted."

"Do you have any idea why these nuts want to pin this on Bruce?"

"No. It makes no sense."

"You said it was dangerous for you to come to the church," Judy said. "Why?"

"You've been helping Bruce. They could come after you, too. I didn't want to lead them to you. I thought it safer to meet in a neutral place, a public place."

"Why meet here?" Judy looked around. "If they're watching you, they probably followed you tonight. If so, they know we're involved."

"I called you from a restaurant in Carnegie. It's where I make most of my calls. After I called you from the phone booth at the restaurant, I made sure I could be seen going into the ladies' room. I climbed through the window and ran to my car. On my drive here, I saw no one following me."

Judy and David stared at Nicole with wide, surprised eyes.

"What's your take on this, Nicole?" asked Judy.

"It's an attempt to warn me off helping Bruce. I take their warning seriously; they most likely killed a man in cold blood. They're determined to make sure no one interferes with the plan to make Bruce pay."

"Are you frightened?"

"Let's say I'm being very cautious. I wanted to meet because Bruce said you believe he's innocent. I figured maybe we could team up, work together to discover who belongs to the cult. If we could find out their names, then we could notify the police. Once the police have them in custody, the case against Bruce will collapse."

David snorted. "You make it sound easy."

Nicole gave him a sharp look. "Nothing about this is easy. Being watched, getting ominous warnings from somebody who very likely had a hand in killing Walter Harris has been anything but easy." Nicole lifted her glass and swirled the Coke.

"So, you work for Duquesne Interior Design?" Judy asked.

"Yes, I work in corporate design."

"You're aware these people may harm you—maybe even attempt to kill you—and yet you still want to be involved? You love Bruce, don't you?"

Nicole looked down at her clasped hands. After a long moment, she said, "Yes."

"Does your mother live in the Pittsburgh area?"

"Yes. She lives in a side-by-side duplex in North Hills. Her younger sister and husband live in the adjoining house."

Judy pressed her to consider staying with her mother, but Nicole said living with her, even temporarily, would not work. Judy inquired about staying with a friend or colleague.

Nicole laughed. "No, thanks. I have some good friends but sharing living quarters has killed lots of friendships. I'll be careful. Thanks for being concerned."

"Nicole," David asked, "do you know where your father's living?"

"Not exactly. Mother told me he's somewhere in southwestern Pennsylvania. She heard he's the minister of a small nondenominational church, but I don't know anything about it or where it's located. Frankly, I couldn't care less."

Nicole leaned under the paltry light from the wall sconce and looked at her watch. "I think I'll head home." She smiled. "Maybe tonight will show the Eye guys I'm not helpless, and that they're not as smart as they think."

"What's the phone number at Duquesne Interior?" David asked. "Do you have an extension? That's probably the safest way to communicate."

Nicole gave him the information, which he wrote on a blank page in his pocket appointment calendar. He omitted her name and the name of the firm. At Judy's prompting, Nicole also gave them the address of her apartment in Carnegie. They offered to walk her to her car.

"No, I better go by myself. Wait five minutes before you leave in case they're out there." She hugged them. "You two are terrific. I'm confident you'll do all you can to help Bruce and me. But please, please don't take any chances." Then, without so much as a glance back, Nicole Palmer strode to the door and was gone.

"What do you think, Jude?"

She turned her sea-green eyes toward the ceiling. "I think I'd like a Manhattan on the rocks. But making one might be above his pay grade." She nodded toward the barkeep.

"You're probably right. Let's go down in the valley to Gillian's." They waited, and he consulted his watch. "Okay, five minutes are up. I want to hear your takeaway over drinks."

• • •

Ten minutes later, after a twisting descent down Fort Couch Road, they pulled into Gillian's. There were few patrons on such a chilly November night.

After the bartender served their drinks, David pressed Judy for her thoughts on Nicole.

"For starters, Nicole may have bitten off more than she can chew. This bunch won't hesitate to put her out of the way if she persists and uncovers something that could tie them to Harris's killing. Nicole's smart, but she may be following her emotions rather than her brain." She retrieved the maraschino from her drink before continuing. "Do you think Bruce loves her?"

"I don't know, babe. During the conversation we had in the jail, Bruce told me her phone calls helped him."

"He does love her. She's not a woman who would risk bodily harm carrying the torch for a guy who doesn't care for her."

David sipped his whiskey and rubbed his earlobe. Like it or not, he and Judy were involved in this. He couldn't neglect or ignore his pastoral responsibilities. Nor could he do or say anything that might jeopardize the safety of his church members. And yet a family friend—his friend—was facing a murder trial, a murder he didn't commit, a murder for which unknown persons for unknown reasons set him up. David couldn't turn his back on Bruce or his mother. In large part, he was who he was and where he was today because of the compassionate help Bruce's father gave him.

"I don't see this as a this-or-that decision," he said. "My ordination vows have a vital claim on my time and talents. Likewise, I can't refuse to help Bruce if I believe he's innocent and there are things I'm able to do to free him. Nicole's willing to put her life on the line for Bruce. Seems to me that I—*we*—ought to put our oars in the water, too."

Judy smiled and looked at David in that special way that always melted him.

"Now that I've decided to join you in the rowboat," he said, "here's a familiar, but as yet unanswered, question. Why do these radical killers want Bruce to take the fall for Walter's murder? The only answer I can come up with is that someone who's part of Naqam knows him. That's the only connection that makes sense, though I doubt Bruce *knows* that he knows anyone in the cult, not counting Walter."

"What about Walter's family? Did his wife hate the MacDonalds because Lloyd was acquitted? The Harrises moved from an excellent school district in Mount Lebanon to Ormsby. It's a small town, more of a blue-collar culture in contrast to Mount Lebanon. Regina may have harbored resentment about the move."

"I never met Regina, but from what I've heard, they moved because Walter lost his job. Seems to me Regina would have more reason to resent Walter on that score."

"What about the two daughters? What was their relationship with Bruce?"

"I never heard Bruce say anything about Carin. As for Allison, he considered her a snoop and blamed her for not telling the truth about the spilled perfume. Other than that, I don't know if he ever had any true interactions with her. Mr. Mac was more involved with the sisters than Lynn or Bruce." He gave a slight head shake. "Allison is seventeen or eighteen now. I wonder how she's doing."

Judy stared across the room with catlike focus. "I wonder if Harris' wife and daughters bought into the fundamentalist doctrine."

"Don't know. If I had to guess, I'd say they didn't sign on willingly. Walter probably laid down the law where that was concerned." David sighed. "None of this answers the mystery of how the killer got Bruce's knife."

"Or why the killer left it behind to incriminate Bruce."

Stymied by the twin mysteries, husband and wife agreed to focus their efforts on learning what they could about the Naqam Malakhim cult—its location, history, and founder or founders.

"Tomorrow, I'll call the Washington County Historical Museum to learn what I can about the cult," Judy said.

"Good idea."

Judy eyed his empty glass. "Can I have your cherry if you're not going to eat it?"

"Sure, cute stuff. Let me settle with the bartender and we'll head home."

At the parsonage, David put the car in the garage. They walked through the enclosed breezeway into the kitchen without switching on a light. As David moved into the dark living room to hang up his jacket, a car glided to a stop across the street. The headlights winked out. He watched from the unlit living room. No one got out.

Upstairs, as they got ready for bed, Judy said, "In addition to contacting the historical society, Carnegie Library will most likely have material on Ormsby and possibly the Avardian cult. Are you still going to Oakland Wednesday to give Mrs. Rogers communion? You could drop me at the Carnegie to research Ormsby's history and its leading citizens."

"Sounds good. And I can join you afterward. I want to reread the newspaper accounts of the Harris murder, particularly the family's activities when they realized he had disappeared. Then we can grab a late lunch or early dinner at Shuster's. What d'you say?"

"That's a terrific idea, all right." She kissed him. "I've got an idea, too. Come here and I'll tell you about it."

CHAPTER 34

Wednesday, November 6, 1963

David and Judy drove out of the dim interior of the Fort Pitt Tunnel to behold the stunning, sunlit view of Pittsburgh's metropolitan center. Below on their right, a tug pushed a string of coal barges upstream on the Monongahela River.

They exited the highway and drove a few miles to Oakland and the Carnegie, adjacent to the University of Pittsburgh's monumental Cathedral of Learning. Judy jumped out and ran up the steps into the library.

David drove on to visit Mrs. Adele Rogers, a feisty octogenarian with a terrific attitude about life—and death.

After receiving Holy Communion, she rose from her chair and said, "I hate to rush you, Pastor Elliott, but my friend George asked if he could have the first dance this evening at the weekly shindig. I've had my eye on him for a while, hoping he might make a move, and he finally did." There was a sparkle in her eyes. "At my age, it takes a bunch of time to get gussied up, so if that's it for your visit, I'll say thanks for coming all this way and hope you'll come again soon."

Politely but insistently, Mrs. Rogers ushered David to the door. He saved his laughter until he was back inside the car.

• • •

Judy had made progress in her research and shared what she'd uncovered about the town of Ormsby, Pennsylvania, founded in the early nineteenth century, and the advent of a small group of rogue Mormons from the Mormon enclave in Kirtland, Ohio.

She riffled through her notes. "Here's where the story gets interesting. In the winter of 1833, the bodies of Amos Rigdon, the founder of Ormsby, and his wife, Sarah, were found under the ice in Chartiers Creek. Their deaths were ruled accidental. Well," Judy paused, "guess who bought the Rigdon house and farm?"

David shrugged.

"The rogue Mormons from Kirtland. They bought it at auction two months afterward."

He started to say something, but Judy put a hand on his arm.

"Guess what else?"

"They established a used-horse dealership and made a fortune?"

"Stop it! The name of the man who headed this little *family* was Avard Fletcher!"

"Yeah? So?"

She pursed her lips and tossed her head. "Don't you remember the 1877 murder of the Scofield family in Ormsby? Or weren't you listening?"

"Oh my gosh! The Avardian Priesthood! *Avard* Fletcher!"

"You're such a brain, David. I also searched some recent editions of a Washington County newspaper looking for any mention of Naqam Malakhim but didn't find any."

"Maybe we need to take a day trip to Ormsby next week, look around, go to the post office where Walter was snatched, check the phone book for familiar names and the street address for the Harrises. I bet we could find some mention of Walter Harris's disappearance. If we're lucky, we talk to someone who knows more than what we've seen on the news." David pulled out his pocket scheduler. "Next Tuesday, there's an Evangelism Committee meeting at seven-thirty, but nothing else. How's that sound?"

"Okay by me." Judy placed her hand on the scheduler. "Remember, Mother invited us to dinner after church this Sunday. She's making her famous pot roast. Dad assured me there will be lots of Heinz ketchup on hand."

David chuckled. His mother-in-law always cooked the meat until there were no juices left.

A stack of newspapers lay on the table.

"I had one of the volunteers bring the editions with accounts of the Harris case," Judy said.

David read the articles referring to the Harris murder. It was all there: Walter failing to return home from the Ormsby Post Office, Regina and Carin's search, the identification of the body, the arrest and interrogation of Bruce, his account of his whereabouts the night of the murder.

For the umpteenth time, David probed his memory for a significant fact he might have overlooked.

"I can't stop thinking I'm missing an important detail somewhere. But enough of this for now. Let's get some food at Shuster's."

The start of evening rush hour clogged the main streets, including the ramps to the Fort Pitt Bridge and tunnel. As they crawled along, Judy suggested buying a bottle of red wine at the shop next to Shuster's. Her sister and husband would also be at dinner on Sunday.

"It's been a while since you've seen JoAnn," David said. "She and Mark weren't able to come the last time your mother had Sunday—"

And just like that, the puzzle piece he'd been struggling to find flamed on the front burner of David's mind. He told Judy as they entered the noisy tunnel. When they emerged into the twilight at the other end, she looked through their research notes and found it.

"It's obvious now that you pointed it out," Judy said.

"Yeah, it's obvious, but is it significant? There could be a simple explanation—an oversight by the reporter or just a coincidence."

"But this wasn't just a coincidence."

"You're right, Jude. This was no coincidence."

CHAPTER 35

Tuesday, November 12, 1963

Midmorning, Judy and David drove on Route 19 to Ormsby, eighteen miles south of Ellerton. The weather had turned a touch warmer. As native Pennsylvanians, they had no illusions. Winter weather would arrive all too soon. The trees on the steep hills bracketing the highway were leafless, the trunks and limbs a dreary gray-black shade. Judy had packed sandwiches for an in-car picnic, maybe when parked in the local cemetery where they planned to look for familiar names.

The town of Ormsby was three miles southwest of Washington—or *Little Worshington* as it was familiarly called by residents of southwest Pennsylvania. Just a block beyond the *Welcome to Ormsby* sign, they pulled up to a phone booth at the side of a gas station.

Judy lifted the phone book dangling from its chain. She jotted the addresses for the Ormsby Post Office and the Walter Harris residence. Ormsby had seen better days. Washington Road, Ormsby's main street, counted four boarded-up, vacant commercial buildings in a three-block stretch.

A yellow-brick Methodist church occupied the corner of Washington Road and Sycamore Avenue. In the next block a fast-food restaurant, drugstore, hardware store, and a locally owned market were doing business. David turned left onto Elm Street. About two hundred yards farther stood the small redbrick post office building. He pulled into the parking area and shut off the engine. A modest but tidy two-story house sat next to the government building, separated by a concrete drive and detached garage.

Judy pointed to a floodlight attached to the roof of the post office. Unless the bulb had burned out, the parking lot, or at least the entrance to the post office, would be brightly lit at night.

"Harris would have parked near the door unless there was another vehicle here the night he disappeared," David said. "So, when his wife and daughter arrived, his car was probably parked near the sign to the left of the entrance."

"There's no outside mailbox, so patrons have to enter the vestibule to deposit mail." Judy walked to the door and scanned the hours of operation. When she returned to the car, Judy reported, "The front door is locked every night at ten o'clock. There's a letter and package slot, plus some rental boxes to the left of the lobby. If Walter came to mail a letter or pick up mail if he had a PO box, he had to do it before ten."

"I don't recall that any of the articles or broadcasts mentioned the time he left home. Assuming Walter knew the closing time and had to get inside, he got here before ten."

Judy and David discussed their observations and ideas. They agreed the open car door either meant his abductors forced him from the vehicle or he left it open while he went inside. Considering the large lighted parking area, which fronted on a busy street, the adjacent house, and other houses across the street, a ruckus or shouts for help by Walter would have been noticed and reported to police.

"Walter either recognized the individuals who came up to him or their behavior didn't alarm him—at least not at first," said Judy.

"What about Allison? If she didn't join in the search for Walter that night, where was she?"

A sporadic flow of cars and pickups moved in and out of the parking lot. A dusty Chevy station wagon rolled in and parked a couple of spaces from the Elliotts.

"Seeing this is helpful. Although, we don't know for—" David jumped at a sharp rap on the window. A tall young man with a gap-toothed smile stooped to look inside the car. His brown hair was in a pompadour and accented by long sideburns. David rolled down the window a couple inches.

"Hi there, folks," the stranger said, still smiling. "I see y'all are from Pennsy. Pittsburgh?"

"Up north," David said.

Pompadour put his right hand on the door handle, casual-like, as if he didn't realize it was there. "Noticed you been parked here for a spell and wondered if you might be needin' help with directions." His eyes flicked past David and focused on Judy.

David kept his voice level. "That's very nice of you, but we're fine. Just resting for a spell in a public parking lot."

"I used to live in Pittsburgh, but I couldn't stand the high taxes." He addressed David but kept his eyes on Judy. "You fixin' to visit someone around here or just movin' through?" Still smiling.

Judy twitched. She grabbed David's arm. Outside her window stood an older man with thinning gray hair and muscular arms.

"Thanks for your concern," David said to Pompadour. "We're moving on." He rolled up the window and turned the ignition key. The men backed away a few steps. David forced himself to exit the lot at a casual pace.

At the next block, he turned right, then right again at the next street. He parked where they had a view of the rear of the post office and part of the parking lot. The station wagon was gone.

"That was weird," Judy said. "They didn't make any threats, but they sure were intimidating."

"No kidding. Did you have a chance to see their license plate?"

"Uh-uh. What do you make of it? Think it has anything to do

with Walter Harris?"

David kept his eyes on the rearview mirror. "Hard to say."

"Neither of them went into the post office. I was looking out the rear window as you drove away. They pulled out and headed toward Washington Road before you got to the next block. I didn't see which direction they turned."

"Just two of Ormsby's many helpful citizens. Let's check out the Harris residence."

They drove west for three or four blocks on Elm. The houses were larger, some of brick construction, two or three stories, several with front porches. The lawns were small. Most of the places featured foundation shrubs and narrow beds of dormant flowers.

"There it is." Judy pointed while David looked ahead, creeping along. "Concrete steps lead to a recessed front door; small, screened side porch; no landscaping; concrete drive on right side of house; detached garage. There's a green Toyota pickup truck parked by the garage."

At the next intersection, Judy said, "Make a left and park, David. I've got an idea. May I have the trunk key, please?"

She got out and opened the trunk lid. After poking around for a bit, she returned wearing a jacket she had brought in case it turned chilly and the daypack holding their picnic food. She carried a spray bottle of window cleaner, a red-and-white-checkered napkin, and a rag. Judy bunched up her hair under the napkin, which she deftly tied around her head. She looked like Rosie the Riveter of World War II fame.

When he couldn't stand it any longer, David asked, "Okay, what's going on in that fertile brain?"

"Hello, ma'am," Judy said cheerfully. "I'm a home products representative for Ezy Kleen household cleaning products. This spray cleaner cleans everything around the home. Oh, I see you have a smudge here on the doorframe." She grinned slyly. "My first and only prospective client is Regina Harris. None of the family has ever seen me, so I can check her out. Your job is to park the car up the street a few houses away and sit tight."

"Oh, no." He shook his head. "That's not going to happen."

"Don't be a stick-in-the-mud. I want to get a handle on how she's doing. Does she seem sad? Tense? How's she dressed? Is she wearing makeup? Anybody else in the house?" Judy rolled her eyes at David's scowl. "Honey, the worst thing that can happen is she decides to buy my product. I'm not going inside."

"No. High risk, low reward."

"I'll stand five feet from whoever answers. And I'm armed. This window spray is powerful stuff. Besides, you'll be near."

"Judy!"

"Sweetheart, do you really think Regina's the type of woman who attacks door-to-door salespeople? Chances are nobody will even answer the bell."

David muttered a warning about the fate of stubborn women. He drove back to Elm and inched the car forward.

"This is close enough, David. Park here. I won't be long." With that, she scooted out and walked briskly to the Harris home.

• • •

David's eyes fixed on his wife as she rang the bell. Because the door was recessed, he couldn't see who she was talking to, but someone had opened the door. Judy went into her act, even spraying a small space on the exterior wood. The exchange was over in less than a minute. Judy turned and walked away.

She slid into the passenger seat with an alarmed look in her eyes. "Let's leave now David. Give it a U-turn."

"What is it, honey? What happened?"

"I'm sure it was Allison who answered the door. I went into my spiel, and she told me they have all the cleaning products they need. When I sprayed and wiped the wood panel, I looked past her and saw a guy in a room at the end of a hall—the kitchen, I think. He wasn't looking in my direction, but it was Pompadour."

"What?" David turned toward her. In the nick of time, he corrected steering to avoid sideswiping a parked truck. "Great Bald-headed Uncle Ed!"

"Yeah, that's what I say. Let's be on the lookout for the station wagon. Also, that Toyota pickup. We need to find the cemetery."

David stopped at a gas station and asked the attendant for directions. In a matter of minutes, they arrived at Green Grove Cemetery. They drove to the farthest point from the entrance onto a one-lane gravel roadway shielded from the street by thick evergreen trees. Judy broke out the sandwiches and thermos of coffee.

"It could have been just a coincidence that Mr. Pompadour was at the Harrises. Maybe he's Allison's boyfriend."

"You don't believe in coincidences, Jude. Neither do I. There are only connections. By the way, why was Allison home? It's a school day. She's seventeen, maybe eighteen, but I doubt she graduated last year."

"Oh, Pastor Elliott, you're so sweetly naïve." Judy grinned at him. "From my brief encounter with Allison, I'd say she knows her way around. She's attractive in a hard sort of way. She looks older than eighteen. Rather tall, blonde, good body, great legs, beautiful blue eyes."

"You didn't see Regina or Carin, but that doesn't mean they weren't in the house."

"I don't think either of them were. There was something about Pompadour being in the kitchen that made me think he and Allison were alone."

"So, you don't think he was doing the dishes as another of his helpful citizen services?"

"Mr. Pompadour doesn't strike me as the volunteer dish-washing type."

"I doubt his buddy is, either. I would not like to meet him in a dark alley. Did you notice the size of his arms?"

"Do you think Pompadour and Muscles belong to the cult?"

"I think there's a strong possibility. They singled us out at the post office. If those two are Naqam members, that's unsettling, to say the least. Somehow, they knew we would be at the post office today. Pompadour's obvious connection with Allison puts an unnerving spin on the situation. What the heck is going on?"

"David, did you mention to anyone we were coming to Ormsby today?"

"I told Jan Sunday in the greeting line after church."

"Who was within earshot when you told her?"

"Um . . ." He scratched the back of his neck. "Claire Jakubowski and their son, Jimmy, stood behind Jan. Next came the Whittakers, although they were talking with the Ralstons."

"Did you tell Jan *why* we were taking a ride to Ormsby?"

"Just that you and I wanted to take advantage of my empty schedule during the day."

"If Claire overheard you tell Jan, do you think she would have mentioned our trip to Jake?"

"I can't imagine why she would've, unless Jake had told her he needed to contact me today."

"The night we got home after meeting with Nicole, you saw a car park across the street near Paulson's. Do you think we're being followed?"

David finished his coffee and wiped out the cup with a paper napkin. "I don't know, but I don't think we were followed on our way today. Traffic was thin. There was a car behind us when we got to the outskirts of Little Washington, but it turned off into a gas station. I'm sure Pompadour and Muscles weren't following us, but they knew we were going to be in Ormsby today. And where we would most likely be? The post office. That means they also knew *why* we were there. What was the warning Nicole got? *The Eye of Naqam sleepeth not.* They want us to know we're under surveillance, that they're aware we're looking into Walter's death, and that they can track us. You must admit their method was clever. Suppose we took our suspicions to the police. What would we say? This guy asked us if we were lost or needed help? That one had biceps bigger than my thigh?"

"But we got the message—stop nosing around or suffer the consequences."

"What I'm asking myself, Jude, is how Naqam knew Walter Harris would be at the post office, and when."

"The Eye of Naqam Malakhim sleepeth not," Judy repeated. "These people are scary-weird. They could have had a lookout watching the Harris house. When Walter drove off, they followed him and grabbed him."

"Hmm. That's probably what happened. It's only four blocks from their house to the post office. Whoever took Walter had to have been in the neighborhood. Otherwise, he would've returned home before they could get there." David tapped the steering wheel. "Seeing Pompadour inside the Harris house with Allison raises all sorts of implications. If he's a member of the Naqam cult, and they arranged to kill her father, what's he doing there? Are the Harris sisters and their mother somehow involved in this?"

"We can't assume Allison knows that her big-hair boyfriend belongs to the cult. We don't even know that ourselves."

"You're right. Pompadour may be nothing more than Allison's heartthrob. Or *hairthrob.* But again, somebody told Pompadour and Muscles our destination and location."

"I think we can take for granted that we're being watched by some of the same bunch of weirdos tailing Nicole. The Eye of Naqam. The connection is Bruce. The more we dig for the truth, the more dangerous they'll become."

"That makes sense. But who's the brain pulling the strings?"

Judy touched David's hand. He turned his head to her. "Honey, how much do you know about Jan?"

"Jan Henry?"

"Yes. What I'm driving at is, she's the only person you told that we were coming here today. As church secretary, she alone knows who calls you and who you call, who you counsel. She has access to your notations of phone calls, your daily schedule, your files. Do you have complete confidence in her discretion, her commitment to your ministry?"

David stared at his wife as if she had cast doubt on a family member. "You can't be serious. Jan's worked with me for six years. I completely trust her. She's never given me a reason to doubt her intentions. And you tell me I jump to conclusions."

"Don't get defensive. I'm trying to look at all the possibilities. Can you say without a doubt Claire Jakubowski overheard you say we were coming to Ormsby today?"

He admitted he could not. The atmosphere inside the car stayed frosty until Judy opened the bag of her always delicious chocolate chip cookies. David's pique dissolved with the first bite.

When the cookies were gone, the Elliotts walked among the nearby graves, peering at gravestones on the chance they might see a familiar name. Since it was the oldest section of the cemetery, few markers were still legible.

David looked at his watch. "Half past one. Tell you what, let's see if Pastor Clark at First Lutheran in Washington is at the church. John's been the minister there for eighteen years. We'll ask him if he knows anything about Naqam Malakhim."

• • •

Pastor John Clark had been a member of David Elliott's ordination examining committee and the only member of that august group of Lutheran theologians who hadn't intimidated him. They parked in front of a door marked *Church Office* and rang the bell. A jovial man in a clerical collar welcomed them and led the way to his study.

David introduced Judy, and after a bit of catching up and other pleasantries, Pastor Clark asked what he could do for them.

"Without going into too much detail, John, we wondered if you had ever heard of a religious cult in or around Ormsby with the Hebrew name Naqam Malakhim."

Pastor Clark tapped his chin. "Interesting name. Too many years since I struggled through my Hebrew classes at seminary. What's the translation?"

"Avenging Angels."

"Naqam Malakhim. Doesn't sound friendly, does it? I have two families who live in Ormsby, so I get down there from time to time. But I've never heard of an active cult operating in the town. If you don't mind my asking, Dave, is this what brought you to my neck of the woods?"

"Yes. They left their calling card at the scene of a murder. The victim lived in Ormsby."

"Oh, yes. Walter Harris. I thought I saw on the news the police had charged a man with his death."

"That's right. Bruce MacDonald. Judy and I believe he's innocent, and we're doing some private investigating."

"So how does this cult fit in? I hadn't heard anything about that."

Judy answered. "The police are keeping details of this from the public, Pastor Clark. One of our members is a detective who asked David to translate *Naqam Malakhim*. That's how we heard the name."

"John, you realize we're revealing confidential information from a homicide investigation, which we have no authority to do. Our only purpose is to seek justice for an innocent man. I know we can rely on you to keep this in complete secrecy."

"Of course, Dave." Pastor Clark leaned back and clasped his hands behind his head. "Well, I've been here almost twenty years, and this is the first time I've heard of Naqam Malakhim, or any religious or nonreligious cult in these parts. At least not in the twentieth century. The Avardians petered out in the late 1800s. Have you heard of them?"

"Yes, we have."

"I'd be really surprised—no, astonished—to find out there is cult activity in these parts. The congregation's very involved in our city, and somewhat less in the surrounding area, but I've never heard of it before now."

"So," Judy persisted, "you don't think they came from here?"

"No, I don't. Of course, if it will help, I'll make some discreet inquiries without revealing the name you mentioned and give you a call if I learn anything pertinent."

David and Judy stood. "Thanks, John, for taking time to see us. You've been helpful. It's great to see you."

After they left, Pastor Clark shook his head. *I hope you two know what you're doing.*

• • •

Judy and David headed north, their car climbing the hill out of Washington.

"This has turned out to be a day of surprises," Judy said. "The two guys in the parking lot who seemed to know why we were there, then one of them shows up in the Harris house with Allison, and now Pastor Clark dumps cold water on the idea that the Naqam cult is based here. Do you think he may be mistaken?"

"I doubt it. He's always struck me as having his thumb on the pulse of Washington County. First Lutheran sponsors several community programs—Alcoholics Anonymous and health services for the homeless, for example. That sort of involvement indicates he and his congregation know what's going on in the community."

After a few minutes of silence Judy said, "We made good progress today. Seeing the layout of the post office where Walter was taken and its proximity to his house was helpful."

"Now that we've seen the post office and the nearby neighborhood, it's clear that Walter's abductors were daring. Or lucky," David said.

"I nearly forgot I was the Ezy Kleen girl when I realized Pompadour knows Allison well enough to be in her kitchen." She exhaled. "We need to find out what we can about Allison's relationship with Pompadour and how he and Muscles recognized our car. I'm still not convinced Naqam isn't based in Ormsby. Pastors, even police and sheriffs, can't know everything that goes on in a place."

"Pastors don't know everything?" David raised an eyebrow.

She punched his thigh. "That's in case you begin to believe you know everything, pal. Here's a thought. What if there is no Naqam Malakhim? What if the killer, or killers, invented an imaginary cult to throw investigators off the scent? I mean, it still doesn't make sense that a religious cult would blame the killing on Bruce."

Neither spoke for some minutes.

"Have you ever heard of Occam's razor?" asked David.

"No."

"It's a theory that suggests you should always go by the simplest or most likely answer that's supported by the evidence."

"Is this why students think you should always choose *C* as the most likely answer on multiple choice exams?"

David stole a glance at her to find out if she was serious. She was. "Yeah, something like that, I guess. Anyway, I think the simplest answer to the problem of how the killer got Bruce's knife is that he or an accomplice knows Bruce. The Harris family lived next door to Bruce. So, the most likely answer is one of the Harrises stole his knife—Allison or Regina. That makes them prime suspects."

"Since it was stolen seven or eight years ago, technically any member of the Harris family could have stolen the knife. So, you're floating the theory that a member of the Harris family killed Walter. That's what Occam's razor would suggest. Am I understanding this?"

"You are."

"What happens when the multiple choices range from *A* to *Z* instead of *A* to *E*? What does that do to the idea of always choosing *C*? Doesn't that blow up the Occam's razor theory? If there are several perplexing pieces of evidence that have to be considered, how can you decide which one is the most likely or the simplest?"

"What evidence do you see as perplexing?"

"For starters, where he was killed. He lived in Ormsby. Why kidnap him and take him to a lonely spot above Chartiers Creek? Why not some vacant lot in Ormsby or right there in the post office parking lot? According to Occam's razor, if Walter's wife or daughter killed him, it would have been simpler to put a knife in him while he slept in his own bed."

David started to say something, but Judy held up a hand. "Wait your turn. Then there's *how* he was murdered. Unless Walter was chloroformed or given a serious drug, he would have fought like a wounded grizzly. And finally, I'm perplexed about the motive. The Naqam manifesto said Walter deserved to die because he was a fornicator. There's no report or evidence that Walter's wife and daughters were Naqam members. If Regina found out Walter was messing around, the simplest, most likely action for Regina to take would've been divorce or separation—not murder.

"I concede that it was likely one of the Harrises who took Bruce's hunting knife. Allison and Carin spent lots of time in Lloyd and Lynn's home. Allison nosed around in their private possessions. Chances are, she's the culprit. But that doesn't prove Allison, Regina, or Carin, for that matter, killed Walter. And we can't prove Allison handed the weapon to the killer, we can only assume she did."

After a few moments, David said, "I don't think Carin had anything to do with any of this. Allison's snooping triggered Walter's false accusation against Mr. Mac. Walter used and manipulated Allison. She had reason to be angry with him. But what unbearable circumstance or event would drive Regina or Allison to assent to Walter's gruesome murder? You've convinced me it wasn't his adultery. There's circumstantial evidence that Walter Harris had previous extramarital affairs. I was told Regina knew about one of them. You're right, Jude, Regina would have cut him loose, not cut his throat.

"And what about Allison?" David asked. "What was she dealing with? Her dad was unfaithful to her mother. Allison would have been angry and sad, maybe ashamed, but unless she's insane, I doubt those feelings would lead her to ask the Naqams to slaughter him."

"What are you leading up to?"

"If Regina or Allison did kill Walter, or got someone to do it, there had to be something else. Something more sinister. Something more terrible than fornication to motivate them to kill him in such a violent way."

CHAPTER 36

Wednesday, November 13, 1963

The morning sky was a fast-moving blanket of low clouds. David walked up the path to Grace Lutheran, which was founded in 1949. It was a typical New England-style church building with a steeple above the entrance, redbrick exterior, stained glass windows on both sides, three steps leading to the altar and pulpit, choir pews flanking the altar.

He entered the side door to the nave and waved to Tom and Ellen Paxton, the sextons who were cleaning and polishing the floor and pews in readiness for Sunday's worship services.

Jan was in a rare black mood, which matched the ink stains on her hands.

"This stupid mimeo. This is the second stencil I've cut this morning and look at the copy! All the closed letters are filled with ink. For some stupid reason, the drum is stretching the new stencils."

"How old is the mimeo?" David asked.

"It was here when I was elected secretary seven years ago. I called Gestetner. One of their technicians is on his way."

"We need to buy a new model. You don't have to put up with this. I'll call Ted and ask him to explore what's available."

Ted Keane, chairman of the Property Committee—or the 'Prop it Up Committee' as he jokingly called it—wasn't available at the lumberyard he managed, so David left a message with his assistant.

Next, he dialed Detective Jakubowski's number at the county police station.

"Yeah, what's up, Pastor?" he barked.

David overlooked Jakubowski's surliness. He told him what happened in Ormsby, about the two men who had intimidated them at the post office, and Judy seeing one of these men in the Harris house with Allison.

"By the way, Jake, did you know we were going to Ormsby?"

"Yeah, Claire said she heard you tell Jan. Sergeant Eggleston and I were not happy to hear that. I'll say this as plain as I can, Pastor. You are interfering in a police investigation, and I'm telling you to stop. In case I haven't mentioned it, Sergeant Eggleston and I are the investigators of the Harris murder. I gotta go."

David considered the rebuke, trying to be objective. Jakubowski and his partner had one goal—to find Walter's killer. Nicole, Judy, and David had only intended to help, though he admitted *their* primary goal was to clear Bruce. He walked to his study window and gazed down on the rooftops of the houses on the street below.

He had told Jakubowski that Nicole was being warned and threatened by people who used the same Hebrew term written on the notice taped to Harris' forehead. Nicole had even mailed Eggleston and Jakubowski the threatening note the Eye of Naqam sent her. David also provided the detectives with potentially important leads about Allison Harris, Pompadour, and Muscles. *How was that interfering? None of us had any intentions of upstaging Jake and the police.*

David returned to his desk. On an impulse, he phoned Nicole at Duquesne Interior Design, wondering how Jakubowski had reacted to the message she'd sent him. The receptionist said Miss Palmer was not in.

"This is Pastor Elliott of Grace Lutheran Church in Ellerton," David said. "It's imperative that I reach Miss Palmer. Did Miss Palmer report for work today?"

"No, sir."

"Did she phone in sick?"

The woman informed him that unless he was a member of Miss Palmer's family, she was not at liberty to answer his questions.

David called Judy. He filled her in on his conversation with Jake and with the Duquesne Interiors' receptionist. He asked her to call Nicole's home number.

"I'll do it as soon as we hang up. If I have any news, I'll call you."

While waiting, David tossed through a stack of papers on his desk, looking for his notes on this Sunday's sermon. *Nuts. Where the heck did I put them?* He started on the next pile when the phone rang.

"I talked to Nicole. Someone broke into her apartment yesterday. She says the place is a total mess."

"Did she call the police?"

"No. The intruder pinned a warning to a closet door with one of her kitchen knives. 'If you contact the police, you're dead.' She said the note had the Eye of Naqam illustration centered at the top of the paper. Nicole figures she has some sort of incriminating evidence the intruder was looking for, but she has no idea what it could be. She's putting things back where they belong piece by piece to see if anything's missing."

"It's possible that he didn't find what he was after."

"Nicole said the same thing. I asked her if she needed my help, but she felt it best to do this by herself. Oh, and by the way, whoever got in had a key to her apartment."

"No kidding? She's a sitting duck. Call her back. Tell her to get her door lock changed and—"

"She already took care of it. Honestly, David, do you think all women are ditzy?"

He had no answer and made none. A wise decision.

CHAPTER 37

Sunday, November 17, 1963

The eleven o'clock worship service ended, and the organist finished the postlude. The ushers gathered behind the locked door of the office, counting and recording the offering. David hung his robe and his stole on a hanger, then walked to the parsonage. Judy was putting lunch on the table just as he came in.

"Lynn MacDonald called a few minutes ago. She sounds exhausted. She wants you to call her. I'll let her tell you the latest news about Bruce."

"Did you tell her about Nicole?"

"No. Lynn doesn't need anyone else to worry about."

"Good thinking, babe."

David called Lynn.

"Bruce was arraigned November 7," she said. "On Meredith's advice, he pleaded not guilty. Bruce's trial will begin Tuesday, February 25, at Allegheny County Courthouse in Pittsburgh. Would you consider serving as a character witness?"

"Of course. Listen, tell Bruce I'll come by sometime this week. Meanwhile, what can I do for you—and for Bruce?"

"Pray, Dave. Pray like hell."

It seemed to David the trial had been hitched to a ballistic missile. Holy smokes, November was more than half over. He counted on his fingers—ninety-nine days till the trial. Ninety-nine days to get the evidence they needed to prove Bruce's innocence. Ninety-nine days to find the answers. He related this news to Judy. They looked at each other. Where *were* the answers?

CHAPTER 38

Wednesday, November 20, 1963

David parked his car near the carriage house and hustled up the familiar steps to the kitchen door.

"It's good to see you, Dave. Or do I call you 'Pastor' on official pastoral visits?" Bruce teased.

"You can call me *thirsty* and bring us a couple beers."

Bruce opened two bottles of Iron City. Bottles in hand, they went up to the sunroom.

"I feel close to Dad here," said Bruce. "Dad and I, Rudy and Nicky, we all worked together in this room a bunch of days."

"How is Rudy? What's he doing these days?"

"He's doing great. He calls me or stops in about once a week. You heard he graduated with a degree in mechanical engineering and landed a job with Pittsburgh Plate Glass?"

"I did. That's great. And he still lives at home with his mom and dad? At least he was the last time I talked with him," said David.

"Yeah, but they gave him an ultimatum—find yourself an apartment, *or else*."

David and Bruce laughed. They both knew Rudy's parents were softies when it came to their son. The ultimatum had little chance to be enforced.

The two friends sat in comfortable silence until Bruce spoke.

"Nicole told me the three of you are working together on this. Thanks, Dave, and tell Judy the same. That means a lot."

"You would have done the same for us," David said. "Nicole's a heck of a strong woman. Intelligent, except for her love for you. But everyone has their weaknesses."

Bruce smiled. "When the subject is Nicole and Judy, we are two fortunate guys." He swigged his beer. "It really helps to be here instead of jail. Mom's been wonderful, and Nicole's visits take away a lot of the anxiety. I can't thank Meredith enough for arranging home confinement. That said, there are still too many hours spent alone. Mom's gone most of every day working for her clients. I read some, and watch stupid soap operas on television. That leaves too much time to think about what's coming at me."

"Tell me more."

"I never could understand Dad's anxiety. He knew he was innocent. He had a strong faith in God. Still, he had trouble sleeping. What I couldn't figure out was why, after a court of law acquitted him, he went into a mental and physical tailspin. Dad had every reason to resume an enjoyable, productive life. After he died, my emotions ranged between rage against the Harrises and anger against Dad. Why couldn't he accept his innocence?"

Bruce walked to a window and leaned on the sill with both arms. He turned his head to look at David. "I blamed God." He bowed his head. "Actually, I blamed Dad for believing God sent him Harris to make him a saint." He pushed himself erect. "Here's the strange part, Dave. I'm in the same frame of mind. I know I'm innocent. Still, the possibility of being found guilty of murder sometimes jolts me awake. Daytime is worse. When Mom's not home, my brain replays the same thing over and over. '*We, the members of the jury, find the defendant, Bruce MacDonald, guilty of murder.*' I've tried everything I can think of to distract my thoughts—old movies, crossword puzzles, cartoons. I've read a thick slice of Plato, and Immanuel Kant's ideas about justice. I didn't get much out of their writings. Yesterday, I started reading *The Ox-Bow Incident*. I like Westerns."

"Trust me, Bruce. you won't like that Western. Put it back on the shelf. Save it for your fortieth birthday. Have you shared all this with anyone else?"

"No. You're it, Dave."

David prompted Bruce to share some more details about his situation. Bruce admitted he'd been struggling with insomnia, drinking more than usual, and skimping on physical exercise.

"Before I came today, I did some research on you," David said. "I already knew you played basketball in high school, but I didn't know that you were a very good player. A star, for gosh sakes. During your senior year, you scored sixty-one points in a game against Bethel Park. According to the newspaper headline, you sank 79 percent of your field goals and made fifteen of fifteen foul shots. You also set a record in 1951 for foul shooting percentage that hasn't been broken since. I was terrible at making free throws. What was your secret?"

Bruce made light of his success as a player. "Hell, that was twelve years ago."

"I'm serious, pal. Okay, so you're at the free-throw line. Three seconds to the final buzzer. You have two shots. Make both, and your high school wins its first conference championship in ten years. So, tell me, what are you thinking as you're standing there with the ball in your hands?"

"Okay, I'll play your silly—"

"It's not a silly game," David said, no-nonsense now. "What's going through your mind?"

"Actually, I started thinking in the locker room before every game. I would go off by myself and visualize the ball going into the basket every time I'd shoot—layups, jump shots, bank shots, free throws. Then when I stood at the foul line during a game, I focused on the front rim and saw the ball falling over the rim and into the net."

"You're saying you practiced visualization techniques. You envisioned a good outcome. Did you ever have a game when, let's say you missed your first couple shots, and you began to doubt yourself?"

"Sure."

"What happened if that doubt persisted for the whole game?"

"I played lousy. But I didn't let that happen more than a few times."

"You didn't let that happen. Think what you just said, Bruce. You controlled your thought process during a slam-bang high velocity game of basketball. You refused to let negative, unhelpful images dominate you."

Bruce tilted his head. "You believe my visualization method can help me now?"

"Yes. Bring it to bear when your mind makes bad assumptions about the future. You're in the locker room. See Jake arrest the murderer. Hear the prosecutor declare that all charges against you have been dropped. Feel the fact that you're a free man. Make it a habit to visualize this every night when you get in bed. It may not change the outcome—you have no control over that. But you do control your thinking, your attitude. And you have a lot of evidence to show how powerful that is."

Bruce gazed out the window. Then he looked directly at David. "Thank you. I'll do it."

CHAPTER 39

Friday, November 22, 1963

David stood at the hospital window, watching the traffic surge toward the business district of Pittsburgh. The morning sun inflamed the windows of buildings across the river. The weather report promised unseasonably warm temperatures, and he hoped it would prove accurate. There were daffodil bulbs to plant and many leaves to rake and scatter over the compost pile. He turned back to the room.

Since four that morning, David had been at Allegheny General Hospital with Christine Delgado and her dying mother. The nurse had given the frail woman something to quiet the roaring pain, but she was restless and uncomfortable. It seemed it was just a matter of time. Christine held her mother's hand.

An hour or so after noon, David stepped out to allow the doctor to examine the patient. A commotion began at the nurses's station. Two nurses sobbed and embraced each other. Another ran toward him, crying.

"The president!" she wailed. "Someone killed Kennedy!"

David hurried to the nurses's station. Medical and cleaning personnel huddled before a portable radio. A reporter confirmed the bulletin from Dallas. John F. Kennedy had succumbed to an assassin's bullet as he rode in an open convertible through Dallas, Texas.

He called Judy from a pay phone on the floor. She hadn't heard. They were shocked, stunned, reluctant to accept the truth. Judy wept. David regretted not being with her.

"I love you, babe."

"I love you, David."

David returned to the vigil over Christine's mother. Christine had heard the news. She looked up at him, pain and grief clouding her eyes.

"Oh, Pastor. Not President Kennedy. It can't be our president!" Christine covered her face with her hands. The tears she had held in check all day burst between her fingers. David held her close, his tears mingling with hers. They grieved for Christine's mother, President Kennedy's family, and their loss as a nation.

Mercifully, the elderly woman's pain ceased forever sometime after six. It was close to eight when David got home. He and Judy ate canned tomato soup and toasted cheese sandwiches while sitting in front of the television. No matter how often the network showed the scene, their shock and horror didn't diminish. Police captured Lee Harvey Oswald, the alleged assassin, but not before he killed a Dallas policeman. Conspiracy theories began emerging from politicians and analysts, their dark thoughts growing like mushrooms, spreading a fungus epidemic.

• • •

Sunday, Grace Church was packed. Thunderstricken, frightened, grieving people yearned for meaning and hope. The worshipers gathered silently, as if approaching the grave of a loved one. They sang the hymns brokenly, with a touch of defiance in some voices. After the final hymn, they rose and left as silently as they had come.

Hand in hand, the Elliotts walked to the parsonage just in time to see Jack Ruby shoot Lee Harvey Oswald dead on national television. Neither had any appetite for food or more news. In the living room,

Judy watched as David mindlessly built a fire in the fireplace.

The year 1963 had been calamitous, charged with death. The horrific, rapidly increasing numbers of soldiers and civilians killed in Vietnam. The slaying of Medgar Evers. The 16th Street Baptist Church bombing by white supremacists that took the lives of four young girls in Sunday School. And now President Kennedy's assassination.

David stared at the crackling flames slowly consuming the Beech wood. Death had slammed into his life, sometimes without warning, sometimes with heart-tearing, creeping inevitability. His dad. Mr. Mac. Christine's mother. Walter Harris. The shadow of the death penalty clouded Bruce's life, and the lives of those who loved him.

"Do you think this country will ever get turned in the direction of liberty and justice for all?"

"It has to," Judy said. "It has to."

CHAPTER 40

Saturday, November 30, 1963

"Hello?"

"Hi, Judy," Nicole said into the phone. "I've got something important to tell you both. Is David there?"

"David's teaching a confirmation class at church. He'll be here a little after noon."

"I figured out what the intruder was looking for at my place. He didn't find it, though. My mother had it."

"Had what?"

"A photograph. Once it dawned on me that was what he was looking for, I drove to mother's this morning and brought it back to my place. It's kind of a long story, and I'd rather tell you in person. The sooner, the better."

Nicole started to say more, but Judy interrupted. "Nicole, where are you?"

"My apartment."

Judy told her to hang up and call back from the restaurant phone booth. Fifteen minutes later, they resumed their conversation. Was Nicole's phone still tapped? Neither woman knew but agreed that assuming so was smart.

"Do you want to get together this afternoon? We could meet somewhere halfway. Not the Green Lantern, though." They shared a laugh. They decided to meet at one o'clock in a bookstore on a side street in Mount Lebanon.

• • •

At noon, Nicole left The Whitfield and walked to the nearest trolley stop. Was she being watched? Nicole expected she was, but if someone had tapped into the beginning of her conversation with Judy, they had been unable to hear the plan she and Judy made when their call resumed. Nicole remembered reading that when a fox is pursued by hounds, she runs in the opposite direction of her den, where her pups lay hidden. *Bruce says I'm foxy. Let's see if I'm a total fox.*

Ten minutes later, she boarded the downtown trolley she rode to work each day. An elderly couple and a young woman with two children were onboard. Nicole took a side-facing seat near the front. The trolley glided from the stop on its way to Pittsburgh. A sea-green car caught her eye as it pulled out from a parking place and traveled about a block behind the streetcar. She didn't know one make of car from another, but she thought it looked like a compact. She smiled. *Do foxes smile?*

Outside the town limits of Carnegie, the trolley line veered away from the street and entered a wooded area for nearly a mile. Nicole pulled the exit cord for the one stop within the woods. On the platform, she waited until the trolley went around a bend, then she jumped down to the tracks and sprinted across to the outbound stop. In less than two minutes, the Carnegie/Mount Lebanon streetcar rounded the bend. She climbed aboard and soon greeted the Elliotts in the bookstore.

• • •

David often patronized the establishment and requested the use of a small, secluded reading room. Behind the closed door, David and Judy listened to Nicole's story. She had promised important information, and she delivered in spades.

"Last month, Lieutenant Jakubowski and Sergeant Eggleston came to my apartment to ask me to verify Bruce's alibi. I couldn't stop looking at Eggleston. I felt sure I had seen him somewhere but couldn't place him. Well, now I know. Let me give you some background. In September 1955, I saved up my pay from Mr. Mac and bought a camera. I shot a roll of film at a coffee hour at church to see what the camera could do, you know? If the pictures turned out well, I planned to show them to the editor of our high school yearbook, thinking maybe he'd give me the assignment to take candid pictures of the seniors. Anyway, here's one of the candid shots I took at the coffee hour."

Nicole showed them a three-by-four, black-and-white photograph of two men. "I made a second copy of this one because I liked the lighting and the kind of tense interaction between the two men."

David leaned in for a closer look. "That's Walter Harris on the right."

"Who's the other man?" asked Judy. "The look on his face is intense. I don't think he liked what Walter was saying."

"His name in 1955 when I snapped this was Charles Craft. Father had recently baptized him. I didn't pay much attention to him. He seemed like a loner. But Craft and Father got together on a regular basis for several months. I have no idea what they talked about. Most likely, Father did most of the talking. Today his name isn't Charles Craft. It never was. His real name is Harry. Harry Eggleston. Sergeant Eggleston of the Allegheny County Police Department."

"Jake's partner!" David blurted. "You're telling us Eggleston joined your father's church in 1955 under an assumed name—the church where it just so happens Walter Harris and family were members? And now he's a lead investigator in Walter's murder?"

Judy whistled. "What do you always say, David? No coincidences, only connections."

Neither he nor Judy had met Eggleston. David recalled a line from *Hamlet*, spoken by the palace guard when he sees the ghost of

Hamlet's father. *"Something's rotten in Denmark."*

"He has a beard," Judy said. "Isn't there a regulation forbidding a policeman to grow a beard?"

"I don't know, but Sergeant Eggleston is clean shaven now."

David frowned. "Do either of you know if there's a regulation forbidding a policeman or detective from working a case where he knows the victim?"

Judy and Nicole both said they didn't.

David pursued the thought. "Even if there's no regulation against it, shouldn't Eggleston have told Jake he knew Walter? Wouldn't the fact that he knew the victim present the possibility of influencing Eggleston's judgment during the investigation? What's the difference between that and excusing a potential juror who knows the defendant or the victim?"

"So, you're convinced Eggleston ransacked your apartment," said Judy. "How do you know Eggleston figured out you had this picture and felt so threatened that he tore your place apart to find it?"

"He had to have noticed me studying him as he read me Bruce's alibi. Eggleston's a trained investigator. My guess is at some point he remembered me taking pictures at Sola Scriptura."

"Okay, but why was he using a fake name back then?"

Nicole shrugged. "Maybe he was doing some secret investigation and needed an alias."

David pulled his earlobe. *If Eggleston used an assumed name at Sola Scriptura Church to do an undercover police investigation, his subject probably was a church member. Walter Harris and Reverend Palmer were likely his marks. But why would Eggleston go undercover to investigate Harris in 1955? It must have something to do with Walter's accusation against Mr. Mac, which the Mount Lebanon police handled. Was Eggleston a Mount Lebanon cop then?*

"Do either of you have a dime? I'm calling Lynn."

When he returned, David told them Lynn was certain Eggleston hadn't been a Mount Lebanon cop or detective when Lloyd MacDonald was being investigated.

"Let's think about this," David said. "You really think Eggleston ransacked your apartment?"

"Who else would it be? Although I don't know how he got a key."

"He may have a set of lock picks or requested a key from the front desk at the Whitfield. There's only one reason he would do it, and that is he realized you remembered him as Craft."

Judy pushed a stray lock of hair from her cheek. "All of a sudden, he recalls you took his picture with Walter. Did he resist you taking his picture at the coffee hour?"

"It seemed like he made sure I didn't get a full-frontal view of his face." Nicole pointed to the picture. "Just his profile."

"That might explain his angry expression."

"Sounds like you and Eggleston had simultaneous *Aha!* moments," David said. "You didn't say anything to him, though."

"Because I wanted to see the photograph to make sure."

"So, Eggleston saw a hint of recognition in your facial expression or body language. When you didn't call him out, he wondered why. Then he's got the answer—you still have that photograph and need to check the picture to be sure."

"And the most likely place you would have the picture is in your apartment," Judy finished.

"This picture incriminates him in some way. Maybe his previous connection with Walter Harris violates police regulations and warrants a suspension or worse. We just don't know how," David said. "Jake has to see this photo right away. But you can't do it. I'll give it to him. Eggleston won't think twice about me talking with Jake."

Judy pointed to the image. "Who has the other copy of this?"

"Regina Harris. After I had the film developed, I pasted them in a small album and put it on a table in the church so people could see them. She asked me to make a copy. I gave it to her the next Sunday."

"Did you take any other pictures of Eggleston that day?" David asked.

"I don't think so. I brought the album back to my place this morning but didn't look further after I found this one of Eggleston and Walter."

A shaft of sunlight found a tear in the blanket of clouds, highlighting a shelf of books. The trio stood, wordlessly acknowledging the light beam as a sign their meeting had ended.

"Gosh, Nicole," said Judy, "you told me you had important information. You undersold it by a mile."

"Come on." David placed a gentle hand on Nicole's shoulder. "We'll take you home."

As they walked to the door of the bookstore, Judy took the picture from David. "I'll take care of this." She put it in her purse. "If this found its way into the Bermuda Triangle on your desk, it would disappear forever."

• • •

David phoned Jakubowski at home and asked if they could meet that evening. Jakubowski declined. He and Claire were going to a movie. David tried for Sunday afternoon, but the detective nixed that, too.

"Look, Pastor, if this has anything to do with the Harris case—and frankly, I hope it doesn't—come to my office tomorrow morning at eleven. I have a meeting at nine-thirty, but I'll be back by then."

"Will Sergeant Eggleston be there?"

"No. If you need him at the meeting, you'll have to come tomorrow afternoon."

David couldn't believe his luck. "Jake, thanks. I'll be there at eleven."

CHAPTER 41

Monday, December 2, 1963

The Allegheny County Police Department stood a block from the county jail on Fourth Avenue in downtown Pittsburgh. There was no chance anyone would mistake this formidable structure for a friendly hotel or department store. The rough exterior's soot-blackened stone accentuated its grimness. The lower half of the windows on the first floor were opaque.

An austere-looking police officer at the admitting desk answered the intercom, and after consulting his log, electronically unlocked the door. He signed David in, recording the name, make and model of his car, license plate, the person he was there to meet, and the time.

Jakubowski's office was on the second floor—room 219. David left the elevator and searched for the homicide office past offices marked *FRAUD*, *THEFT*, and *VICE*. About a mile down the hallway, he took another left at the corner. *HOMICIDE 219.*

He knocked on the opaque glass door. A man's voice said, "Come in, Charlie. The door's open!"

David entered. A man sat at a desk, his back toward him.

"It's not Charlie, sir. I'm—"

The man swiveled around to face David. "Oh, sorry about that.

I'm Sergeant Eggleston. What can I do for you, sir?"

"I'm . . . uh . . . looking for the fire and arson division. Can you—?"

"Third floor," Eggleston said, standing, his eyes on David's visitor badge. "Didn't they tell you at the desk?"

"Yeah, they did. I thought they told me 219. Sorry I bothered you. Thanks."

David turned and hoped he wouldn't fall or faint before he got out of there. He pulled the door shut and was almost to the corner when he heard a door open behind him. He glanced over his shoulder.

Eggleston stood outside 219, watching.

David waved. "Thanks again!" He turned the corner. At the elevator, he hit the UP button. *Did Eggleston follow?* He couldn't risk a look. The elevator doors opened. Jakubowski stood inside. He took a step forward, but David shoved him back into the elevator. Then he pivoted and pushed the button to close the doors.

"What the hell are you doing?" the detective yelled. "Are you crazy?"

The elevator rose to the third floor.

"Sergeant Eggleston's in your office. I didn't think he'd be here. I expected that you and I would meet privately."

"Why? You're not making sense."

"Jake, you have to listen to me. There's a photograph Nicole Palmer took in 1955 that you must see. It's a picture of Walter Harris and—" The elevator cruised to a stop, and the doors glided back. Jakubowski and David stepped out into the hall.

"Not here in the hall," David said quietly. "I need someplace where we won't be interrupted."

"This way." Jakubowski waved him along. Halfway down the hall, they entered the men's room. A man had just finished drying his hands and walked out. The place was empty.

David showed the photo Nicole had taken, explaining the circumstances of when and why she had snapped the picture. Jake studied the photo, a frown creasing his forehead.

"Would Sergeant Eggleston have been doing detective work at the church?"

"No. In 1955 he was a patrolman. Why?"

"Because he told Reverend Palmer and the members of Sola Scriptura his name was Charles Craft."

Jake leaned against a toilet stall. He looked like he'd been punched in the face. He stared at the photo. "Did Eggleston appear to be suspicious when you showed up in the office?"

"He seemed more puzzled than suspicious. He tried to read my name on the badge, but I don't think he got close enough. He had to have noticed my reaction when he swung around and introduced himself, though. He watched me until I turned the corner toward the elevator."

"Okay. I want you to get back to your car right away. Don't linger getting out of the building. Turn right out of here. Use the stairs. They're at the end of the hall." Jakubowski opened the door and scanned the hallway. "It's clear."

"What about you?"

"I have to report this to the commanding officer."

David hustled to the stairs and took them at a gallop. On the ground floor, he started for the door—then stopped. Eggleston stood at the admitting desk, looking at the sign-in book.

David darted into a side hall, looking for another exit. He saw right away it was a dead end. He knocked on a door marked *Maintenance*, but there was no response. He tried the door. *Locked.* He went back to the corner and peered at the desk.

No sign of Eggleston. He moved quickly.

"You need to sign out, sir."

David pretended not to hear the officer at the desk and kept going. The officer yelled. David quickened his pace.

He was about six feet from the door when Eggleston came up the short flight of steps from the street and drew his gun.

"Get your hands in the air, Elliott! Face the wall! Put your hands on the wall and spread your feet!" He pressed the barrel of his gun against the back of David's neck. "Outside!" He twisted David's right arm behind his back and pushed him toward the steps. "Why did you want to see Jake?" he hissed in David's ear.

"Harry, that's no way to treat my pastor."

Eggleston lowered the gun. David looked to his right as Jakubowski walked toward them. Another man circled to the left; his eyes riveted on the sergeant.

Jakubowski held the photograph in his left hand above his shoulder. "Is this what you're looking for, Harry? Holster your piece, Sergeant. Very slowly, please. Now step away from him . . . I said NOW, Harry!"

The other officer moved closer as tensions escalated. David's mouth was the Sahara Desert.

Eggleston released David and stepped aside.

"Thanks, Pastor. See you in church," Jakubowski said.

David fled without a word. Outside, rain drizzled. He stood beside the car, head bowed, hands squeezing the door frame. Involuntarily his mind flashed back to Las Cruces, New Mexico, 1954. *David saw the man he had trusted level the gun at him. Felt his muscles tense to receive the kill shot. Heard the gun blast close beside him. Watched, uncomprehending, the man crash backward against the phone booth and fall dead. Turned and saw his companion holding a smoking revolver, staring at the body.*

David trembled, fighting to blot out the image. The visual terror faded, then disappeared. Spent, and thoroughly wet, he swung himself into the car. He put his head on his crossed arms against the steering wheel for several minutes. *This hasn't happened since my final year in college. Mr. Mac called it shell shock. But why now?* David reached back. His fingers touched the place where Eggleston had jammed the gun barrel.

When his breathing returned to a normal, he sat up and drove back to the church.

He entered the narthex and smelled a strong chemical odor. Inside the church office, the smell was suffocating. Ted Keane and Jan watched a salesman demonstrate the Ditto machine.

In answer to David's question about the dizzying aroma, the salesman explained it was methyl alcohol, the chemical catalyst that guaranteed legible copies quickly and cheaply. "Perfectly harmless," he assured as he rotated a handle. Copies of the bulletin emerged in purple letters from the innards of the Ditto.

Something routine—exactly what I need, David thought, warming to the task.

"Sir, will you excuse us for a couple of minutes while we discuss this?"

When the office door closed, David opened the window and switched on the overhead fan. He swiped a handkerchief through his still-damp hair. "Jan, it's your call."

"Well, it costs less than a mimeograph, and it does a good job of copying."

"I vote no," Ted said. "I have a headache from the smell after only ten minutes. Jan would be unconscious before she finished the weekly bulletin run. And can you imagine the complaints you'll get about the purple paragraphs? I'll tell him we're not interested. We need to get a premier model mimeograph and get with the times."

David leaned back in the chair; his hands clasped behind his head. *This conversation beats a gun at your neck, every time.*

• • •

Late that afternoon, Jake dropped by the office. David thought he looked ready to drop.

"It's been rough," he admitted. "Harry and I have worked as partners for three years. Two men from Internal Affairs interrogated him after confiscating his official files and the contents of his desk. In one of the drawers, they found a crime scene bag containing a comb promoting a barbershop in Ormsby. He claims it's his, that it fell out of his pocket while we conducted the crime scene investigation.

He's been charged with evidence tampering, which is a felony. He's in jail for now, but his attorney will post bail. Harry hasn't admitted anything. Obviously, his relationship with Walter Harris raises a ton of questions. I phoned Nicole Palmer. She verified that she took the photo of Harry with Walter Harris at a church social event in September '55. That's it for now." He rose to leave.

"Thanks, Jake, for pulling my fat out of the fire this morning. I'm sorry about Sergeant Eggleston. I can't imagine how tough it's been for you. Let me know if I can help, Jake."

"I appreciate it, pastor. Give my regards to Judy."

CHAPTER 42

Tuesday, December 3, 1963

David put his untasted cup of coffee on the saucer. The front-page story of the *Post-Gazette* held his attention. It detailed David's ordeal at Allegheny County Police Department, including the arrest of Harry Eggleston. The story intimated that David had given evidence pertaining to the Harris murder. The story identified him as the minister of Grace Lutheran Church.

Rats! This was not going to go well.

Judy agreed. It wasn't long before the phone started ringing.

"Let me get it." Judy rose and picked up the phone. "No, Pastor Elliott isn't available. . . . No, I don't know when he may be. . . . Yes, I'll tell him you called. . . . You're welcome."

When the phone was back on the hook, she said, "That was a producer at KDKA. He wants to interview you."

The phone pealed again before Judy got back to the table.

"Hello? Oh, hi, Chuck. . . . Yes, we read it. . . . Yes, it was scary for him. . . . Sure, here he is. . . . Thanks. You have a nice day, too."

Chuck Roper was president of the Grace Lutheran church council and a long-time member who occasionally forgot that he didn't own the church. On the best of days, David and Chuck rubbed each other the wrong way. This was not one of those days. Roper wasn't interested in discussing this over the phone, declaring he would be at the parsonage in thirty minutes. He arrived in twenty-eight.

Never one to mince words, Chuck got right to the point. He reminded David that he was not paid to spend time "messing" in a murder case, nor did the job description include having the pastor's name and the church "plastered" all over the front page.

He played the former-pastor card, declaring that Pastor Hahnrot—"may he rest in peace"—never caused any trouble in all the years he served Grace.

"And mind you," Chuck went on in his gravelly voice, "I'm not the only member of the church who's upset, believe me. My phone's been ringing off the hook. I've called a special council meeting tonight at seven. You'll have the opportunity to explain your actions."

Chuck stood, shook David's hand, and hoped he would have a "nice day."

Judy came down the stairs when she heard Chuck start his car. She hugged David and kissed his cheek. "You okay, babe?"

"Yeah, I'm okay. I'm going upstairs to do some thinking. How are you doing, kid?"

"I'm ticked off! Chuck really had to do this tonight, the night before Thanksgiving? He couldn't wait until next week? Jeepers, it's not as if you committed a crime or publicly renounced your faith in God! Damn it, hasn't he read the parable of the Good Samaritan? God calls us to love and serve all people, not just the ones in your congregation!"

David wrapped his arms around her. "You're so beautiful when you're ticked off. Change of subject. What did Mother ask you to make for dinner tomorrow? I hope the ingredients don't include cayenne pepper. You've got enough pepper in you to season a hundred Cajun roasted turkeys."

He went upstairs to his study and sat in the old blue easy chair. Outside the window, the bare branches of a towering beech tree rocked in the wind.

Is this what God wants me to do? he wondered. *Am I supposed to pretend that what's happening in this country and in the world isn't part of my calling? If some member of Grace was accused of murder, would that make it okay for me to get involved, but only then? The Christian Church can't sit around proclaiming love for God but be indifferent to the sufferings of the imprisoned, the afflicted, the oppressed, or the injustices done to the others."*

David acknowledged he couldn't stand the pettiness, the politics, or the exclusivity of the organized church. Pastors and priests who preached or acted on their opposition to the Vietnam war, who supported civil rights for all, might find themselves looking for employment.

If this was what being an ordained minister entailed, he didn't believe he'd be staying in this for the rest of his life.

Why am I having this pity party? David asked himself. *Ordination vows and marriage vows alike don't offer a lifetime guarantee against difficulty and conflict. For better or worse. In sickness and in health. I'm conveniently dismissing historical disputes I learned in church history classes. Luther's break from the Roman Church, the separation of the Lutheran Church into ethnic enclaves. German, Swedish, Finnish, Hungarian. The theological conflicts over baptism, original sin, the Trinity to scratch the surface. And I'm ready to throw in the towel because of this trivial dust-up?*

• • •

A full moon skated above wispy cirrus tendrils. David made his way to the church. The dark shape of a small animal lumbered across the path and disappeared in the weeds. *Probably a skunk.* Inside the church, David went downstairs, not knowing what to expect, but ready for whatever happened. He entered the room where the council always met. All members were present—eight men and one woman, Lydia Barkley. The usual pre-meeting sociability was limited to a few nods and a brief smile from one or two.

"Pastor," said Chuck Roper, "please lead us in prayer."

David opened every council meeting with a prayer, but this seemed inappropriate.

"Chuck, if you don't mind," Lydia said, "I wish to pray."

Bless you, Lydia.

True to his word, Chuck gave David the opportunity to explain himself. David said he regretted that the incident had made the papers. He explained that he had information that was vital to Jim Jakubowski's investigation. He said if the same or similar circumstances presented themselves in the future, he wouldn't hesitate to take the same course of action. No one asked a question. Bob Minnick, church council vice president, asked each council member if he or she had heard complaints that David was neglecting his pastoral duties and responsibilities. No one had.

Chuck Roper replied that many had expressed their dissatisfaction with the pastor's ministry, "and not only in this instance." Bob asked for their names. Chuck declined, saying they had spoken with him in confidence. That went over like a lead cloud.

Minnick said that until those people came forward and aired their grievances face-to-face with the pastor and the council, there was nothing more to say, and moved to adjourn. The motion received a prompt second, and the meeting ended.

As David locked the side door and started to walk home, Lydia Barkley stepped from the shadows and asked to speak with him.

"Pastor, I'm a friend of Lynn MacDonald. She told me you and Judy have been doing whatever you can to clear Bruce's name. To me, helping others in difficult times is what Jesus calls us to do. Thank you both."

CHAPTER 43

Saturday, December 7, 1963

David looked out the bathroom window. Low slate-gray clouds plastered the sky. It looked as if it would rain any minute. Nuts. At least the weather report had hinted at somewhat mild temperatures. A sweater or light jacket would do.

Ken McGilvireid, associate pastor at Mount Lebanon Lutheran, and David had planned a Luther League retreat for their high school kids. Eighteen teenagers had signed up. David had reserved the pavilion at Ellerton Park. The group wouldn't get wet while eating, but most of the activities were scheduled outside of the roofed pavilion. Two couples from Grace had volunteered to make lunch.

Some of the kids knew each other. As it turned out, David knew one of the girls from Ken's church, though he didn't recognize her until she introduced herself—Cissy Ellsworth, the daughter of Jim and Bev Ellsworth, good friends of David's parents and the MacDonald family. Cissy had been about nine or ten the last time David had seen her.

Cissy and David briefly caught up on family matters. She had just finished her junior year at Mount Lebanon High School. David noticed Cissy had inherited her mother's friendly personality.

Pastor McGilvireid had put together a stimulating and thought-provoking program. The final activity asked the assembled kids to write on a slip of paper one sin they had committed during their life. Pastor Ken instructed them to fold the paper and tell no one what they had written. He told them that God's forgiveness is complete and given without conditions. He assured them that by acknowledging their sin and being sorry for it, they need not be troubled by that sin ever again.

Ken gathered the group around a charcoal grill. He instructed them to place their folded paper in the fire and watch until it burned to ashes. Then he offered a prayer, thanking God for His love and forgiveness.

As the kids walked back toward the pavilion and the parked cars, Cissy hung back and fell in step beside David. "Pastor Dave, can I talk with you in private? I need to ask you a question."

"Sure, Cissy." He gestured to a picnic table, and they sat.

"I had a good time today. I met two kids from your church—Barb and Susan. We plan to keep in touch. Maybe get together at Christmas."

David smiled. "Barb and Susan are great. Lots of fun. Barb sings in our choir and in her brother's rock band. Susan's a huge baseball fan. Loves the Pirates."

Cissy traced a finger over initials carved into the tabletop. "I read the story about you in the paper. About what happened to you at the police station. It said you had some evidence about the murder—the Walter Harris murder. Are you . . .? I mean, do you work as some sort of private investigator on this case?"

"Nothing as exotic as that," said David. "We just want to do whatever we can to help Bruce."

Cissy nodded, then took a deep breath. She held out a folded piece of paper. "I didn't throw this in the fire, 'cause I'm not sure what I should do about it—about something I know."

A girl hailed Cissy. She and the others were ready to drive back to Mount Lebanon. David told Cissy he'd take her home if she needed more time. She waved the other girl away.

"That will be great. Thanks, Pastor Dave." She unfolded the paper and studied it. "Is it a sin if someone tells you something really bad and you don't tell anyone about it, not even your parents or your pastor?"

"What do you think, Cissy?"

"Well, if someone makes you swear never to tell anyone about it, and you agree but then later on decide against that because it's really bad, I don't see that as being sinful."

"Will telling this secret be helpful or harmful to the person who made you swear?"

She looked him right in the eyes. "Helpful. To her, and to me."

The wind had picked up. The sky darkened and promised rain. David disliked interrupting her just as she had decided to confide in him, but he did. "Let's go to the pavilion, Cissy. It looks like we could get wet."

They ran for it, and the rain held off.

"So, when I was a kid," Cissy resumed, "I got to be friends with two girls, Tiffany Lewis and Allie Harris. Tiffany kind of drifted away to other kids, but Allie and I stayed friends, even after she moved to Ormsby. Anyhow, one rainy day before they moved, Allie was over to my house, and we were playing checkers. I had just taken her last checker. All of a sudden, she swiped the checkerboard, spilled the checkers onto the floor, and called me a . . . a son of a—"

"A son of a bitch?" David supplied.

"Yeah." She nodded sheepishly. "So, I asked her what was wrong, and she started crying, not loud, but real soft-like, which for some reason was even worse. I closed my bedroom door so Mom wouldn't barge in. Finally, she choked out that her dad made her do things she hated, but he forced her."

Cissy looked at her clasped hands and took a breath. When she lifted her face again, there were tears on her cheeks. "Allie said . . . geez, Pastor Dave . . . she said that, uh, her dad made her put her mouth . . . um—"

"That's okay, Cissy. I understand. How old were you both when she told you?"

"Nine. I had a Bible on my bookshelf, and she made me swear on the Bible not to say anything to anyone. She was afraid her father would kill her if he found out."

David looked out from the pavilion. Lightning blinked briefly. Thunder cleared its throat far to the west.

"After she and her family left Mount Lebanon, we didn't see each other, but we wrote letters about school—you know, kid stuff. She never said anything about her father. Later, when we were in middle school, she wrote that she hated living in Ormsby. She said she'd flunked algebra. Allie is smart, Pastor Dave. I couldn't believe she'd flunk any subject, especially algebra. Then last May, I was shopping downtown at Kaufmann's and ran into Allie in the cosmetics department. She had a doozy of a shiner around her left eye. Her dad still molested her but had begun to abuse her too—you know, punch her, stuff like that. Anyway, Allie said she did something to her dad that prevented him from assaulting her and he slugged her." Cissy shook her head. "She said her mother believed all the lies her dad told her about the black eye." Cissy twisted the ring on her right hand.

"I begged her to tell the police, but Allie laughed. She asked me if I thought the cops would believe her or her parents. She said her mother had known for years what her dad was doing but feared he'd kill her if she didn't say or do what he wanted." Cissy gazed at the folded paper. She remained silent for some time. Cissy looked at David. "Anyway, now that he's dead, do you think it would be a sin for me to tell the police about this?"

"No, it's not a sin. Telling the police is the right thing to do, Cissy."

David tore a blank sheet from his appointment book and wrote Jim Jakubowski's name and phone number. "Lieutenant Jakubowski is investigating Mr. Harris's murder. He's a good policeman, and a good man."

Another lightning flash and thunderclap came, but closer together this time.

"Come on. We'd better run before we get soaked."

They almost made it. Machine-gun blasts of rain and hail smacked the car windows. When the brunt of the storm had passed, David drove Cissy home. He thanked her for confiding in him and suggested she think about telling her parents, too.

"Cissy, do I have your permission to share your brave story with my wife?"

"Sure, Pastor Dave." Then she thanked him and dashed to her front door.

David headed home through the downpour. Irony of all ironies—Walter Harris falsely accused Lloyd MacDonald of sexually molesting Allison, whom Harris had forced into a depraved incestuous relationship for years.

This had to make an impact on the Harris murder investigation. At the very least, it hung a plausible motive on Allison. *Which means what, exactly? Bruce had a plausible motive to kill Harris, too. Come to think of it, if Regina discovered what Walter was doing with Allison, then she had a strong motive to kill him as well. But having a motive doesn't necessarily lead to murder.*

• • •

David pulled into the parsonage driveway and put the car in the garage. Inside, Judy stood at the gas range, tending a soup pot. He wrapped his arms around her waist and peeked over her shoulder at the contents of the pot.

"Boy, the chili smells terrific, honey."

"It seemed like a day for chili, with the rain all afternoon. How did the retreat go?"

David shared some highlights of the gathering, cutting it shorter than it deserved. He couldn't wait to tell her what Cissy had shared with him.

Judy opened the fridge and took out a block of cheese. "Hon, while you fill me in on the rest, will you grate some cheddar? Maybe a cup? I'm going to top our bowls with it."

While he grated, David recounted in detail the conversation with Cissy. Horror, sorrow, and rage spread across Judy's face. She turned to the stove, lowered the flame under the chili, placed a lid on the pot, then wiped her hands on her apron. She pulled out a chair and sat.

"No wonder Allison killed that . . . that—"

"Judy, what Allison suffered from her father doesn't mean she killed him."

"Oh, yes," she said. "Yes, it does!" She looked at her husband. "David, you can stop grating. We need one cup of cheddar, not one quart."

"Sorry. I was wondering about something. I've read stories in the papers and watched TV news reports about rapists charged and convicted for violating more than one girl or woman. Do you think it's plausible that a degenerate who violates a close relative might do it to another relative?"

"I wouldn't put it past Walter Harris."

CHAPTER 44

Wednesday, December 11, 1963

The first item on David's agenda was to call Matt Arnold, editor of the *Ellerton Eagle* daily paper. During the six years David had been pastor at Grace Lutheran, he had come to admire Arnold's professionalism as a newspaperman.

Matt answered David's phone call—proof that the *Ellerton Eagle* wasn't the *New York Times*.

"Good morning, Matt. Dave Elliott here. Do you have a minute? I'll be brief. I need information on Walter Harris, mostly vital statistics—specifically, when and where he was born, names of parents, siblings if he had any, where he was educated, date and place he married Regina . . ." David laughed. "No, it's not material for a sermon. If anything comes of it, I may have a news story for you. . . . Next week will be terrific. Thanks very much."

• • •

The Wednesday morning Bible study had concluded its first session on the book of Revelation. As he walked from the church to the parsonage for lunch, David kicked himself for choosing the last book of the New Testament to study.

The class had quickly dissolved into an argument between

Mildred Bates and Marge Detwiler as to the identity of the "angels who did not stay within the limits of their proper authority."

David had informed them they were discussing a verse from the first chapter of the book of Jude, which was on page 334, *not Revelation,* which began on page 336. However, this correction didn't deter Mildred or Marge, and before things simmered down, someone wanted to know if it was true that one hundred angels could dance on the head of a pin.

Quit grousing, Elliott. They showed a lot of interest. Would it have been better if they'd sat there like pasteboard cutouts or didn't show up at all?

In the kitchen, Judy's eyes shone with eagerness to share some news. "I just got off the phone with the curator of the history collection at the Washington County Historical Society. He really knows the history of this area. No surprise there. I'm going to suggest to Marge Detwiler that we schedule him for a future program for the Women's Auxiliary."

"What a simply angelic idea."

"Huh? What on earth are you talking about?"

"Nothing. What did he say?"

Judy produced her notes. "He said *Wapakonee* was the name of the Indian wife of Pierre Chartier, who had a trading post near the creek named for him. Pierre named the only oxbow on the creek Wapakonee to honor his wife.

"And listen to this. In the nineteenth century, the Avardian cult practiced blood atonement killings in the high field above the oxbow—the very place Walter Harris was killed. Historical documents reveal the Avardian victims were killed with a dagger while standing erect. After their bodies bled out, they were placed on a precise east-west axis with their heads to the east.

"What's more, the Avardians placed a detailed account of the sins of each victim of blood atonement near the body." Judy looked up from her notes. "Walter Harris's execution followed the script of the Avardian blood atonement ritual from beginning to end in every detail."

"Does that mean the Naqams are descendants of Avard Fletcher?"

"No, not according to the curator."

"Maybe someone in the Naqam cult came across the history of the Avardian method of shedding the blood of a sinful member. This fit their delusional theory, so they adopted it."

"That wouldn't have been too difficult. The curator told me the *Encyclopedia of Blood Atonement* includes an entire section on the Avardians."

Judy had fixed herself a salad with homemade Italian dressing and a banana stuffed with peanut butter. David made a sandwich of a thick chunk of cheddar cheese and a thick slice of onion and poured a glass of cold milk.

"Cheese and onion?" Judy grimaced. "You have a pre-marriage session at four with Beth and Fred."

"The onion smell will be gone by that time."

"Let's hope."

David took a bite. He held the sandwich at arm's length. The onion was eye-wateringly hot. Judy shook her head and smiled.

"Okay, so, the night we met Nicole at the Green Lantern, she mentioned something about seeing an illustration of blood atonement in one of her father's books. Maybe it was this encyclopedia the curator cited. Nicole said the caption went something like, 'Blood Atonement at Wapakonee Oxbow, Chartiers Creek.' That's a strong indication Nicole's father had a copy of the *Encyclopedia of Blood Atonement*."

David enjoyed his sandwich while listening to Judy.

Her nose wrinkled. "Gee, David, why didn't you go for broke with Limburger cheese and onion?"

"I don't like Limburger. Besides, we don't have any."

"A small plus for Beth and Fred."

Undeterred by her sarcasm, David theorized, "It's a safe bet Reverend Palmer did have that book in his library. What's more, it's not far-fetched to presume he dug into the history of the Avardians and admired their deluded theory of redemption."

"If so," Judy spread her arms for emphasis, "Reverend Palmer may be smack-dab in the middle of this."

"Tomorrow I'm going to be in Oakland visiting Mrs. Rogers at Presbyterian Hospital and Dorothy Tromans at Montefiore. Since I'll be in the neighborhood, I'll go to the Carnegie and look at the *Encyclopedia of Blood Atonement*. It may have some additional information Jake can use."

"What's wrong with Mrs. Rogers, hon?"

"I spoke with her daughter. Apparently, she sprained her knee dancing with her squeeze, George."

"Oh dear." Judy giggled. "Sorry. A sprained knee isn't funny, but the circumstances are kind of cute."

"I know what you mean. Hey, if a woman her age sprains a knee, better to do it dancing than slipping on a rug." He looked at his watch. "I'd better get back to the office. The sermon still needs work. Maybe I'll get it written by four o'clock." He kissed Judy.

She leaned back. "Thanks for sharing your cheese-and-onion sandwich, particularly the onion."

David took the hint. After brushing his teeth and using a liberal dose of mouthwash, he kissed her again.

"Much better," she reported. "Not perfect, but much better. If you don't smooch Beth or Fred, you'll be fine."

• • •

David found his sermon notes in one of the piles on his desk. Jan only worked mornings on Wednesdays, so he had the place to himself.

The writing went well, and by three o'clock, the sermon had come together. He put it on top of the nearest stack to polish and revise tomorrow.

The phone rang.

"Pastor Elliott? This is Jake." As if anyone could mistake his voice for another. "I got a call Saturday night from Cecile Ellsworth, nicknamed Cissy. She said you talked with her that afternoon at a retreat. Miss Ellsworth told me she had some important information to give me about Allison Harris. We met Monday morning. Her mother came with her. My new partner and I consider her story vital to our investigation of the Harris murder. Thanks for advising her to see me about it."

"Sure, Jake. I'm glad she decided to tell you."

Jake said nothing for a long moment.

"Jake? Are you still on the line?"

"Yeah." More silence.

David waited.

"Listen, Pastor, I called the state police barracks in Little Washington and asked them to pick up Allison Harris. I got a return call from them today. They're unable to locate her. Mrs. Harris and Allison's younger sister stated she never came back from a weekend fishing trip. They didn't seem too worried, according to the officers who went to the home. Allison dropped out of school this year, and her mother said she's been difficult ever since. I talked with Mrs. Ellsworth just before I called you. She assured me if she or her daughter hears anything about Allison's whereabouts, they'll get in touch right away. On the off chance that you hear anything about this turn of events, get hold of me."

"I will."

"Gotta go. Thanks again for having Miss Ellsworth contact us."

The line went dead.

A "*turn of events,*" Jake had called it. A weekend fishing trip? David doubted Allison Harris ever went fishing in her life. An idea came to him—call it man's intuition. He picked up the phone receiver and dialed a number.

"Hello, Mrs. Ellsworth? This is Pastor Elliott. . . . Okay, Dave. . . . Yes, Lieutenant Jakubowski just told me. I'm confident the police will locate Allison. Actually, I called to speak with Cissy if she's available."

After a moment, Cissy's voice came over the line. "Hi, Pastor Dave."

"Hi, Cissy. You must be worried about Allison. The police have excellent resources for this sort of search. . . . Right, I'm sure he'll let you know right away. But I need to ask you, did Allison ever mention she liked to fish, or do you know if she's ever fished before? . . . Yes, that's what I thought, too. One more question. It's very important. Your answer may be a big help in finding your friend. After we talked and you decided to notify Lieutenant Jakubowski about the horror Allison suffered all these years, did you call Allison to tell her? . . . No, Cissy, calling her was not the wrong thing to do. You didn't want to blindside Allison. . . . Yes, I will. Peace be with you, Cissy."

And with you, Allison.

CHAPTER 45

Thursday, December 12, 1963

David finished his hospital visits, glad to see Dorothy and Adele were mending and in good spirits. He decided to walk the few blocks to the Carnegie Library on Forbes Avenue. Finding another parking place would take more time than hoofing it.

The building towered above pedestrians approaching the stairway to the main entrance, especially the eight massive columns above the three entrance doors. The construction contractor engraved Andrew Carnegie's motto—at least his motto for libraries—*FREE TO THE PEOPLE* in the stone above the doors.

At the reference desk, a helpful staff member brought David the *Encyclopedia of Blood Atonement.* He sat at a table in the reference room. The index had three references to Chartiers Creek, and the first one contained the graphic illustration Nicole had mentioned. He read the accompanying text. Then reread it. He sat back in the chair, wondering. *Had he, Jake, Nicole, and Judy gone off in the wrong direction from the beginning?*

David read it a third time, then asked the woman at the desk to make three copies of the page. He then phoned Jakubowski from the booth in the library lobby.

"I ran across a piece about 19th century blood atonement executions on Chartiers Creek while reading a reference in the library," David explained somewhat disingenuously. "It throws some interesting light on what happened to Walter Harris and may be an important lead to his killer. . . . Sure, Jake, I can be there in fifteen minutes."

• • •

David showed the detective a copy of the page from the encyclopedia without preamble.

Jakubowski placed it next to the manifesto found with Harris. The wording was identical. He looked quizzical. "What are you driving at, Pastor?"

"A couple of things about this got me thinking. John Clark, the longtime pastor at First Lutheran in Washington, told me he had never heard of a religious cult named Naqam Malakhim—or any cult—operating in Ormsby or anywhere in the area."

"With respect, Pastor, so what? That may or may not eliminate that neck of the woods as the operational base for Naqam. A professional criminal investigator"—his emphasis on *professional* wasn't lost on David— "doesn't depend on the supposition of one person, even if he is a clergyman."

David checked his impulse to respond with a devastating comeback, which wasn't difficult, because he couldn't come up with one.

He pressed on. "A month ago, Nicole Palmer mentioned to Judy and me that when she was a teen living at home, she snuck into her father's study, randomly opened one of his books, and came across the captioned illustration you have there. I think Reverend Palmer made up this Naqam Malakhim stuff to sidetrack us—I mean, the investigation. As you know, the Harrises were members of Palmer's fundamentalist congregation, and I wouldn't be surprised if they joined his church in Ormsby when they moved."

"Calling the small group of fundamentalists who meet with Palmer in an Ormsby diner a *church* stretches the definition," Jakubowski said dryly.

David ignored the comment. "The relationship between Nicole and her father has been awful for years. When Nicole was a teen, he forced her to confess her sins every day before she was allowed to eat dinner. Her father begrudged her friendship with Lloyd MacDonald. After Lloyd's death, Nicole and Lloyd's son, Bruce, became close friends. Palmer didn't like that relationship either. The two dated for a while but broke it off. They stayed friends, though. I think Nicole's father used the Eye of Naqam to scare his daughter into giving up her efforts to prove Bruce's innocence. Instead, it made her more determined."

Jakubowski picked up the two papers, tapped the edges on his desk to align them, paper-clipped them together, and put them in a file folder. "You're strapping Nicole's father to the electric chair on the basis of a book in his library, a possible sexual relationship between Nicole and Bruce MacDonald that Reverend Palmer disapproved of, and his resentment of a friendship she had with Lloyd MacDonald eight years ago?"

"No. But I think Palmer's involved in this somehow. What's your reaction to the identical wording of the two manifestos?"

"I want to think about it for a bit. I will say, the charge of fornication fit Walter Harris. We located and interviewed three women who admitted to affairs with him." Jake stood. "Sorry to push you out, but I've got a meeting with my team in a few minutes. Thanks for bringing this. It may turn out to be important."

David stepped past him into the hall. "Jake, one last question. What's the significance of the fact that Eggleston knew Walter in 1955?"

"We're checking both of their backgrounds. I've got a theory that looks solid, but there are some loose ends to tie. Okay, I gotta get to the meeting. Take care, Pastor. Thanks again."

CHAPTER 46

Saturday, December 21, 1963

At the end of Saturday morning confirmation class, David asked himself who disliked Saturday classes more—he or his twelve-year-old students? *I do,* he admitted. Four days before Christmas, the kids were not focused on Luther's interpretation of the Apostle's Creed. Nor was he, to be honest.

He searched the piles on his desk for the typewritten copy of tomorrow's sermon. *Doggone it. Where the heck is it?*

The phone rang. David picked up, and the *Ellerton Eagle* editor, Matt Arnold, began by expressing how surprised he was when Judy told him David was at the church. He had always believed ministers only worked one day a week. David clarified. "Ministers are *paid* for only one day a week."

"You got me, Dave." Arnold laughed, then got to the point of his call. "My research guy uncovered some interesting information about Walter Harris. I mailed you his findings. You should get it today. Here's a brief preview to intrigue you: Being the excellent researcher that he is, Gordon worked back from the date of Harris's killing. Walter Harris moved to Mount Lebanon in June of 1955 from Shaker Heights, Ohio, an eastern borough of Cleveland. He married

Regina Douglas, a resident of Cleveland, in 1945. Their daughter Allison was born in 1946, and her sister Carin in 1948.

"Previous to this point, the life of Walter Harris becomes unusual. Before 1942, there was no one named Walter Harris."

"What?"

"The county clerk of Cuyahoga County—the county includes Cleveland—recorded that in 1942, when he was eighteen, Harris' name was legally changed from William Hargrove to Walter Harris. His mother and father didn't change their surname."

"Are you saying that—"

"Hang on, Dave. There are more surprises.

"In Parkersburg, in 1941, seventeen-year-old William Hargrove raped his thirteen-year-old cousin. Hargrove was arrested and charged, but his attorney somehow got the charge reduced to statutory rape. Fortunately for Gordon, our research whiz, and for your purposes, newspapers in those days carried lots of personal, extra-legal details. Apparently, the girl's father wanted Hargrove to rot in jail. However, his wife, perhaps out of misplaced family loyalty, persuaded him to drop the charge altogether. Although there's no report of it in the Parkersburg paper, evidently all agreed that if the Hargroves left Parkersburg on the next stage, so to speak, and agreed to have no contact in the future, the girl's family would discontinue legal action. To lend weight to this, Gordon unearthed a classified ad listing the Hargroves' house for sale.

"Violet, the cousin Hargrove raped, lived a brief, tragic life. She became a drug addict and died of an overdose during the heroin epidemic of 1952.

"Here's the final chapter, Dave. Violet's parents were Frank, who also died in 1952, and Victoria, who still lives in Parkersburg. Violet had a younger brother named Harold, born 1932. Guess the family name, Dave."

"Eggleston."

David didn't remember thanking Matt or hanging up. "Great

Bald-headed Uncle Ed!" he shouted. He dialed Jakubowski's home phone number.

"Hello, Claire. Is Jake available?"

CHAPTER 47

Friday, December 27, 1963

David was upstairs reading the opening chapter of Shirley Jackson's novel *We Have Always Lived in the Castle* when Judy shouted from the den.

"David!" she hollered. "Come down! Oh my gosh! Jake's on the news!"

Standing behind the KDKA microphones were the mayor of Pittsburgh, the chief of the Allegheny County Police Department, Lieutenant Jakubowski, and an unidentified fourth man. David and Judy listened attentively to the police chief's matter-of-fact delivery, which contrasted remarkably with what he disclosed.

"The murder of Walter Harris has been solved," he said. "Former Allegheny County Police Sergeant Harold Eggleston has confessed to killing Mr. Harris. He has been charged with one count of murder in the first degree. Named as accomplices are Edward 'Eddie' Mercury and William Mitulski, both of Ormsby. They remain at large.

"A warrant for the arrest of Allison Harris, Ormsby, daughter of Walter Harris, has been issued. Miss Harris is wanted on charges of aiding and abetting, and accessory before the fact of murder. The search for the suspects is ongoing, with the full support of

Washington County division of the Pennsylvania State Police and the Ormsby Municipal Police Department. We'll take your questions."

Jakubowski and the county police chief fielded a torrent of questions from reporters. When the number of shouted inquiries decreased, the fourth man stepped to the microphones. He introduced himself as the Allegheny County District Attorney.

"In light of this evidence, the county of Allegheny has petitioned the court to dismiss all charges against Mr. Bruce MacDonald and hereby order his immediate release from custody."

Judy and David jumped up and hugged, whooping and laughing and dancing.

Their phone rang. Lynn MacDonald cried *and* laughed. "Bruce called to give me the news before it went on the air. There are some legal formalities to be completed, which Meredith said she'll oversee. You bet we're going to have a party! What a Christmas gift!"

Nicole Palmer called. She was over-the-moon happy. "After I convince Bruce to marry me, will you perform the wedding ceremony at your church?"

• • •

The news had not yet reached the Harris home on Elm Street in Ormsby. Allison Harris, who had been in hiding for two weeks, had slipped back home that afternoon. She looked at the revolver and box of shells that sat in the open glove box in Bill's Toyota pickup. Allison had watched him load the gun several times. *How hard can it be?* she thought. Making certain the safety was on, she carefully loaded the six chambers.

Allison had tired of Bill Mitulski many weeks earlier. She thought his pompadour made him look like a vain, swaggering high school kid. He had always disgusted her during sex. Sex revolted her, often made her physically sick. But having sex with him had been a necessary cost of carrying out her objective. Since she had achieved at least the first part of her goal, he had become expendable.

When Bill shot at targets, he held the gun in both hands. Allison had asked him on one occasion to let her shoot at the bottle he set up as a target. Her first shot was nowhere near the target. Bill had scolded her for *pulling* the trigger. "Squeeze it, dummy!" he'd said. Her second shot had shattered the bottle to smithereens.

Allison checked the time. Bill would be there in forty-five minutes. He'd told her that he and Eddie Mercury, the muscle-bound old goat, had to take care of a couple things. Allison had suggested that when Bill got back, they might have a few beers at the Pink Tango and then have sex back at the house. Predictably, he had fairly drooled at the prospect.

She slipped the gun into the pocket of her jacket and walked toward the back door. Allison's sister was at the movies with her boyfriend. *What will happen to Carin?* The moment of consideration for her sister faded. Allison opened the back door and entered the kitchen.

Regina was sitting on the sofa in the living room. A movie flickered across the television screen. Allison closed the drapes, but her mother didn't appear to notice. She did notice when Allison switched off the television.

"Allison, turn that back on, please. I was watching that."

Allison stood in front of Regina. She smiled at her mother. Allison had never felt so happy, so peaceful, so sure of herself. "I'll turn it back on in a few minutes, Regina. I have something to discuss first, something that's been on my mind for quite a while. First, some news. Walter wasn't murdered by some wacky cult members. I had him killed."

Regina bolted upright. Her jaw twisted. "What? No." Realization dawned on her face. "NO!"

"Remember Charles Craft, the guy who joined Reverend Palmer's church when I was a little kid? He's a cop. He practically begged me to let him kill Walter. Isn't that hilarious?" Allison sneered. "And why did I have him kill that model of morality and marital fidelity? You know why, don't you, Regina? Yeah, you know why. You've known since the start. Your wonderful husband raped me every Goddamned week of my life from the time I was nine years old. Nine!

"You knew what was going on during those *private times*. And you knew Mr. Mac would never have touched me or hurt me, but you kept your mouth shut so Walter wouldn't take it out on you. Instead, you let him take it out on me. And when you realized our whole family scandal would come out, you begged him not to let me be a witness at Mr. Mac's trial. So, a good man, who liked and respected me and Carin, died a broken man. You and Walter might just as well have shot him."

"No, Allison. It wasn't like that! I loved you!" Regina smiled weakly.

Allison exploded. "SHUT UP!"

Allison lowered her voice. "Ever since Bruce told Walter I snuck into his house, I've hated Bruce, because Walter used it as an excuse to increase the number of private times he forced me through.

"When I found Bruce's knife in our yard, I hid it to get back at him. Then, when I arranged to have Walter killed, I gave Eggleston the knife and ordered him to use it and leave it at the scene of the crime. Now Bruce is going to feel what it's like to be punished for something he didn't do, just like I was punished for eight years!"

Allison switched on the television and turned up the volume.

"I'm so happy, Regina. Look at the smile on my face. I want you to remember me smiling at you, Regina." Allison picked up a heavy sofa pillow. She took the gun from her pocket.

Regina shrank into the sofa, throwing both arms in the air in front of her, her mouth open in a soundless scream.

Allison covered the gun muzzle with the pillow and shot her twice. The first shot killed Regina instantly. Allison clicked on the safety, turned down the volume on the TV, and went back to the truck to wait for Bill.

• • •

The lights from Eddie's car reflected in the rearview mirror. Bill climbed out and said something to Eddie, who backed out of the driveway and pulled away. Allison swung open the driver's door.

"Gotta take a piss first," Bill said to her, and headed for the kitchen door.

Allison scrambled out, releasing the safety. She caught up to him as he stood in the doorway of the living room.

"What the hell?" He turned toward Allison.

Her shot caught him in the left temple. His body jerked back against the doorframe and fell like a tree into the living room. She made sure he was dead, then took his car keys and wallet.

A neighbor stood on the sidewalk as Allison backed out the driveway. She rolled down the window. "I heard a loud noise over here. Everything okay?" the neighbor asked.

"Yeah. Bill's stupid truck backfired. Sorry I disturbed you. See you later." She smiled cheerily.

• • •

Allison drove to her destination. Thirty-five minutes later, she parked the pickup in a grassy parking area. She climbed out, then locked the doors and threw the keys and wallet into the creek. Standing motionless beside the truck, Allison listened. The only sounds were the burble of creek water and the metallic popping of the cooling engine.

Satisfied, she made her way beneath the overhanging bare-branched trees to her chosen place. Although she had no flashlight, Allison walked without hesitation into the open field, feeling exhilarated. Allison lay on her back and looked up at the stars. They seemed close enough to touch. *How beautiful.* She listened to the gurgling water. The insect chorus. *So peaceful.* The soft hooting duet of two owls in a distant tree floated in the night air. Allison smiled.

Then she took out the gun. She clicked off the safety. She put the barrel in her mouth and remembered to *squeeze* the trigger.

REFERENCES

The Impact of Being Wrongly Accused of Abuse in Occupations of Trust: Victims' Voices, Carolyn Hoyle, Naomi-Ellen Speechley, and Ros Burnett.
University of Oxford Centre for Criminology, 2016.

The Spiritual Exercises by St. Ignatius of Loyola
Vintage Books, Knopf-Doubleday. 2000

The Jesuit Mission: Seeking God in all Things
Georgetown University. 2018

The Legal Concept of Evidence
Stanford University. 2015

A NOTE FROM THE AUTHOR

The Girl in the Orange Maillot is the darkest and most sinister of my murder mysteries. It was also the most difficult to write because the tragedy depicted in this book happened to a close friend.

Although my friend emerged from the hell of a dastardly false accusation rightfully judged before the law as an innocent man, he was broken emotionally, physically, spiritually.

My notes and observations of this fatal disaster remained in my files for more than twenty-five years. Those years provided the distance needed to write his story. His widow graciously gave her approval.

Unfortunately, my friend's experience is not unique. Innocent children, men, and women continue to suffer the consequences of sexual molestation and of lies that change their lives forever.

It is my fervent hope that those who read this book will do what they can to fight this moral stain on families and communities.

ACKNOWLEDGMENTS

Most especially I am deeply thankful for Karen Dumont, my wife, best friend, and alpha reader, who knows exactly when I need a good listener and when I need a kick in the butt.

What would a writer do without beta readers? Not much. Thanks for your helpful suggestions and tough love, James R. Bennett, Thomas Burton, Susan Joanis, Barbara Jones, Carolyn Pizzuto, Greg Pizzuto, and Ann Winkle.

Heartfelt thanks to my editors. Kerry Stapley helped me to better understand the nuances of voice, character development, pace, and structure. And Chelsea Cambeis, comprehensive line editor, whose unerring eye and expertise on copyright law saved me a ton of embarrassment. Together they made this book so much better in so many ways.

To Linda Witkowski, who challenged me many moons ago to write a murder mystery about a kumquat (yes, a kumquat): each story I've written continues the challenge. And that's a good thing. Thank you, friend.

Special appreciation to attorneys Tom Wagner and Susan Joanis for patiently helping me with legal matters.

Finally, my profound gratitude and admiration for the real Lynn MacDonald. You know who you are.

CPSIA information can be obtained
at www.ICGtesting.com
Printed in the USA
BVHW032106060322
630779BV00005B/41/J

9 781646 636150